ALSO BY EMMA DIBDIN

The Room by the Lake

THROUGH HIS EYES

EYES

EMMA DIBDIN

HEAD
of
ZEUS

First published in 2018 by Head of Zeus Ltd
This paperback edition published in the UK in 2019 by Head of Zeus Ltd

9 7 5 3 1 2 4 6 8

A catalogue record for this book is available from
the British Library.

ISBN (PB): 9781786694089
ISBN (E): 9781786694058

Typeset by Divaddict Publishing Solutions Ltd

Printed and bound in Great Britain by
CPI Group (UK) Ltd, Croydon CR0 4YY

Head of Zeus Ltd
First Floor East
5–8 Hardwick Street
London EC1R 4RG

WWW.HEADOFZEUS.COM

THROUGH HIS EYES

PROLOGUE

You have to know when to say no. That's one of the first things they tell you about journalism, when you're young and hungry and everything feels like the last step before your big break. You have to know when to let a story go, or a hunch, or a dream. This business is dying and being reborn into a form nobody understands, or so they tell you, and when the stakes feel so high it's hard not to cling to everything. This is doubly true when you write about Hollywood.

I said yes. From the first day I arrived in Los Angeles from London, chasing a dream I didn't yet understand, I started saying yes and never stopped. Every yes feels like one step closer to the inside, to being embraced by the untouchable.

People talk about star-fuckers and hangers-on and fangirls with derision, as though it's shameful to crave proximity to the famous, and not the most natural thing in the world. Celebrities are less like gods than drug dealers, delivering us into a more narratively perfect world in which everyone is beautiful and nothing is irreparable. This is a city built upon an industry built upon our collective need for escape, and the sheer force of all the stories that have been told here gives the city a glow, some nights, when you're paying attention.

I have never been able to say no to the glow.

1

On that particular sun-bleached winter morning, the morning everything changes, I am beyond tired. I haven't had more than three hours of sleep in any single night for weeks, and my edges are starting to fray. I woke up this morning fully clothed, my head at the foot of the bed, face down and I've never been able to fall asleep face down. I have no memory at all of how I got home last night, and this is no longer uncommon.

This is what it takes to break in, I tell myself in my weaker moments. The field has never been narrower for aspiring journalists, between the proliferation of unpaid internships and barely-paid work, the disappearance of staff writer jobs and the prioritization of *clicky content* over good writing. But the truth is that I've never cared much about journalism per se, because it's a means to an end, a way to be inside. I've never wanted to be an actor, or to be famous, but to be a part of the world in which beautiful people tell stories for a living.

And so I hustle. Starting at five each morning I log on to work a three-hour shift for an up-and-coming entertainment website whose name I hardly remember, aggregating news stories about celebrity weddings and feuds and wardrobe malfunctions. They will likely fold within a few years, but for now they're still in the high-hopes deep-pockets phase of the startup life cycle, throwing resources at the wall to see what sticks, and as a result they're paying me far more by the hour than they need to.

During normal work hours, I'm covering maternity leave for the assistant editor of Nest, an online home decor brand. I've spent the last six weeks pretending to care about interiors, because the company that owns Nest also owns Reel. Once the glossy monthly magazine I always dreamed of working for, Reel now exists mostly online, and is the home of movie industry news, interviews and features, straddling the divide between a trade journal and a mainstream consumer brand. They'll cover acquisitions and distribution deals, but also run reviews, lavish photoshoots, in-depth recaps of television episodes, profiles of actors and directors and the odd writer. Jobs at Reel are scarce and sought-after, but now I'm within grabbing distance for the first time.

My evenings and weekends are for freelance assignments, and though I'm pitching hard and eking out the odd byline here and there, most of what I end up being assigned is video. Go to a red carpet and get a clip of so-and-so talking about something buzzy that we can make ad money on. Go to a junket and get a news line that will make people watch our YouTube channel. It's far from what I imagined when I made the decision, spontaneous and yet thoroughly planned, to board a flight to Los Angeles and become a movie journalist, to get nearer to the beating heart of everything I love.

I've been here for three years, and this is the first year in which I've even felt close. I'm making enough money to pay rent, and buy food, and pay down my debts a little bit more each month, and I'm doing it in proximity to what matters. And so it doesn't matter how tired I am in this moment, or how impossible the prospect of carrying on like this seems, or that my right eye has developed a convulsive twitch which I hope isn't noticeable. I'm close.

And so I get out of bed after my shift, put on something resembling officewear and refuse to fall asleep on the hour-long bus ride along palm-tree-lined boulevards from Echo Park to Fairfax. Instead, I apply my makeup on the journey, starting with the fifteen-minute routine I've developed to hide the dark crescents under my eyes. I had my long dark hair cut into a fringe last year, on the charming recommendation of a video editor who told me it would make my face look less 'harsh' on camera. I hate to admit that she's right; the fringe softens my angles and emphasizes the bright blue of my eyes and makes facing the world easier on mornings like this.

'You look like hell,' a sardonic voice murmurs in my ear when I finally make it to my desk. Justin is the creative director across several brands at this company; he has a dry wit, a filthy mind, and is the only person here I trust.

'Feel like it. Thanks.'

'Did you go out last night?'

'I had a hot date with the Shorty Awards.'

'Oh Jesus, who made you cover that?'

The Shortys are essentially the Oscars of streaming video content, honouring the best and brightest YouTubers and social media influencers. They are everything I hate about my job. I don't answer, because I'm not technically sure I'm supposed to be taking freelance assignments during my time here, and though Justin won't care you never know who else is listening.

'Why don't you sit in on this today?'

He's gesturing towards the conference room, where the weekly editorial meeting is about to begin. As a temporary contractor I'm treated as two levels up from an intern, and do not usually warrant an invite.

'Are you sure?'

'Don't get too excited – I may need you to cover for me if she asks for ideas.'

I nod and follow him in, already brainstorming in my head.

'All right, what's everybody got?' Jackie Smart, the pixie-cropped, quietly formidable editor of Nest, asks. 'I know I don't need to remind anyone of this, but we've fallen just short of four million unique users for the past three months, and I want us to get over that threshold this month. Justin, want to start us off?'

'So the high-res Rita Ora shots are in – I'm still not convinced anyone cares what her condo looks like but I guess we're gonna find out. She's agreed to share it on all her social channels, so we should get a decent spike out of that. We have talent lined up for the next three weeks of home tour videos... Oh, so we're still looking for someone to take on whatever this Clark Conrad thing is.'

'Clark Conrad?' I say, trying to sound casual after almost choking on my coffee.

'The one and only, although given the amount of restrictions on questions it's gonna be hard to tell who the interview's with.'

'Why would Clark Conrad agree to an interview for Nest?' Nest is where people go for a window into a more perfect world, be it Jackie Kennedy's childhood home or Jennifer Lawrence's first Santa Monica mansion. Nest allows you to tour the houses of people who will never know you exist. Nest is not publishing exclusive interviews with one of the most media-shy A-listers in Hollywood.

'Because he's very excited to talk all about the inspiration behind the remodelling of his Laurel Canyon home,' Jackie replies. 'It's his post-divorce crisis pad – he's gut-renovated it, added a new wing for his daughter, made the whole thing eco-powered. I get the sense he's trying to rebrand himself as a cool single dad, divert attention away from the fact that his last movie bombed and America's favourite marriage is over.'

The Conrad family as a unit are almost more famous than Clark himself: Clark and Carol, their two beautiful blonde daughters Sarah and Skye and their golden retriever Banjo. They were on-screen lovers first, starring together in a late-nineties romantic comedy which is now remembered solely as the movie where they got together, rather than for its delightfully off-kilter plot about a woman who chases her ex to Texas in hopes of reconciliation and winds up becoming a rodeo star. Carol was the lead in the movie, but Clark was the breakout – playing the roguish cowboy who shows our heroine true love – and that dynamic held true in their marriage. As his career flourished, hers faded, and despite tabloid speculation that Carol's first pregnancy was an accident, she seemed more than happy to transition into the full-time role of wife and mother. 'I'm a Southern girl at heart,' she would say in interviews for lifestyle magazines, in between glossy shots of her relaxing at home with Clark and the girls, stirring a big pot of chilli on the stove. 'I've always been a homemaker.'

The Conrads had it all; they were wholesome enough to appeal to middle America, effortlessly glamorous enough to own every red carpet they attended, and just enigmatic enough to keep their tabloid appeal alive. The loss of them out of nowhere felt like a tangible blow to pop culture; so much so that the magazine I was working for when the divorce announcement happened declared an unofficial Day of Mourning, and let people drink at their desks as they wrote up coverage.

'His architect is also thirsty as hell,' interjects Justin. 'Conrad is doing this guy a favour, from what I can tell. He's desperately trying to become a thing, have you seen his Instagram?'

'Wait, you need someone to do the interview?' I said this too fast, I realize, too eager to make sure I'm not misunderstanding in my brain fog. 'I'll do it.'

'Don't get too excited,' Justin tells me. 'We're not going to get anything good out of him. He won't do any video, so the tour is just going to be ten minutes of this architect nobody cares about. We're scheduled to be at the house for four hours, we'll shoot all the various rooms, and you'll get colour quotes from the architect for each one, super-detailed. Then you'll get twenty minutes with him, which they've negotiated down from an hour.'

'I can make it work.'

A silence, as Jackie exchanges a glance with the features editor, and I clench my fists under the table. There's no way they will actually give this to me. It's way above my pay grade, way above my experience level. How has some veteran profile-writer not already swooped in to take this? An interview with Clark Conrad is like a unicorn sighting in the world of movie journalism, for anyone, even for people who haven't idolized him since puberty.

'I'm not sure we should—' the features editor whose name I can never remember begins, then cuts herself off. 'Maybe we hold off on making a call on the writer. I have a couple of freelancers I'd like to run it past.'

'We're really down to the wire on this,' Justin says. 'How fast can you get a freelancer onboard?'

'I'm a little confused as to why we still don't have a writer assigned,' says Jackie softly. She is the kind of woman who never raises her voice, never needs to, because people lean in to catch every word. She turns to the features editor. 'Eleanor, could you clear this up for me?'

'We had Jim Rothman assigned, but he pulled out when we told him about all the restrictions on questions, and it's been hard to—'

'Okay,' Jackie interrupts. 'I don't need to hear excuses, I need a solution. The interview is happening this week, yes?'

'Friday,' Justin confirms.

'All right, Jessica. Let's give you a shot. Send your notes and your transcript to Eleanor when you're done, and the two of you can work together on the angle. Do you have any clippings of similar pieces that you've done before, anything long-form? In case Clark's rep asks.'

We both know that this has nothing to do with his rep. They want to vet me, and though there's a part of me that bristles, I know they're right to do so. I'm a nobody being handed an absurdly huge assignment.

'Definitely. I can send you some clips today. I've written interviews before.' This is true, but only with studio executives, indie directors, the odd supporting actor. No one on the level of a Clark Conrad, not even close.

'She's a pro,' Justin says. 'You don't need to worry, she's way overdue for an assignment like this.'

I glance gratefully at him.

'All right, sounds good.' Eleanor smiles, tightly. 'Jessica, we can go over your questions in more detail later, but maybe try to get a line from him about *Loner*. The fandom for that show is still really engaged, even though it's been off the air for so long, so anything he says will get picked up.'

As if I don't know this.

'And obviously anything he says about the divorce will be buzzy. I'm not expecting much, but it's the whole reason for this midlife crisis renovation project, so even anything he says about the house that sounds like it could be about Carol if you read between the lines…'

'I'm still not over it,' Justin says mournfully. 'The downfall of America's golden couple. Love is dead, chaos reigns.'

The strangest part of Clark and Carol's breakup has been Carol's complete disappearance ever since. All anyone knows is that she moved to New York with the couple's elder daughter Sarah, that she has retired permanently from acting, and that she's been spotted a few times hiking in the Adirondacks. She has given no interviews, no statements, and has barely been photographed since the move. It's not for lack of trying – almost every week, a gossip magazine will run some variation of the cover line 'Why She Disappeared', promising to finally reveal the truth about Carol's new life, and to explain why she took Sarah with her and not Skye. There's a persistent rumour that she cheated on Clark and is now quietly shacked up with the mystery beau, possibly pregnant with his child. Another impressively detailed theory says she's joined a cult based in upstate New York, risen swiftly through the ranks of this 'new religious movement', and has now indoctrinated Sarah despite Clark's best efforts to stop her. But the actual stories are always filler, a cobbled-together mess of old quotes and speculation from unattributed sources. Carol has become an enigma, which is all the more reason why any quote at all from Clark will be breaking news.

Later in the day I send over my meagre list of meaningful clippings to Eleanor and Jackie, trying to ignore the dismissive remarks already ringing in my head. I'm imagining all the ways this assignment could be taken from me before I ever had it, all the clear, undeniable reasons for me not to get invested in this. There's no way I will be at Clark Conrad's home in the canyon two days from now for an exclusive interview. Replace his name with the name of any other star and I might believe it, as an extreme but still plausible twist of fate. But not him.

I refuse to entertain the thought, for the rest of the day. I write the captions for a gallery of 'The 19 Best Colours To Paint Your Bathroom, According To Instagram', and outline a draft of '10 New Year's Resolutions For Your Home' for tomorrow, anything to distract myself from thinking of Jackie and Eleanor currently evaluating my clips, holding my dream in their hands without even realizing it.

On my way out of the office Jackie calls out to me and I spin on my heel, go running.

'I just wanted to say, your clips are good. You're a strong writer, sharp and concise and voicey. I'm happy to have you do this piece.'

'Thank you so much. This is a real honour.'

'Justin's filled you in on the tight turnaround, right? You're going to his house this Friday, you have a half-hour with him, and we need the piece to run before the end of next week.'

'That's not a problem. I can get it done. I'm already pretty familiar with his work.' All my energy is focused on staying calm, keeping my voice steady, not revealing what is happening inside me. Do not seem like anything more than a rookie eager for her big break.

'Great. So here's my one tip for you: go in with a headline already in mind. It can change, of course, but don't walk in there without an angle. You may be there for Nest, but you're still a reporter.'

'A headline?'

'I know, it's probably anathema to everything you've

been taught. Never decide what story you have before you have it, follow the facts, all of that. But we have so many restrictions on this that I'm concerned we're going to end up with nothing. Clark Conrad is a star, obviously, and we want this article to have breakout potential beyond our regular audience. I want people to read this piece even if they don't care about interiors. So go in with an angle – something good, something people will click on even if they don't care about Clark Conrad – and then whatever non-answers he gives, at least you'll know how to direct the conversation.'

Again, I bristle. She's so certain that I'll get nothing, that Clark Conrad will play the PR game and I won't have the skills or the guts to draw anything out of him. But I smile, and thank her, and leave with headline possibilities already bouncing around my mind.

Back home, I try to settle in for a normal evening, a quiet evening, but I barely remember how. This is the first free night I've had in weeks and it's only free because I forgot to respond to the editor who asked me to cover a red carpet. This would normally drive me crazy, the idea of missing out on an assignment, but now everything feels distant and I'm still not quite allowing it to sink in, the reality of what I am doing two days from now.

I run, finally, because it's been a couple of days and my muscles feel twitchy and tightly coiled. I do not miss a workout, not ever, not until recently when there haven't been enough hours in the day, and I have to find a way to make it work because without exercise, my thoughts spin out and become uncontrollable. I know this, have learned this, but still it's an effort. Three years in LA and I still haven't adjusted to how much planning it takes to go for a run here, how the sidewalk drops away unexpectedly to remind you that this is a city built for cars, not for people, not for human movement. Being so reliant on mechanical cocoons to get around makes me anxious, and so I opted for Echo Park, with its relative walkability and its lakeside running loop.

A popular myth holds that the Echo Park lake used to be full of bodies – murder victims from back when gang violence still had a strangle-hold on this area. I believed it for most of my first year here, until l looked more deeply into the local lore and learned that while there's a lick of truth to it, the bodies were mostly drownings and suicides. Now the lake is my favourite thing in the city, a picture book gem dotted with sailboats and lotus flowers and palm trees, a perfect view of the downtown skyline spread out behind its glimmering surface. Some days, it's the only thing that makes living here bearable.

After seven laps of the lake I feel wrung out and blissful, and finally I allow my thoughts to go to him. Clark Conrad. Back in my apartment I start streaming *Loner*, the beloved NBC drama which brought Conrad his breakout role, and after five seasons gave him the springboard to become, against the odds, a movie star. I have every boxset on my shelf, of course, their cardboard corners tattered from years of use, but nothing to play them on since my DVD player finally died last year.

Loner centred on a seemingly amoral, ambitious lawyer who moonlighted as a do-gooder vigilante. It was essentially a superhero show before they were in vogue, though the network would never dream of selling it as that. Loner was 'a lawyer with a dark secret', defending scumbag suits by day and saving lives by night, aided by his otherworldly ability to sense death around him. He could sense if someone was about to be hit by a car, or killed by a mugger, or burned alive in a fire, and wherever possible he would intervene, save them, always in disguise to avoid any link between his two lives.

Of course, there was a tragic backstory driving him to do all this saving, a horrifying childhood trauma that left him an orphan, and my favourite episodes were always those that delved most deeply into the angst of his past. There's something comforting about a hero who has endured unthinkable pain and survived in spite of it.

Loner is probably no longer the role that most people know Clark Conrad for; he's been a bona fide movie star for more than a decade, one of the few actors whose name alone can still get a film financed. But to me this will always be who he is. *Loner by name, loner by nature*, and yes, of course this tagline is absurd, almost as absurd as the fact that the character's literal name was Richard Loner. The kind of thing TV could just barely get away with in the nineties. People talk about this show now with affectionate scorn, as a corny oddity, but there's a reason its fans have stayed so engaged and are still clamouring for a reboot. The thing is there's nothing insincere about *Loner*, and after a few moments of watching Clark's performance you forget the silliness of its concept.

Netflix reminds me that I'm midway through an episode – season three, episode twenty, the episode I've re-watched enough times that I can probably recite it – but I opt to begin the entire show again from the beginning. I watch his face, the face that has been an endless comfort to me through so much, listen to the voice that has been a mainstay when everything else in my life is collapsing, and think about what's to come. What I'm going to ask this man. How I can possibly communicate, in the space of twenty minutes, what he has meant to me, how he came to represent for me the idea of what a good man looked like. Most people get over their teenage crushes, but he is my exception.

Not that I'm there to communicate any of this to him. I'm there to ask him the kinds of questions that will prompt newsworthy answers, because I am not a fan, or rather I am no longer just a fan. I'm a reporter.

I know I should be taking notes because there are ideas coming to me, questions, angles, but I'm too tired to hold my head up. I'm out cold before the sun has even gone down, the words of the show circling my mind as I'm drifting off, Loner's dry one-liners following me into my dreams. This is not the first time he has lulled me to sleep.

2

'Angela! Angela! Turn this way!'

'Towards me, Angela!'

'Angela, what happened with Jason? Are you guys getting back together?'

'Angela! To the left! Angela!'

'WE LOVE YOU, ANGELA!'

'Hey, Angela, five minutes for *Us Weekly*? Angela!'

'Angela, what's your perfect breakfast?'

'ANGELA! ANGELA! ANGELA!'

'Angela, right over here! Over your shoulder!'

There are few things more soul-destroying to me than a red carpet. Angela Jackson, a twenty-something TV actress currently in the tabloids for breaking up with her co-star, is posing for pictures as photographers, reporters and fans vie for her attention, their demands overlapping each other until it's all a meaningless din. But she's a pro, she keeps smiling and posing and turning even as the photographers shout conflicting instructions at her, begging her to grace their lens with one perfectly sellable angle.

My editor specifically wants me to get a quote from Angela but I have too much dignity, or fear, to scream at the top of my lungs to try to attract her attention, and in any case it's pointless. I suspect the reporters who do this are just trying to feel less useless, because if the star's publicist doesn't want them to speak to you, they will not speak to you. I flag down the only publicist I know here as she barrels by, a phone in either hand and a clipboard under her arm, and thankfully her face lights up in recognition.

'Jessica, hey, do you want to speak to Logan?'

And within a few minutes he is there in front of me, the baby-faced supporting actor with a rabid teenage fanbase, and I'm trying desperately to get him to say anything interesting about this film we both know is bad. I ask him softball questions, the fundamentals in any PR training exercise (what drew you to the role? Who's your biggest career inspiration?) and watch him with a sinking heart.

'Yeah, you know, it's just a really exciting project to be a part of, and obviously Bryan is such a legendary director, it was a no-brainer for me.'

'What was the most challenging aspect of the role for you?'

He furrows his brow, evidently not having prepared an answer even for this.

'You know, I guess it was all challenging, in terms of the work, but I had such a great team around me that it was just a real honour to be there every day.'

I'm going to get nothing from this guy.

'Great! Thanks so much for your time.' I smile, and he is ushered along to the next hopeful. The carpet is winding down now, the four big-name stars of the movie all whisked away at once in time for the start of the premiere, and already the sense of anticlimax is settling in. A group of fans across from me brought homemade signs declaring their love for the franchise's leading man, who glided straight down the carpet without a second glance at either them or us, completing a single interview with *Entertainment Tonight* before disappearing into the movie theatre. One of the fans is crying now, being consoled by her friends who are clearly still recovering themselves.

My feet are aching from hours of standing, but this isn't the end of the night. The carpet was a wash, but I'll try my luck at the afterparty, maybe sidle up to Angela with recorder in hand and get her talking. The art of the cold approach is something I'm still learning, but if I start drinking now, I should be in the right frame of mind when the time comes.

The party is not due to start for another hour, at a hotel rooftop across the street from the theatre, but the doorman waves me into the lobby and I slip into a booth there, relishing the darkness and the relative quiet. I text the social media editor of the site I'm here for tonight, send her a couple of carpet clips I think could make good Instagram fodder, then pull out the notecards on which I've been trying to perfect my questions for Clark. The interview is tomorrow, and I should have spent this evening preparing, should have said no to this assignment. Anxiety is fluttering softly at the edges of my throat, not constricting but just unsettling, making it hard to think straight or to sit still, and I steady myself by reading over my questions again, the draft version of them. How many questions can I ask in twenty minutes? How long will his answers be? How much time should I allow for follow-ups, for unexpected tangents? These are the calculations you always make before any interview, but this is not like any other interview.

I order an Old Fashioned from the bar just off the lobby, and on an empty stomach it takes effect almost instantly, slowing things down just enough for me to plan.

We had our final pre-interview meeting today, myself and Justin and Jackie and Eleanor and the videographer and the photographer, during which all the things that I can't ask about were impressed upon me again.

'Nothing about Carol or the divorce, nothing about the bad reviews for *The Silver Circle*, nothing about his personal life—' Justin interrupted himself, reading from the publicist's email. 'Basically, you can ask about the house and you can ask about his work, but only the well-reviewed stuff.'

'I liked *The Silver Circle*,' I said, though this isn't entirely true. It was a misconceived adaptation in which Clark played a hardened CIA analyst who's drawn into a supernatural adventure involving a prophecy and a cult of hooded demons. He was miscast, but still mesmerizing.

'Will Skye be there?'

'Yes, but just for the photographs. We're expressly forbidden to ask her any questions, like we even need to. If we want to know what she thinks about anything, we can check any one of her fifty-six pensive Instagram posts this month.'

'Is she still dating that terrible boyband person?' asked Jackie, with the confidence of someone who knows she's out of touch and doesn't care.

'Of course! Their love is indestructible,' Justin replied, drily. I tuned out at this point, as I tend to from any conversation about the world's most exhaustingly omnipresent pop star, Brett Rickards. In truth I don't have much interest in talking to Clark's younger daughter Skye either, though I know she's a tabloid mainstay, a socialite ten years too late for that to be an actual career path, a nineteen-year-old already infamous for her nightlife and her striking transformation from good girl to goth. I should try to get something from her, something I can sell to *People* or *Us Weekly* and make enough to pay my rent for a month, but I simply don't care. Skye Conrad is not who I want to write about.

The lobby bar is beginning to fill up with glamorously dressed guests, the first arrivals from the premiere across the street, all of them heading towards the elevator to the roof. I join the throng, wishing I'd had the foresight to bring a pair of heels to change into, wishing my dress were longer and less clearly from H&M, wishing I could blend.

Upstairs, the line for the bar is already insane, the space too small for the number of attendees, guests and their plus ones jostling for attention. It's clear that this is not the real afterparty, this is the pre-afterparty where everybody important makes an appearance before departing to find the real action at Soho House or the Chateau Marmont or, more likely, somebody's mansion. Even behind the velvet rope, there are always more ropes.

'Oh my God, Tom?'

I could be hallucinating, except that I finally had a decent night's sleep last night, and no, that is definitely Tom Porter grinning and striding towards me, one of my oldest friends from back in London inexplicably here at this glossy, half-empty party.

'Hey, Jess,' he murmurs into my ear, squeezing me tight, fitting against me like he always has.

'What the hell? How long have you been in town? Why didn't you call me?'

'I emailed you, a couple of weeks back. Don't have your US number, so I just thought…'

And yes, now I remember, the email landed in my inbox on some breathless afternoon in between a junket and a CrossFit class and coffee with a publicist I've been trying to befriend for months, and there was no room for it. I read it and immediately failed to retain it, not because Tom is not important to me but because I don't know how to process him any more.

'Ugh, you're right. Sorry. This month has just been completely insane, with work.'

'I assumed. Are you still doing eleven jobs?'

'Just two. Plus freelancing in the evening, hence this whole situation.' I gesture around at the room. 'How come you're here? Please tell me you finally made the big move.'

Tom has been talking about moving to LA since we were at university together, seven years and a different life ago. I made the move myself without telling him, without telling almost anyone, keeping the goodbyes to a minimum when I packed as many clothes as I could into the largest suitcase I owned and booked a flight, never looking back over my shoulder for fear I'd be frozen in place.

But unlike me, Tom had something to leave behind in London. An actual career, albeit an inconstant one; stints at the Globe and the RSC; a supporting role in a West End musical; most recently the lead in a six-part BBC adaptation that got enough attention from its Stateside airing that he's of interest to casting agents here.

'Are you here for pilot season?' I ask, as a passing waiter refills our glasses with more champagne we could never afford.

'So many auditions.' He nods. 'And so. Few. Callbacks. They say ninety per cent of an actor's skill-set is absorbing rejection, so I'm just honing. But I'm going in for a studio test tomorrow on this new teen drama for The CW, the one about the twins.'

'Oh yeah, they're hot twins and one of them's a ghost, right? So you'd have to play two roles?'

'Yeah, y'know, I thought I'd start out with something low-key and easy.'

'Well, congrats on passing their hotness test. That is a high bar.' The CW is a network traditionally geared towards young female viewers, and its actors are known for being a particularly ludicrous kind of hot – there's regular pretty and CW pretty, and there is no mistaking the one for the other. Tom is not what I would call CW pretty; he's always been unconventional looking, with a long face and longer hair that he refuses to cut shorter than shoulder length. Back home he was perfect for Shakespearean roles, and got cast as a lot of grunge rockers, but he's never going to be a leading man.

Still, no woman has ever managed to pin him down for longer than six months, and our run lasted less than two; two winter months in which I flung myself into his orbit and abandoned my own and let myself think I was in love. Two months of huddling together in the cold dawn as we lined up outside West End box offices for cheap day seats, of running through torrential rain from the tube station to his house, of kissing hard outside stage doors. He is still the closest I've ever come to falling comfortably into a relationship, the way I've seen people do around me throughout my life. The only time I've woken up in someone's bed and stuck around for breakfast instead of slipping out at dawn was with him. He's the only person I ever thought of a future with, but that's long in the past.

LA may not have seasons, but it's still January and still night-time and I forgot to bring anything to wear over my dress, so Tom lends me his suit jacket. As it turns out, he shares an agent with Logan, and seems unsurprised when I tell him how boring he seemed on the carpet.

'Wait a minute, this is off the record,' he tells me, interrupting himself right before an anecdote is about to get juicy. 'Do I need to watch myself around you now? Are my bitchy stories going to end up on TMZ under a pseudonym?'

'I would never. Come on.'

And so he tells me how Logan is a nightmare to work with, how he showed up late and high and had to be fed his lines on this film we're all here to celebrate, and how he would have been blacklisted by now if it weren't for his social media following.

'That trumps everything now. Being talented, being hardworking, knowing your lines, sure, that's all good. But if you're an influencer? You're basically untouchable.'

'So, get yourself an Instagram. You could easily be an influencer, all those BBC fans? The crowds who waited for you at the stage door after *Much Ado*?'

He rolls his eyes.

'I don't want to do that shit. Put my life out there as a commodity. That's the opposite of what acting is supposed to be. The less people know about me, the better. How are they supposed to buy me in a role if all they're thinking about is the avocado toast I ate for breakfast three days ago?'

'You know The CW is probably going to make you get an Instagram if they cast you,' I tell him. 'And a Snapchat. And whatever other social media platforms the kids are using that I'm too old to know about.'

'And you're two years younger than me.'

I smile at him.

'And this is why I love hanging out with you. Eternal youth. Although I actually do have to get to bed early tonight.'

'Big day tomorrow?'

I take a breath. He's the first person I'm telling, and his reaction does not disappoint.

'Clark Conrad? Jesus, how did you pull that off? I thought he never did interviews.'

'He doesn't, really.' I explain about the home renovation, the fact that it's for Nest, the architect friend he's doing a favour for. 'Plus I guess everybody loved him and Carol together so much, he has to try and get himself out there as a single guy now. Pimp his bachelor pad.'

'So do you have to interview his architect too?'

I nod with a grimace. 'How much do you think I can learn about interior design by tomorrow morning?'

The reality of tomorrow is pressing in on me now, too urgent to ignore, and so at ten-thirty I reluctantly order a Lyft, promising Tom that we'll catch up properly this weekend. I have so few real friends in LA, so few people with whom I share history, that I'd forgotten how it felt to be known. And as we're parting ways he looks at me, holds on to my hand for long enough to make me wonder.

Speeding through the night back towards Echo Park, I try not to feel the ache too profoundly, try to refocus my energies back towards the impossible day that awaits me in the morning.

My apartment looks so much worse at night. By day it can pass for cosy, enough sunlight flooding in from the single south-facing window to offset the gaps in the skirting boards and the grubby off-white walls, and it's occurred to me before that this place would be fine if it were always morning. Cockroaches don't come out as much in daylight.

I find a dead one on its back beside the cooker, and when I spray it with Raid to be sure it's not playing dead its legs twitch feebly, just enough to turn my stomach. I wrap its body in three layers of kitchen towel and walk all the way down the hallway to throw it directly into the trash chute, as far away from my bed as possible, as though it matters. As though there aren't hundreds more waiting in the walls.

'You're taking on too much again,' my mother warns me, when I finally steel myself to return her call from beneath the covers, trying to make excuses for why it's taken me this long. 'Getting lost again.'

She makes an art form of this. She has a sixth sense for when things are going well for me, and picks those moments to make thinly veiled reference to the worst time in my life. I moved five thousand miles away and she still won't let me go.

'This isn't like before. I'm fine. I'm taking on exactly the right amount.'

'Have you signed up for your insurance yet?'

'Yes.' I have to let her believe that I make enough money to afford monthly health insurance.

'You sound strange.'

'I'm just tired. I'm about to go to sleep.'

'I wish you would phone me when you actually have time to talk.'

'You're going to be waiting a while if that's your condition.' Then, because I can already hear the wound in her reply before it comes, 'Sorry, I'm just really busy this week. I have a big interview tomorrow.'

I'm too tired to explain to her why it's big, why it matters, why she should pay attention to my career for once instead of simply worrying. Instead, I lie and say my battery is dying and then hang up on her, and go to sleep running through Clark's filmography in chronological order in my head.

3

There are parts of LA that are closed off to me. As a non-driver in this city you are always navigating around your own limitations, adjusting your plans based on where you can and cannot reach, calculating in your head how many bus transfers it will take to get you within three miles of your actual destination.

'You're basically disabled,' a colleague once scoffed to me, a broad-jawed slick-haired bro who thought he was hilarious, and despite his wildly offensive choice of words, he isn't wrong. Not driving in LA is a deficiency around which your every plan revolves, and there are parts of the city you will simply never go. For example, the Hollywood Hills and the canyon neighbourhoods within, their tucked-away streets winding up and up and up into secret kingdoms, hidden gardens and wonderlands deliberately segregated from everything in the city below. The hills are a mystery to me, but not for much longer.

'The GPS is going to give out soon,' says Tanya from the driver seat, our video producer and de facto manager for the day. I've never met her before, but she greeted me outside the office today with a smile that didn't reach her eyes, and has ignored everything that I've said since. I'm squeezed into the backseat between Justin and Nick, the laconic photographer who smells of cigarettes. 'You sure we know where his place is? I thought he lived in the Bird Streets.'

'No, he's way into the mountain,' Justin replies. 'I have it pulled up on Google, we want to take Wonderland Avenue.'

'I hate these roads— Jesus.'

We slow down sharply to allow a car to pass in the opposite direction, driving altogether too fast for the narrowness of the space.

'Who chooses to live here? Why would you put yourself through this every day?' Tanya mutters, glaring at the driver as he roars past. 'This is like driving in a funhouse mirror.'

'The craziest people in the city live in Laurel Canyon, right?' replies her assistant producer, Chloe, whose unkempt hair has been distracting me all day. It looks like she hasn't styled or even brushed it in months, and she's wearing baggy boyfriend jeans and a plaid shirt with a button missing and yet somehow, on her, the look works. The disorder looks deliberate.

'I would kill myself if I had to do this drive every day.'

'I don't think Clark Conrad drives himself anywhere,' Justin says.

'Oh no, he does,' I reply. 'He has a motorcycle and drives that everywhere unless he's going to an event or something.

Then he uses a driver, but he tries to be low-key as much as possible.'

'Is he still dating Amabella Bunch?' Tanya asks.

'Ugh, please do not talk to me about Amabella Bunch right now, I skipped my beta blocker this morning,' Justin moans, and I smirk. I've been in denial about this particular element of Clark's life, so much so that I've left it out of my interview preparation entirely. His girlfriend of just under five months, Amabella, is an influencer, a failed actress who has now made an actual career of sponsored inspirational Instagram posts, whoring out every moment of her life for public scrutiny through just the right filter and in just the right lighting. Amabella posing with a green smoothie. Amabella doing Pilates in an exotic location. Amabella looking wistfully into the sunset. She gets paid more money per post than I'll make in a year, probably, and she goes home to Clark Conrad every night. I've always found envy to be a waste of time, but sometimes it's unavoidable.

'Wait, didn't the Manson murders happen somewhere near here?' Chloe says vaguely, squinting out of the window as though expecting to see some evidence of a fifty-year-old massacre.

'Okay, no, that's Benedict Canyon, and can we lighten up?' Justin reprimands her. 'Like, for example, Joni Mitchell used to own a place here. Isn't that nice? I think that's nice.'

I tune them out, thumbing through the index cards on which I've written down more questions than I will have time to ask. I'm usually good at prioritizing topics, but here there are so many variables that I'm struggling. In theory, I am to ask him mostly about the house with a few tangential questions about his work, his trajectory over the past two decades, the Oscar and Golden Globe nominations he has just received for a biopic about Neil Armstrong. In practice, I need to get him to talk about the divorce, if only in passing, if only in the context of his new home. Jackie wants this to be more than a Nest article about a celebrity home; she wants wide pickup, recognition for the brand, and the first post-divorce exclusive with Clark will do that in spades.

'He's gonna win, right?'

'What?'

Justin gestures down at my notes. 'For *Armstrong*.'

'Did I invite you to read my questions?' I ask snappily, but he's unfazed.

'I doubt he even cares, he already has an Oscar,' Tanya says.

'Yeah, but he's never won Best Actor, and he's been nominated for it a bunch of times,' Justin points out. 'You know actors care about that shit, it's all about the tiers. Supporting is good, but it ain't the real prize— Wait, I think that's it, see that house coming up on the left?'

I crane my neck upwards trying to see, but then we take a bend and all at once there it is, unmissable, a sprawling rooftop nestled into the canopy of trees just hinting at what is hidden. A modern castle carved impossibly into a hillside.

'How do we even get up there?'

'Just take Wonderland for another few minutes, and the email said there'll be a gate coming up at the corner of Crescent Drive with an intercom.'

Sure enough, a few winding moments later we arrive at the gate, and are buzzed in up the steepest driveway I have ever seen, so steep that I'm briefly afraid the car will stall and we'll skid uncontrollably back out into the road. The house is not as large as I imagined but it is taller, its three storeys stacked high and its bright white walls standing out a mile amidst the wilderness.

'Is that… a moat?' I ask pointing towards what looks like a swimming pool surrounding the house.

'All the A-listers have moats these days,' Justin says. 'You're British, you should be into the castle vibe.'

'That's his wraparound pool,' Tanya replies, as though this is the most obvious statement in the world. 'It's literally the signature part of his whole renovation – that, and the climate-controlled art cellar. Did you even read about the house at all before we came here?'

I ignore her, appreciating Justin's covert eye roll.

Jerome, the architect, meets us at the top of the driveway. Dressed in a crisp white shirt and chinos, he has the pressed, edgy energy of someone eager to be seen. I hang back as he welcomes the others, walking a few paces around the driveway and scribbling down as many colour notes as possible onto my lined pad (water features, miniature rock garden, two cars out front).

'Hi!' chirps a polished brunette to my left, sticking out a hand for me to shake. 'I'm Peyton.' Clark's publicist, newly hired. Until recently, he was one of the most famous people in Hollywood without one. I exchange pleasantries with her as we follow Jerome and the others inside, nodding politely as she reiterates once again that I will have twenty minutes, that I am to ask no personal questions, that Clark will not participate in the video shoot, that the interview will take place at 4.40 p.m. and that we need to wrap at five on the dot. Wrap meaning: get the fuck out of Clark Conrad's house.

'All sound good?' she concludes with a razor-sharp smile, and I beam back and say, 'Absolutely. Can't wait.'

'So, Clark wanted to leave the place exactly as-is, show you the lived-in house,' Jerome is saying, leading us through the foyer towards the light-flooded kitchen. 'But I persuaded him to clean up a little, y'know, because Nest doesn't need to see the bachelor pad reality. Let's keep it aspirational, right?'

'It's cosy, though,' Tanya notes. 'It doesn't have that sort of too-vast minimalist thing that we see a lot of.'

'Right, Clark is all about that, the homey vibe as opposed to something very functional. He always said from day one that he wanted it to feel like a home, not a residence. So here, for example, you'll see we went for something more traditional with the kitchen where the focal point is this beautiful dining table, not an island like you'd see in a lot of more modern designs. Instead of an island, we did this outsized breakfast bar. He's big on entertaining, so we still wanted the food preparation and dining areas to be integrated, but this just feels more rustic, more welcoming, and that's really the direction we went with throughout the house.'

Our next stop is a sunken living room with three walls of windows, looking out onto a deck and the canyon wilderness beyond. Three steel-grey couches sit at right angles around a coffee table that looks carved out of driftwood, while the fourth wall of the room is lined with cluttered bookshelves, horizontal volumes stacked on top of vertical rows, ornaments and wooden sailboats dotted haphazardly in front of the books. Here I see the cosiness, the clutter without which this room would feel sparse.

Upstairs a library room, lined with more overflowing bookshelves and a cabinet of awards: two Emmys, a Golden Globe, an Oscar, a collection of glass plaques from lesser ceremonies. After all the times I've been forced to ask Hollywood's most inane question ('Where do you keep your Oscar?') I'm seeing the reality at last, the fact that these are physical objects that are stored in someone's home, and must be accommodated like any other knickknack. This room is tucked away at the end of a corridor, almost hidden from the main house, and I make note of this, planning to use it as a lead-in to talk about Clark's humility, his everyman thing, his infamous unwillingness to act like a star. Clark Conrad does not need every guest in his home to see his trophies.

'So do you guys know what shots you want to get first?' Jerome asks, as the tour concludes back downstairs.

'Let's start in the reception room, that conversation pit is great.'

Chloe and Nick surge into motion with their equipment, manoeuvring lights and cameras around me and I try to find somewhere unobtrusive to stand, suddenly deeply aware of my superfluity here. There are few situations quite like this, when you've been invited into someone's house not as a guest, but as part of a business transaction.

'Jessica, you wanted to speak to Jerome for your piece also, right?' Peyton asks. 'While they're getting their photos, do you guys want to grab a corner, maybe go back through any rooms you want extra details on?'

This, at least, I am prepared for, having asked Jackie for some basic interior pointers. I ask Jerome about the finishings on the wood and the colour scheme across each of the bedrooms, the elements of mid-century architecture preserved alongside modern renovations, the reclaimed oak furniture and sea-grass rugs, because as it turns out Jerome is both architect and interior designer.

'Am I right in thinking that there's a whole separate wing of the house, with its own entrance?' I ask, deliberately vague.

'Oh, yes, Skye's suite. I would love to show you around there, but you know—' Jerome gives me a conspiratorial glance. 'She's a teenager. Not big on hospitality. Probably still asleep.'

Undoubtedly. I saw paparazzi images of her on the Daily Mail this morning, weaving her way out of The Abbey in the small hours, cigarette in hand, Brett and his posse in tow. Jerome takes me outside to point out the exterior of Skye's wing, the edge of her patio visible through its surrounding hedge. She has her own semi-private section of the wraparound pool, one side of its C-shape ending right outside her bedroom, and it strikes me that father and daughter could both swim in the same pool without ever encountering one another.

It takes me longer than I expect to run out of questions about the house, but finally it happens, and although Jerome seems as though he could talk for ever with or without my prompting, Tanya eventually calls him away to consult on a shot in the bedroom. And so here I am again, at a loose end in Clark Conrad's house, trying to find a way to look busy.

I wander down a hallway which turns out to be a dead end, a locked door which must lead to Skye's domain. I imagine her somewhere inside, maybe just waking up still fully clothed from last night's excesses, that flowing blonde hair strewn over her pillows, maybe alone or maybe not. This renovation setup makes it clear that Clark respects her privacy, and I wonder if she has any concept of how lucky she is. To be simultaneously free and protected.

This house is a maze, and I'm now not even sure how to get back to the foyer to find the others, so I take the opportunity to look again at the rooms we rushed through before, the ones in which Jerome took little interest because their renovation was minimal. Upstairs, I pause on the threshold of the library room, looking again at the cabinet of awards.

'Hi there.'

I spin around and he is there. His salt-and-pepper hair slicked up into a quiff, his sharp jaw offset by just the right amount of stubble, wearing one of his signature three-piece suits, the Tom Ford numbers that have – along with his name – earned him the title of Throwback Man, a matinee idol flung out of time. He smiles, and I'm dizzy.

4

'Are you the reporter?'

I look around wildly, waiting for someone else to introduce us, but there is no one. This is happening.

'Yes! Hi,' and I move quickly to him, shake his hand and try to smile and hope he can't feel me shaking. 'I'm Jessica, it's such a pleasure to meet you.'

'Great to meet you too, Jessica.' He beams, shaking my hand while squeezing my wrist with the other, his eyes as kind in person as they are on film. 'Want to come on out to the deck? I know you're into interiors, but the view is probably my favourite part of the house.'

I want to tell him I'm not into interiors, that I'm here because I love his work, but I can't imagine a version of this that doesn't sound pretentious.

'Sorry I wasn't here to meet you,' he says, leading me onto the deck, which faces directly out into the canyon and its tangle of trees. Even now in winter, with some of the branches bare, the greenery is impenetrable, spiralling downwards. When I first moved to Los Angeles I scarcely knew what a canyon was, but they are as foundational a part of this city as highways or beaches or narcissism. The ravines cut into the land create entire neighbourhoods.

'Not a problem.'

'Had a few meetings up in Burbank and got caught in traffic on the way back down. Naturally.'

'Of course.' I laugh, and it comes out high and forced. 'Should we wait for Peyton? I think she maybe wanted to sit in…'

'Oh, right…' He looks vaguely back into the house. 'I'm fine with this if you are. Always feels strange to me having a third party hovering around during these things.'

'I couldn't agree more.' The fact that he's calling his publicist a third party suggests to me that they're off to a rocky start. And there's no way he knows I'm supposed to have only twenty minutes with him. At Clark's direction I take a seat on a wooden arbour as he settles onto a loveseat opposite me.

'So I'd like to start with a few questions about the house, if that's okay with you. The renovation, the thinking behind it…'

'That's okay with me.'

'You've owned the place for a long time, correct?'

'Yes, I bought it back in '01, right around the time my show was wrapping up. I'd just hit my thirties and I knew I wanted something more permanent, something that felt like a home and not a crash pad, but it was a bit of a fixer-upper. I liked the idea of having it as a project, but I never really had the time to put into it, and so I would just lend it out to friends when they were visiting, you know, stay here sometimes at weekends. For long stretches I would forget I owned the place at all.'

'You used to live more in the city, right?'

'My ex-wife and I had a place in Beverly Hills.'

'So why the canyon? It's not the most obvious choice.'

'Well, no, but I guess it's the ultimate embodiment of ego, isn't it? The desire to be segregated yet superior, to look down and see everything spread out beneath you. To be in the city but outside of it, and, of course, above it. All of which is a long-winded way of saying that I wanted some space, for myself and for my daughter.'

'So you're enjoying the seclusion?'

'So far, although I do keep a two-bed condo in the city, for when the silence gets too loud. It's another world up here.'

'I definitely see the appeal.'

'Where do you live?'

'In Echo Park.'

'Is that a safe neighbourhood these days? When I first moved to the city, back in the late eighties, it was kind of a warzone over there. Lot of gang violence.'

'Oh yeah, it's pretty gentrified now. They did this huge renovation on the lake there, the year before I moved in, and that's what convinced me. The cheap rent, too, but mostly it was the park. I used to live in West Hollywood and I was just miserable because—'

'There's nothing natural within a five-mile radius, right. And you're stuck in your car all day, driving from one concrete cage to another, never really seeing the world. LA can be hermetic.'

'I actually don't drive. Growing up in London, it just never occurred to me to learn.'

I don't know why I'm telling him this. This interview is not about me, and I try to remind myself that he is only flattering me by feigning interest.

'You don't drive?' He blinks at me. 'How long have you lived in Los Angeles?'

'Three years.'

He lets out a long, low whistle between his teeth.

'That might be a record. I'm not sure anyone's ever lasted that long in LA without a car. How on earth do you do it?'

'It's actually not as bad as you'd think. There's buses, and Uber.'

He nods, and I'm conscious that I haven't got a single usable quote from him in the last minute.

'So, can I ask you about some of the features of the house? What inspired you to finally get to the renovation, after all these years?'

Clark pauses, looks out into the canyon as if considering whether to answer.

'Well,' he begins, finally, speaking very deliberately. 'You may have heard that I went through a divorce last year. And any time a relationship comes to an end, I think it should force you to re-evaluate. For me, the re-evaluation came down to a realization that I want to be more present in my daughter's life, and more present in my own life. I know that it's become very faddy to talk about mindfulness, and meditation, but I cannot overstate how important it's been to me. So being out here in the canyon, up above the fray of it all, just felt like the right move.'

'But the house wasn't right before.'

'Yes, it was… It needed some love. That's how Jerome put it, and I think it's accurate. We didn't change much structurally, except that we added the separate wing for Skye. It was really more about knocking through some walls, turning two small rooms into one big, bright one, like in the living room.'

'Why the wraparound pool?'

'I wanted to see if it could be done.'

There's something about this attitude, the careless audacity of him, that's breathtaking. To do something simply to see if it is possible. This is power.

'Do you interview a lot of actors about their homes?'

'You're the first. Although I did a lot of research online about the craziest amenities that celebrities have built into their homes.'

'Oh, I know. Vitamin C-infused showers, private jet pads… that's a little much for me. The wraparound pool serves a purpose, you know. I thought about just building a little lap pool, which would have got the job done, but I have a strange pet peeve about having to turn around mid-lap. It always feels like slamming on the brakes to me.'

'Is swimming your workout of choice?'

'Yeah, I used to be a runner, but it's too tough on my knees now. I do the treadmill, but it's not really the same.'

I'm not here to ask him about his workout regimen, much as I want to reply by telling him how much I also love running, how much I also hate the treadmill, how alike we are in this respect. Don't make it about you, an editor's voice echoes in my head, from long ago. Don't try to impress them. Don't kid yourself into thinking you matter to them. An interview is a transaction, and that's it, even if sometimes it's well disguised as a regular conversation. I remember wondering, even then, if she was right or if she was simply bitter that she personally had never managed to make the transition from interview to real conversation.

'So, the wraparound pool is about 150 feet end-to-end, in this horse-shoe formation,' he continues, 'and you can really get a good sustained swim without having to stop. Once I get going, I don't want to stop unless I'm forced.'

'Just for swimming, or is that a general life philosophy?'

'Both.'

'You mentioned *Loner* before – I'm a huge fan of that show, by the way. You had your breakout role in television, back when TV was still considered sort of lesser than movies. That's completely changed now, and movie actors are going to TV in droves. Have you thought about going back?'

'Oh, sure, I'm always just looking to go where the good scripts are. I actually had a great meeting with Bob Fleischer at HBO a couple of weeks back, I'm looking at developing something over there – but don't print that, if you wouldn't mind, nothing's finalized.'

'Sure.'

'Television's in such an exciting phase right now, and a lot of the creative talents I worked with in movies ten years ago are now going over there, because TV is more willing to take risks. Or not even risks – just try things that aren't known quantities. The kinds of movies that I made when I was first starting out after *Loner*, your mid-budget dramas, your romances, those are all pretty much gone. Now if you're not making a multi-million-dollar blockbuster, you're making an indie, and most actors like to live somewhere in the middle ground.'

'You've made a lot of blockbusters, but never a superhero franchise. There are so many of them, you must have been offered roles, right?'

He shrugs.

'Sure, I've had conversations. I was actually in talks for one of the DC standalones, but I had to turn it down. There's a lot of strings attached there, and the idea of signing on for a six-movie commitment just doesn't appeal. Maybe because I feel as though I've already covered a lot of the superhero territory with *Loner*. I mean, that character wasn't a superhero, but he was this guy who wore his daytime face as a mask, and lived with a secret burden of responsibility.'

'Yeah, he was a vigilante, an orphan—' I nod, thrilled that he's validating my long-held theory about *Loner* as a superhero narrative.

'Driven to this fight for justice by this pain in his past, right – you really are a fan. And I always liked the idea that by day, he had to be this sort of hollow suit, and associate with these real high-powered New York scumbag types, because that's what power looks like in ordinary America, that was the kind of power his father had, and with that kind of power comes an almost unlimited capacity to get away with things. That show really tapped into things that I don't think it always gets credit for.'

'It was ahead of its time in a lot of ways,' I offer. 'I mean, the golden age of the TV antihero sort of arrived a few years after *Loner* ended, with *Mad Men* and *Breaking Bad* and all these narratives about deeply flawed men you kind of root for anyway.'

'Right. And because we were on a broadcast network, we were never going to have the freedom to go to quite the extremes we might have wanted to. But as I say, I'm enormously excited about where TV is right now, and I certainly hope to go back to the small screen if we can find the right character.'

'Would you ever consider doing a revival of *Loner*? Pretty much every nineties show is coming back at this point...' I trail off, as he's shaking his head.

'Absolutely not. This industry needs to learn how to let things lie. This constant drive to revive existing properties because there's theoretically a built-in audience, it's so short-sighted and so motivated by fear. We have to keep making new things, because at some point we are going to run out of things to revive.'

'Yeah, I think there's a lot of frustration about that.'

'It's a strange time to be an actor, you know, because the other thing that has happened over the past ten years or so is that actual acting talent, and training, has been steadily devalued. A young actress told me a story recently that has really haunted me: she went to audition for a role in something, I won't name the project but let's say it was something for a young adult audience, big money, an adaptation of a very popular book. She'd put herself on tape, gone through several callbacks, done a chemistry read with the male lead, and was down to something like the last four or five girls. And by the way, this young woman is going places – she's truly the real deal, she has got something electric. But she didn't get the part, and in confidence, the feedback her agent received was that her social media following wasn't as big as the other actresses'.'

I nod, thinking of Tom.

'Can you believe that? This young woman is, like I say, the real deal: Juilliard, off-Broadway theatre, years of well-regarded work on television and smaller pictures. Imagine being passed over for an acting job because you're not a social media... maven? What do they call that, someone with a huge following on all these platforms?'

'Oh, an influencer.'

'An influencer!' He snaps his fingers derisively. 'What a term. What a complete bastardization of a term.'

If I had the balls, I'd point out the irony of the fact that he's dating one of the most shameless 'influencers' in the business. But I suspect he has no idea what Amabella really does for a living; she probably lets him think she's still a struggling actress, lets him pay for everything while she's raking in millions in spon-con.

'Is the movie in production right now?' I ask, trying to figure out which YA adaptation he's referring to.

He side-eyes me with a wry smile.

'I'm not here to pick a fight with anyone. That's all I'll say, but that anecdote has really stayed with me, because it shows me what new actors are up against these days. If I'd had to impress casting agents with my following when I started out, there's no way I'd even have got in the door.'

'It feels so anathema to the old idea of a movie star, this very enigmatic, glamorous figure who was sort of unknowable by design.'

'Precisely. Maybe I'm just old school, but I don't believe that sharing the minutiae of your private life is helpful if you want the public to believe in you as a character. But I'm also not sure that some of these kids who are coming up now really care about playing characters. There's a difference, in this town, between people who want to create things and people who just want to be seen.'

'Every actor wants to be seen, though. Right?'

'Maybe,' he says, in a tone that suggests what he really means is no. 'I've personally always found a good character to be a fantastic place to hide. Giving a good performance is really the opposite of being seen.'

I swallow, but I have resolved to ask this.

'You said once, I think on *Inside the Actor's Studio*, that you started acting at a young age because you had experienced some loss. A lot of loss. And that you were drawn to *Loner* because you related to your character as an orphan.' I pause, watching his reaction closely, but he's unreadable. 'Has that early experience affected your idea of what home means? Or the way you approach making a home?'

He is silent, still impassive, and everything in me clenches.

'That's interesting,' he says at last, and I feel my shoulders sink in relief. 'I haven't really thought about it, but I suppose everything that happens to you, certainly before the age of ten or so, affects the kind of man you grow up to be. My parents' passing certainly unmoored me, to a degree, and ever since then I've lived a pretty rootless existence, as a lot of actors do – nomadic. I would say that with this renovation, my goal was to create a house for the first time

46

that really felt like a home, as opposed to a temporary base—'

'There you are!'

We both turn to see Peyton is pacing towards us with a fixed smile.

'This is unexpected,' she says, bright and terrifying. 'Jessica, I thought you knew the interview was due to start at 4.40.'

'My fault,' Clark says smoothly. 'I asked her if we could get started right away—I've gotta be out of here in a half-hour, something came up.'

'When did you get back?' she asks him, in a less accusatory tone than she used with me, more subservient.

'Just about twenty minutes ago.'

'Well, we need you downstairs for a few profile portraits. Jessica, you have what you need here?'

I open my mouth to say no, because I haven't got through even half of the questions on my notecards, but Clark answers before I can.

'Yeah, I think we're about done here, right?' Like a gut punch. That's it. One minute we were having a conversation, getting towards something real; the next it is over. A transaction.

'Absolutely. Thanks so much for your time.'

He shakes my outstretched hand but barely meets my gaze, his attention now elsewhere. I have made no impression on him, of course, and why would I have expected otherwise? This is a man accustomed to life among the stars, and one of his greatest skills is making ordinary people feel as though they might be able to know him.

He and Peyton walk ahead of me, and I let them go, busying myself with saving the interview recording to my iPhone, immediately emailing a copy to myself. I'm trying to retrace our conversation in my head, trying to identify a headline, but my thoughts are scattered and I can't process the fact that this interview is already over, that I assumed I would have more time, that I completely failed to follow Jackie's instructions and go in with a headline. I'm not even sure that I have an article.

'I'm just going outside to make a quick call,' I say to no one in particular when I get back downstairs, and head for the front door, away from the hum of activity in the back yard where Clark is now about to pose for a series of portraits by the pool. The sun is setting now, the winter sky almost purple over the canyon, and I breathe in deep to try to rouse myself back to reality, taking a few final notes on the front yard though I know that I already have more than enough details on the house.

The front yard extends further than I expected, and I find myself close to the perimeter of Skye's private patio, where the wraparound pool ends. I can only see glimpses of it through the hedge, the water that perfect chlorine colour that does not exist in nature, and there's a pink tinge creeping into the blue of the water, reflecting the sky.

I blink, look again, because those aren't sunset colours. Chlorine blue tinged pink, a flash of red on tile, and blonde hair. And suddenly there's a knot in my stomach and something thrills through me as I move, trying to find a better view, and finally there is a gap in the hedge large enough for me to see. Skye Conrad is lying on the steps of her pool in a beautiful one-piece cut-out swimsuit, the same one she was photographed wearing in Malibu with her squad, her hair spread out beneath her on the terracotta, and none of this is out of place except that her veins are open, and blood is flowing into the water from both her wrists.

5

For a while after I find her there is perfect silence, while I try to remember how to speak and imagine this situation as though I am outside of it, and somehow above it. It strikes me what an unbelievable story this would make if it were real, the starlet daughter of the beloved actor dying by suicide at the age of nineteen surrounded by a camera crew who had no idea she was there. I must watch her bleeding for a full minute before I make a sound.

One minute there's silence and the next there's chaos, and I realize distantly that I must have made noise, loudly enough for everyone to come running.

Everything seems fuzzy and when Justin asks me, 'What's going on?' I can't speak, but by now Jerome has seen the same thing that I saw through the hedge, has muttered 'Oh Jesus' under his breath and raced out of sight, around the hedge and towards the gate to Skye's patio, Clark a heartbeat behind him. Without thinking, I follow them and nobody stops me.

The gate hangs open, creaking just slightly against the force of the evening breeze, and the sun has slipped below the horizon leaving everything in a dusky soft focus. It's almost too dark now to see the blood in the water, but on the tile it is unmistakable, pooling beneath her now she has been dragged fully out of the water as Jerome applies pressure to both her wrists. Beside her Clark looks folded in on himself, clutching her head in his hands, silent.

'Is she—' I ask, but no one is listening. Behind me I hear Peyton's voice shuddering as she speaks to 911, trying not to give away Skye's identity or Clark's, telling them only that a nineteen-year-old has been hurt badly. Has hurt herself badly.

'What are you doing?' Tanya hisses at my side, her hand tight on my shoulder, dragging me away from the gate. I shake her off, but she's right of course. This is not mine, this thing that I stumbled onto, however much it feels that way.

We stand in silence after that, not looking at each other, not looking back towards the gate, intruders in someone else's home witnessing the worst moment that will ever take place here, a point of no return for this family. We should not be here, but by leaving we would only draw more attention to ourselves, and so we stay as still as possible. I pull out my phone on reflex, eager to look busy, but quickly realize that it looks even worse to be thumbing through Twitter at this moment and so my phone stays in my hand, held at my side like a talisman. I strain to hear the paramedics but they're too far away, and when they whisk Skye and Clark and Jerome away in an ambulance we all look away, modestly.

'You all need to go,' Peyton says, waving us towards the house, but Tanya and Chloe are already emerging from the front door with their equipment in tow, ready to leave.

As we're driving away the first news trucks pass us in the opposite direction, somehow already tipped off, racing to stake their spots outside Clark's house.

'Do you think she's dead?' I ask, knowing that nobody has the answer, and that someone will try nevertheless.

'Didn't look good,' Justin replies. 'I heard one of the EMTs say he couldn't get a pulse.'

'God.'

'She had to know there was press there, right? She did it on purpose,' Chloe pipes up, gratingly loud.

'I don't know,' I reply. 'Her patio is pretty hidden away, I don't think anybody would have noticed if I hadn't—'

'She was bleeding into the wraparound pool.' Nick, the photographer, speaks for the first time. 'Right? She was hoping to bleed enough for it to spread through the water all the way around to the back yard, fuck up the photographs.'

None of us can think of anything to say in response to this. It seems absurd, and yet not.

'TMZ already has it,' Justin says, lifting up his phone to show me the tweet. 'Story Developing.'

'Of course. They have a source at the hospital, probably more than one.'

I tune them out after this, only dimly aware that they're still talking. My thoughts are consumed by Clark now, by the unimaginable pain he has to be feeling, by the possibility that he has already lost his daughter, suddenly and violently just like he lost his parents. There's a physical ache in my chest at the thought of him, riding beside her in the ambulance and clutching her hand, maybe praying, maybe sobbing, maybe silent. There are so many images of him in my head in extremis, every emotional conclusion played out on-screen in one scene or another: his long-building mental breakdown in the third season of *Loner*, his violent temper in the gangster movie *Fall Guy*, his quiet vulnerability in every role. I want to be more present in my daughter's life, he said to me, barely two hours ago, and now what?

'What if they need me for something?' I whisper to Justin. 'Huh?'

'Like, what if the police want to talk to me? Don't they have to investigate, with something like this?'

'I don't think there's a lot of ambiguity about what happened.'

Already I'm casting myself in a role within this drama – the key witness, the one who found her – but even if the cops get involved, I have nothing of value to tell them. I saw what everybody else saw, only first.

It takes us less time than I expect to reach the office, and once we're all piled out onto the sidewalk the banality of everything sinks back into me, the impossibility of returning to normal now. The others all disperse too quickly, almost without a goodbye, with no acknowledgement of what we have all just witnessed.

I want to ask Justin to come and have a drink with me, but we haven't yet reached that stage of colleague friendship where spending time together outside of work becomes a given, and I don't have it in me to breach the divide now.

So I smile and wave to him as he leaves to meet someone, probably his boyfriend, probably someone with whom he can share.

'You gonna be all right?' he asks, half-distracted.

'For sure. Have a good night,' I say with a smile. And he's gone.

This is one of those rare times that I have not accounted for, the times on dark winter nights when my own solitude closes in and I haven't buried myself in enough work to stave it off. I'm busy enough that my lack of true friends is easy to mask. There are always publicists to network with, acquaintances to sit with at screenings, events where I can get through the night on small talk. I made poor choices in friends when I first moved to LA; most of the fellow expats I knew back then have either switched coasts for New York or given up on the American Dream altogether, ground down by the striving and the competition and the endless hidden costs of everything.

I go to a bar alone, a generic hole in the wall with drinks too expensive to qualify as a dive, and of course the saga is already unfolding on the TV screen above the bar.

'Tonight's top story: Skye Conrad has been taken to hospital following a 911 call from her father's residence. Early reports say she's in critical condition following an apparent suicide attempt. We'll have more updates on this story for you as they come in.'

But in lieu of more updates, the network goes into what already feels queasily like an obituary, describing Skye's upbringing in Beverly Hills, her modelling stints for Urban Outfitters and American Eagle, her admission to USC after graduating high school, and then her decision – announced on social media – to drop out of college before the end of her freshman year, and take the time to 'figure herself out'. The newscaster reads out her last Instagram post, sent at 3.31 a.m. – 'Let's just be wild while we're young', alongside a selfie of her and two models I dimly recognize, all of them making exaggerated kiss-faces at the camera. They look glossy and vicious and invincible.

'Pretty awful, right?' the barman says, watching me watch the TV. 'Super nice guy.'

'You know him?'

'I do a little body double work.' Of course he does. Everybody in LA has a second job in the industry. 'Worked on *The Tie-Breaker*, so I got to meet him a few times. Super, super genuine.'

I nod. Everybody says the same, and my fifteen minutes with him today did nothing to make me inclined to disagree.

'The daughter's a hot mess, though,' the barman continues, now addressing me and three other solo patrons who have all looked up from their drinks, thirsty for insider gossip. 'I heard she OD'd.'

I don't contradict him. Quietly, I reach into my bag and start my digital recorder, without entirely knowing why.

'Did you ever meet her?' I ask him.

'Oh yeah,' he replies with a nasty laugh. 'Yeah. I used to work at the Chateau doing valet parking, and everybody hated her. She literally threw her car keys at me, and she never tipped a cent. One time, she had a full meltdown in the bar and broke a bunch of glasses – and apparently, I wasn't there, but apparently Clark showed up the next day and wrote a cheque for everything, personally apologized to the staff. She chilled out after that.'

'Aren't you meant to keep everything that happens at the Chateau a secret? Code of discretion, and all that?' I ask mildly, with just enough of a smile to show that I'm not actually judging him. In fact, I'm taking notes on my phone in case I can use any of this on background one day.

'Yeah, well, that's why I *used* to work there.'

Once he finally gets called away to serve other customers, I scroll through Twitter to get a sense of people's reactions: mostly sympathy, some snark. Several outlets are already running with 'overdose' in their headlines regardless of the truth, which leads me to wonder if somebody at the hospital is deliberately feeding out a false story. More likely, Skye's reputation precedes her.

I stop breathing for a second when I see the headline. 'Skye Conrad Dead At 19', but it's a screen grab of an article that has already been deleted. A mistake. Somebody at that outlet is getting fired, but was it really a mistake? Maybe that reporter had a source nobody else did.

I can't stay asleep for more than an hour at a time that night, the alcohol and the anxiety jolting me, and so I refresh my feed at two and three and four and five in the morning, seeing if she is still breathing. I dream of her in a hospital bed, her hair a frantic halo, not a spot of blood anywhere on her.

By the next morning there is still no new news, only endless filler from outlets desperate to cash in on this opportunity for clicks – galleries showing Skye's progression on the red carpet from adorable child to awkward tween to racoon-eyed socialite, articles speculating about her relationship with Brett Rickards – did he dump her? Did she cheat on him? Did he give her the drugs she overdosed on? I never thought I'd feel bad for Brett, but that was before I saw the photographs of him dashing from his car into the hospital late last night, trying to hide his face from the cameras, perhaps for privacy or perhaps because he is clearly crying. He's even younger than her.

The office feels cold and far away to me when I arrive, but it's not until I'm almost at my desk that I realize why it's so empty. It's Saturday. The bus took longer to come than usual, the roads were so much emptier than usual, but none of this registered with me. I have nowhere else to be, and so I end up staying to transcribe my interview with Clark, forcing myself to simply type without engaging with the memory. Partway through my cellphone rings, a number I don't recognize. This has to be it. This has to be news.

'Jessica, hi, it's Jackie.'

'Hi!'

'Sorry to call you so early on a Saturday.'

'No, it's fine, I'm actually—' I cut myself off before telling her I'm in the office. It's weird. 'Just doing some work anyway.'

'I just wanted to touch base, obviously, and see how you're doing.'

'I'm fine.'

'I'm sure yesterday must have been disturbing.'

'Yeah, it was.'

'Tanya spoke to the publicist this morning, and it doesn't sound like there's anything conclusive yet on how she's doing.'

'There was a lot of blood.' I say this without realizing that I'm going to. 'I don't know if...'

I can't remember whether the cuts on her wrists were vertical or horizontal. How could I forget a detail this important? Already the mental image I have of the scene has been corrupted, fading a little more every time I bring it to the surface. If the cuts were vertical, opening a vein, then surely she would not have survived the night.

Jackie sighs.

'I can't imagine how jarring that must have been. You'd already completed the interview before this happened, yes?'

'Yeah, I did, but I got even less than twenty minutes. It was all a little messed up, we sort of started early and then finished early – the relationship between Clark and his publicist seemed a little off.' Then, realizing that I sound like I'm making excuses, I add, 'But I got some really great stuff. He was very open, he talked about his work, he brought up the divorce, some of his frustrations with the industry...'

'That's good.' Jackie's tone suggests otherwise. 'But we're in a delicate situation now given what's happened. Tanya obviously didn't push on this too much when she spoke with the publicist today, but it doesn't sound likely that we can move forward. I want you to transcribe your interview and your notes, and then I want you to prepare for the very real possibility that we'll have to spike the piece.'

'Really?' This isn't a surprise, not rationally, but the idea of yesterday being all for nothing is impossible. 'I mean, I understand. It's just…' I trail off, because there's no way of saying 'wasted opportunity' in this situation without sounding monstrous.

'I know it's frustrating. But we can't afford to look tasteless, or like we're cashing in on tabloid gossip. It will seriously impact our reputation and our ability to get access in the future, and I just don't see a version of this piece that wouldn't look tacky, even if we just run it as a house gallery.'

'What if I could get a follow-up with him?'

'What?'

'Obviously, if Skye survives. If she's okay. What if I could get him to acknowledge it, incorporate it into the piece in some way?'

She is silent for a long beat.

'What makes you think that's a possibility?'

'I don't know. He talked about her during the interview, how he wanted to be more present in her life. He built this whole additional section on the house just so that she could have privacy.'

'And she tried to kill herself there,' Jackie says. 'This is not a decor story any more. There's no version of this that we can run on Nest.'

I keep forgetting what site I'm writing for.

'Right. And it's not like I can take this elsewhere, because—'

'Because he granted the interview to us, and we own it,' she interrupts, sharply.

'Of course.'

'Look, if you can persuade him to do a follow-up, let's talk then.' Every syllable laced with scepticism. 'But for now,

I would transcribe your interview, type up all your notes, and then try to forget about this for the weekend. Take a hike. Get some air. Take care of yourself. All right?'

She might be genuinely concerned, but it's hard to tell beneath all the patronizing. I don't even know what I'm arguing for – I don't want to write this story for Nest. I don't want to pad out Clark's quotes with colour description of his house and quotes from Jerome about the finishings. I don't know exactly what story I want to write, but that's not it.

'Okay. Thanks, Jackie.'

She is almost certainly right. Two realities co-exist in my mind now more or less harmoniously: one reality in which I'm delusional, an idiot attaching significance to an encounter Clark will already have forgotten, scarcely better than those red carpet fans who weep over a two-second glance from their favourite. The other reality is one in which Clark and I shared something, something genuine and rare that will endure, and that will force me back into his memory no matter what happens next.

During the endless bus ride home along Sunset, I choose the latter reality.

6

I need a new story.

This becomes clear to me three days after the interview, the Monday, when at four-forty in the afternoon it's growing dark and I realize I have accomplished nothing. There are two galleries due up on the site tomorrow which I haven't started. Everything since the canyon feels irrelevant, laughably so, but I only have three weeks left at Nest and I can't afford to slip now. I need to use this as a springboard to something else.

Skye will live. The cuts on her arms were horizontal, the blood loss severe but not fatal, and now a throng of reporters and paparazzi have set up permanent residence outside the hospital, accosting everyone who emerges on the off-chance that they know something or have seen something.

I saw him for the first time in pictures, emerging from the hospital on Saturday evening looking shattered, his eyes bloodshot and his gait hunched like he'd aged twenty years in as many hours. He seemed smaller, and though I loathed myself for it I couldn't resist watching the twenty-seven-second video clip of him, lit up by camera flashes as he darted from the hospital doors alone, trying half-heartedly to shield his face. It was his ears that needed shielding as they peppered questions at him like rifle fire, trying to get a rise.

'Clark! How's Skye? Is she alive?'

'Mr Conrad, was this a suicide attempt?'

'Was it because of the divorce? Are you in touch with Carol?'

'Any comment on the nude photo leak?'

This story has been around for weeks, as it turns out, but through some kind of wilful ignorance I had managed to avoid it until after that Friday, when I really began Googling Skye. There are supposedly nude pictures of Skye online, barred from publication by any legitimate outlet but still easily available for anyone with rudimentary knowledge of the internet's darker corners. Pictures allegedly taken by Brett Rickards, the creep I actually let myself feel sorry for the other day. His team issued a denial, of course, but there's no real doubt that it's him. Given too much wealth and privilege, too young, he now sees women as just slightly less than human, as something to be consumed.

I'm less interested in the pictures than in the other new development, which is that Carol and Sarah haven't been seen at the hospital once. Initially it was speculated that they were using a secret side entrance to avoid the cameras, but then candid photographs emerged of them in New York: Sarah buying coffee in Washington Square before her day starts at NYU, Carol leaving a yoga class in Brooklyn, the two of them attending a Broadway premiere together. Up until now they have avoided being photographed, which suggests that they've started calling the paparazzi. Whether deliberately or not, these photographs spell out a clear message of lack of interest in Skye, and now all the questions I failed to ask Clark are deafening in my mind.

I've been ignoring Tom's texts for the past three days. He wants to know, of course, what happened at the house and how much of this unravelling scandal I witnessed first hand. But I've barely processed the thing myself yet, and the idea of describing it to him is draining.

The person I did not ignore when they texted, desperate for dirt, is my sort-of-friend Faye, who I met on a red carpet my very first month in LA. It was an unspeakably hot and shadeless afternoon, my first real (though unpaid) assignment as a film blogger in the city, and though she was a fan who had somehow lied her way into the press pen, we felt like equals. She was there simply to see stars up close, to gather their autographs and take selfies so as to have permanent proof that she was physically in their presence, and though I was there as an ostensible professional our goal was the same. To get close. To get almost inside.

The film was an early spring release; a blockbuster planned as a tentpole release until the first test screenings made it clear that this was not a crowd-pleaser. March is not called 'the dead zone' in film release parlance for nothing – it's after awards season and before summer blockbuster season, a no-man's-land of mediocre money-pits and misunderstood indie gems. But both Faye and I were there to meet the same actor, a curly-haired former Broadway star who was the lead in a cable drama we were both obsessed with, and in that first conversation I could tell that we shared something. The need to cling a little too hard to fiction.

It's like waiting for a fever to pass, the feeling of being truly enmeshed in a fictional world, so overwhelmed with it that reality is grey and small by comparison. All you can do in the throes of it is wait it out, distract yourself, do things that force you to be physically in your body. As dissimilar as we are in every other respect, Faye is one of the few people I have ever met who understands this.

I give up on getting anything done at 5 p.m., and head out into the too-dark night though it's too early to be seen leaving. I need to rediscover the part of myself that cared about impressing people here.

'Hey, love!' Faye is an explosion of curly bottle-blonde, her voice high and always childlike, but I'm warmed by how genuinely thrilled she seems to see me, how tightly she hugs me. How she hesitates for a second, but does not say the most predictable thing: you look tired. I do. I couldn't sleep last night, and when the jittery feeling of lying in bed trying to force myself unconscious finally became unbearable, I turned instead to Netflix and lost myself in him.

'You need to tell me every single thing that happened on Friday,' Faye almost yells, once we're seated on a low couch with twin Cosmos in hand. So I tell her, realizing as I do that this is the first time I've really laid it all out and tried to make sense of it for someone else.

'Wait,' she interrupts when I'm almost to the pool. 'It sounds like you got a legit amazing interview with him. Like, I've never read anything where he got this personal.'

'Yeah, it was going really well until his publicist showed up!'

'Stitch that on a cushion, honestly,' she says, clinking her glass against mine. 'It sounds to me like he was enjoying talking to you, just as people, but then his publicist showed up and turned it back into a work thing.'

'Maybe.' I can't stop the corner of my mouth from turning upwards.

'Anyway, sorry, go on.'

I tell her the rest, now distracted by the memory of just how good that interview actually was, and watch Faye's eyes gradually widen as the story reaches its climax.

'Have you heard anything since? Like, has anyone kept you in the loop?'

'God, no. I'm just reading the same as you online.'

'The poor guy,' she sighs. 'So he was as nice as everybody says?'

'Yeah, he was just... normal. He didn't act like he was one of the most famous people in the world and I was a pleb being graced with his presence.' I take a hard sip of my drink. 'But I mean, it doesn't matter. Nobody's ever going to read the interview because Nest is never going to run anything that actually risks being newsworthy.'

'Burn,' Faye purrs. 'I mean, just take the story somewhere else if they're too basic to run it.'

'I don't think I can do that. He and his publicist agreed to Nest specifically, because it's fluff.'

'And? You're sitting on a goldmine here – I mean, Clark Conrad's last interview before his daughter's suicide attempt? Are you kidding? Who cares what the editor of Nest thinks of you once you get that published?'

'Yeah, but I also don't want to…' I stop.

'You don't want to piss him off,' Faye finishes for me.

'I mean, he just almost lost his daughter. It's traumatic enough without some reporter trying to milk it. And who knows when he might be useful to me in the future? It's not worth it.'

'Fair.'

'I do need something, though. A story that's industry-focused, something I can pitch to actual culture editors and be taken seriously.'

'Does it have to be an actor? I mean, obviously that's the most fun, but would you consider something with a producer or an exec?'

'Sure. That might actually be better, because I need to get a foot in the door at Reel. Why, do you have something?'

'You know Ben Schlattman is leaving Scion?'

The Schlattman brothers are two of the most powerful producers in the industry, but their company has been struggling for years, losing money – haemorrhaging, by some accounts – on a series of high-budget gambles which only just broke even. But the brothers' power is in combination; they come as a unit, a one-two punch. I've heard them referred to as good cop-bad cop, Ben the charmer who reels you in, and Bill the hard-nosed tycoon who comes in at the end to make the deal.

'Wait, really? I thought that was just a rumour.'

'Nope, it's real, he wants to go out on his own. They had a blowout, I guess. He plays golf with my uncle,' Faye continues casually. 'I can get you his email address, if you want to ask for an interview. He's kind of a nightmare, but—'

'That's perfect.'

I order us another round, already feeling less adrift, imagining my Q&A with Ben Schlattman as the lead story on Reel.com, maybe even a page in the print edition.

'Wait, I can't believe I didn't ask you this before,' Faye exclaims, clutching my arm. 'Was Amabella Bunch there? Clark's still dating her, right?'

I nod with a grimace. Amabella has been by Clark's side in every photograph coming or going from the hospital, looking directly at the cameras with a practised smoulder as he shielded his face beside her.

'She wasn't at the house, and he didn't mention her. But I had to write a post about her this morning, actually.'

'Ugh, you're still doing those 4 a.m. news shifts?'

'It's just for this month. Probably.'

'They've gotta be paying you enough at Nest that you don't need to take this extra stuff.'

'Barely.'

'You're a workaholic.'

I smile. People say this as though it's a bad thing.

'I mean, having to write about Amabella's "hashtag fitspo" post this morning definitely gave me second thoughts about carrying on.'

'She is always doing the most. I don't know how much that raw food brand pays her to shill for them, but her Instagram is fifty per cent sponsored content at this point.'

'They pay her a lot,' I reply. 'And I mean, fair enough – if you have no discernible talent except taking selfies you've got to hustle.'

'Your burns are on point tonight.'

'I'm sorry, I'm actually being unfair to Amabella. After all, she did have a supporting role in that YouTube original drama series last year, the one where she played the cheerleader who got eaten. That was a pretty nuanced part.'

'She has her own lifestyle brand now too, and a fragrance, because of course. Also, I don't want to be slut-shamey, but—' Faye lowers her voice conspiratorially. 'She was married to that Silicon Valley guy for, what, four months? Are they even divorced yet?'

I shrug. This is an aspect of Clark I simply do not want to know any more about, the part of him that sees any value in Amabella Bunch. The man I met would see through her right away, especially given his distrust of influencers, but maybe she's a better actress than I'm giving her credit for.

'She's garbage,' is all I say to Faye, with a smile.

Back at my apartment, another roach corpse awaits me in the kitchen, and I suppose I should feel blessed that they're always dead now when I see them. The exterminator warned me this might happen – 'It's the chemicals, dries 'em out, draws 'em into the open to die' – but the sight of them still jars me so violently I have to soothe myself afterwards with a shot of whiskey. And, of course, with *Loner*.

This is how I spend my evenings, now. Watching him, one episode after another after another, murmuring the dialogue under my breath as I cook, exercise, clean my apartment. As

I sleep too, probably. Once it finally begins to sink in that I may not see him again, that my Friday afternoon at the Laurel Canyon house will soon start to feel like a memory, I have to hold on somehow. This is how I used to feel close to him.

7

When I tell people what I do for a living, they sometimes get a fervent gleam in their eyes, as though I can unlock something for them. Who's the most famous person you've ever interviewed? they ask. Do you get to go to premieres? What's it really like on a film set? And sometimes I enjoy it, their awe bringing back a spark in me that's been ground out over the years, a reminder that this really is a dream job. Other times, I force a smile and wish I could be honest about how unglamorous the whole business really is.

A case in point, tonight. I am going to the Golden Globes. The unofficial beginning of awards season, one of the few ceremonies that celebrates both movie and TV stars in one evening. Half of the most famous people you can name will be there, either as previous winners or current nominees or presenters. I've spent close to three hours getting ready, which is so foreign that it's warped my entire sense of time. I rented a dress, the kind of full-length gown I have no reason ever to own, and it's so tight around my hips and waist that

I had to practise sitting down. I watched a YouTube tutorial on cat-eye makeup and followed it to the letter, and will now spend the entire night paranoid that the liquid liner will run. I went to the salon that only does blow-dries, and got my hair polished and smoothed and twisted into an intricate up-do that required forty-seven pins to secure. I don't understand the mechanics of it, nor how I will undo it later, but all that matters is that it looks sleek and will require no maintenance from me through the evening.

This is my first time at the Globes, and though I won't have a seat at the actual ceremony, I am covering the red carpet, and then the backstage press room, and then the afterparty, assuming Ben Schlattman was serious. He emailed me back within an hour, responding to my three-paragraph interview query with a single lower-case line: 'sure. come find me after the globes. will put you on the list.' The Scion afterparty is not an easy ticket to get, so this in itself seems hard to fathom. But all of this depends on whether I can even get near the building.

My Uber driver has been attempting to drop me off for the last fifteen minutes, only to be blocked at every turn by men in high-visibility vests waving him onwards and yelling 'No stopping!' The Beverly Hilton is a fortress at the best of times, a nightmare labyrinth of driveways nestled at the intersection of Santa Monica and Wilshire boulevards, and now even the actual entrance is cordoned off, the entire complex reworked and lined with impenetrable security.

My driver looks expectantly back at me, as though I might have a solution to our quandary. As though I have any idea what I'm doing. I'm anxious already, my chest tightening, and I hold in my next inhale for several beats before slowly letting it out. 4-7-8, inhale, hold, exhale. You've got this.

'You can just let me out wherever there's a place to stop,' I tell the driver, ready for this ride to be over. 'I'll figure it out.'

He gestures to our left as we crawl up Wilshire, pointing out a gas station, and I try to suppress a laugh at the perfect anticlimax of this. I clamber ungracefully out of the backseat into the parking lot, restrained by my gown, and walk from the gas station to the red carpet. No one in the parking lot so much as looks twice at me, and I think maybe I'm not the first.

I'm waved inside by an unsmiling security guy once I flash my purple MEDIA lanyard at him, and walk cautiously onto the red carpet as though there might be a tripwire waiting. I keep expecting to be stopped, maybe searched, maybe told that I'm going the wrong way or maybe simply turfed out because I so clearly do not belong here. But nobody gives me a second glance, and as I reach the press pen I realize just how early I am.

My spot is at the lousy middle section of the carpet, sandwiched between a newswire organization and a blog from Germany I've never heard of, and I shoot off a quick email to my editor warning her to lower her expectations. Every carpet has its own kind of internal logic, and it's always a waste of time trying to figure out whether being near the entrance is a good or a bad thing, but being this far from either the start or the end of a very long carpet is not auspicious. I'll be lucky if I get three interviews out of this, and even luckier if they're with anyone who matters.

The pens are still an hour away from being locked down, and so I take a walk all the way to the glossy end of the carpet, the feted place where the major trades and the TV networks are positioned. Rectangular shrubs are lined up to form a hedge around the perimeter, interspersed with golden blocks that read 'Golden Globe Awards', as though anyone could possibly forget where they were.

Way up at the other end of the carpet is the public pen, the place where onlookers and fans can gather to wave autograph pads and memorabilia and scream for their favourites, hoping for a few precious seconds in their orbit. I move closer, pretending to be absorbed in my phone, until I can hear their conversations, overlapping and frantic.

'Do you think she'll sign a DVD?'

'I heard he's only doing the step-and-repeat and then they're going right inside, but if he sees our sign—'

'We're in a good spot right here, everyone has to come past us, I think we have a really good shot of him coming over.'

'I heard she's really weird about selfies, but I want that so much more than an autograph, like who even cares about a scribble on some paper?'

'I just want him to see the sign, honestly, like even if he doesn't come over at least he'll know we're thinking of him.'

I glance over at the girls discussing their sign, and my suspicions are confirmed; they're here for Clark. 'WE LOVE YOU, CLARK' blares their homemade sign in black and gold, a red crayon heart in place of the O, and a part of me wants to forsake my spot in the press pen and join them.

Finally, the process begins. Celebrities are dropped off by limos and SUVs in a holding pen, from where they are escorted down the carpet for a procession of carefully scheduled photo ops and interviews, and the whole thing becomes a blur of tuxedos and satin and shimmery makeup. The German blogger next to me turns out to be a stunning blonde who has brought a cameraman with her, and tries to position herself on the carpet with a microphone until a security guard sternly tells her, 'You're not approved for on-carpet, ma'am, please walk back behind the barrier.' Her name is Hilda, and Hilda eventually proves herself useful because she has no shame in screaming out the names of every celebrity who passes, openly begging them to come over and speak to her. And I, meek opportunist that I am, get to ride on her coat-tails with the few that do come over.

Thanks to Hilda, I speak to a former leading actress from a network drama about her character's unexpected recent death, and to the writer of an indie movie which broke out at this year's Sundance. Most excitingly for me, I speak to the producer of Clark's Neil Armstrong biopic, and get a few quotes on his performance which I can use as supporting colour for the profile I still want to write.

But soon, the carpet is too full for us to get anyone's attention. There's something uniquely bizarre about watching some of the most famous people in the world being herded along like cattle, in a space that's rapidly proving itself too narrow. I'm getting claustrophobic just watching, and now a cluster of publicists is making it impossible for anyone to stop for us even if they wanted to.

'This is a fucking nightmare,' I hear one hiss, seemingly unaware or uncaring that she's within earshot of the press. Over their heads, I see two first-time Best Supporting Actress nominees being shepherded towards the doors by their handlers, arms linked as though they're afraid to let go of one another. I can't blame them. I'm trying to look out for Clark but it's pointless, the carpet now six-deep as everyone rushes to get inside in time for the 5 p.m. show start time, and he probably came as late as possible on purpose, the better to keep his head down and avoid the cameras. He might even have been sneaked in early, or through a side entrance.

Every time I cover a red carpet, I swear to myself it's my last – they're a relic, a throwback to a bygone time when there weren't thousands of online outlets scrabbling for the same access, and a time when stars weren't media-trained to the point of being useless. But I'm nowhere close to the point in my career where I have the luxury of opting out.

Though I picked the lowest pair of heels I could find, the balls of my feet are still killing me, and I'm grateful to find actual seating in the backstage press area, along with a full buffet – salads, charcuterie, two kinds of pasta, a wan-looking cheese plate. I haven't eaten all day, and if I thought about it for long enough I would probably be hungry, but I also haven't been able to work out in days and so I limit myself to Diet Coke and a few kale chips before hurrying in to reserve a spot in the winners' room.

When you win a Golden Globe, you pay the immediate price of being led backstage into this cavernous ballroom where a seated throng of journalists will ask you basic-yet-confusing questions, and your responses will be filmed and uploaded to the internet for immediate dissection. Everyone in this room is hoping, on some level, that at least one winner says something controversial enough to become a story, and to justify all of our being here. It's always possible, too, that someone will make an inspirational speech. The two major currencies of the internet: outrage and joy.

Two hours later, and not a single newsworthy thing has happened in this room. The winners have emerged and given earnest responses to earnest questions, and confused responses to confused ones. The word 'blessed' has dropped dead from overuse. 'What's the first thing you're going to do when you get home tonight?' is a question that keeps being asked, along with, of course, 'Where are you going to put your Golden Globe?' I know I should have the balls to get the mic myself and ask a question, instead of just complaining inwardly to myself about how stupid other people's are, but I'm exhausted and distracted and have no clear assignment here. And Clark, in what's already being described as a 'shock upset', did not win Best Actor in a Drama.

Armstrong was beaten in every major category by a lavish historical romance called *Idyllwilde*, whose poster is laden with quotes calling it 'stirring' and 'heartbreaking'. I found it neither, but its heavy-handed script and showy lead performance are pure awards bait, and though most pundits had predicted a win for Clark and for *Armstrong*, *Idyllwilde* sneaking in has always been a possibility. I try to keep the resentment off my face as the lead actor fields press questions, his answers more smug and contemptuously boring than the average. The only good news here, from my perspective, is that *Idyllwilde* is a Scion production, and so its unexpected Globes triumph throws Schlattman's departure into an even more newsworthy light.

I deliberately kill a little extra time once the ceremony winds down and the last press call is over, so as not to arrive at the afterparty too early. This hotel is not so much a hotel as a complex, housing multiple restaurants and bars and ballrooms which allow most of the various Globes afterparties to take place just steps from the main event. As ever, the real party is the after-afterparty; these do not involve lists or RSVPs and most certainly do not involve journalists. Their locations are secret, usually the home of a celebrity or a discreet private room at the kind of club that knows how to protect its patrons' privacy. Faye somehow got herself into an after-afterparty for last year's Grammys, held at an unidentified millionaire's house in Bel Air, but as far as I can tell she spent most of the evening taking surreptitious selfies and failing to inject herself into conversations between famous friends.

The Scion party is inside one of the hotel's many ballrooms, its dated seventies carpet and beige vibe transformed by lilac-hued lights and candles and champagne flutes into something that feels exclusive. The women here are all lithe and polished and radiant, the men neat and broad beside them, the collective angles of everyone's cheekbones exhausting. The un-chosen few among us are easily discernible, the journalists and publicists and assistants who made it in here as accessories, necessary addenda to the glowing, shining core of this town.

And of course, I know nobody at this party. Except, I suppose, Ben Schlattman, who really did come through and put my name on the list but is nowhere to be found inside. I'm not even convinced that I remember what he looks like, and pull up his face on my phone to be sure before accepting my first glass of champagne from a passing waiter. Then a second. Three is usually the number it takes for me to feel capable of striking up a conversation with strangers, and so I sip my third glass while looping the room, glancing casually from one side to the other as though searching for my companions. Keep moving. This is the most important rule I've learned from years of covering these things alone; don't stay still for too long, don't hover for long enough to make it obvious, don't look desperate.

On my third loop, I finally accept that nobody I know is going to spring out magically from behind a decorative plant to save me. But Melody Harmon is here, the rising star now turned Best Supporting Actress winner, and she's engaged in a conversation that looks non-committal enough for me to cut in.

'Excuse me, Melody?' I ask smoothly, what I think is smoothly, and she turns to me with a sculpted eyebrow barely raised. I remind myself that she's hardly a star, that before this Globe nomination she was recurring on a CBS sitcom, that she's the same age as me and I do not need to be intimidated by her. 'I'm a reporter with Reel, could I ask you a couple of questions?'

She blinks at me, almost smiling.

'No,' she says, then, 'Sorry,' in a tone that suggests that she's only sorry our paths crossed to begin with. And then she is gone, her golden dress a blink in the distance as she shoots away to tell, presumably, everyone else at this party to stay away from me.

I spend the next several minutes in line for the bar, the better to face forwards. If my skin were capable of turning any colour but alabaster, it would be flushed. On my way back, an Old Fashioned in either hand (the line was long and I'm planning ahead), every eye that catches mine feels accusatory, every glare confirming that word has already spread around the entire room. Melody knows everyone here, inevitably, and maybe it's bad form to chase interviews at an awards afterparty, maybe these events do not work like most of the industry parties I've attended. Maybe I've breached some invisible but sacred line, my indiscretion solidifying the fact that I do not belong here.

I get a wall at my back and pretend to be texting frantically, then realize there's an actual text I should be answering. Today marked Tom's fourth unanswered message, this one tinged with an unmistakable, understandable passive-aggression. 'Got some big news... call me if you ever get time. T x.' Right after I've sent off my long-delayed response promising to call Tom in the morning, I spot Ben Schlattman, his face newly clear in my mind. He's in a roped-off VIP area of this VIP party, and as I move towards the rope my path is blocked by a security guard.

'Miss, this is—'

'Mr Schlattman?' I say loudly, and he looks over, as do the three people he's surrounded by. Two power producers in suits, a pinched older actress I recognize from *Idyllwilde*. He's bigger in person than I imagined, both taller and wider, his thinning hair slicked back and beard trimmed short, his suit clearly tailored yet somehow slightly too small. 'I'm Jessica Harris, with Reel. Faye's friend, you—'

He nods, waves me over with a quick nod to the security guard, and the rope is pulled back for me.

'Congratulations,' I tell him as I shake his hand. 'Five Globes, not a bad omen for the rest of awards season.'

'Did you like the picture?' he asks, and I barely hesitate.

'I did, very much.'

'So you're not one of those reporters calling it "hackneyed" and "obvious" and "the easy choice"?' His tone is light, even jovial, but something in his eyes makes me suspect he's serious.

'It wasn't my favourite of this year,' I allow. There's no point in lying more than necessary. 'But I thought it was elegantly made and told a powerful story well. The cinematography was stunning.'

'Roger's a gem.' He nods. 'All right. Not your favourite, but powerful. I'll allow it.'

I laugh, a little too loudly, and let him introduce me to his three companions, all of them feigning interest when he tells them I'm a reporter.

'I thought about being a reporter,' the younger of the two producers tells me.

'Really?'

'Yeah, back when I started out I thought I was gonna be a newspaperman, dig up scandals in Washington, speak truth to power, all that stuff. I was in the mail room at the *Post*, and then the copy desk for a while.'

'Why did you give it up?' I ask.

'Too much work for not enough money,' Schlattman answers for him. 'Toby straightened out his priorities along with the rest of us.'

'Smart move, I can attest,' I say ruefully, and raise my glass in a mock-toast.

'Do you love it?' the producer asks me, as the other two drift away to join a more compelling circle. 'Reporting?'

'I love writing,' I say honestly. 'Using words to try to get at the truth about somebody, or something. I'm not sure I love reporting in the same way, but you have to do the one to get to the other.'

'Not if you're a critic. Then you just get to watch the movies, churn out a few hundred words, pass judgement without having to create anything of your own...'

'Toby's still sour from his last round of reviews,' Schlattman murmurs, and Toby grimaces. His last project, I think, was *Only the Good*, a neo-western blockbuster which got savaged upon its debut at Cannes, drawing boos and walk-outs and a wave of reviews so brutal that it was reportedly re-cut before its eventual release. I never saw it, so can only smile sympathetically.

'So, what can I do for you?' Schlattman asks me. I'm taken aback, and since I'm not sure whether the news of his leaving Scion is common knowledge, I reply with caution.

'Like I said in my email, I'd love to profile you. A little bit of a retrospective on your career to date, obviously, how Scion was formed, the awards success of *Idyllwilde*, and a look into the future. Where you see the industry going, where you see your own work going.'

'A look into the future,' he says, contemplative. 'All right. Let's do it, Jessica.'

The VIP area is growing full, and Toby slinks away in the direction of the bar, presumably punctured by the memory of *Only the Good*. I follow Schlattman over to a low sofa beside his reserved table.

'We don't have to do this now,' I say hastily once we're seated, suddenly realizing he may think I want to interview him immediately. 'Just let me know when's good for you.'

'Want to meet me in the lobby restaurant here tomorrow for breakfast? Bright and early, that'll keep you out of trouble tonight.'

'Sure. Sounds great.'

I watch him, as he continues to ask me questions about my job, my background, why I got into the industry. It's curious, the mismatch between his body language and his apparent interest; he's angled almost away from me, his gaze distant and his face impassive. Anyone watching from afar would assume he was annoyed, or at the very least not enjoying our interaction, and yet he's the one pushing the conversation forward, so much so I feel as though I'm being interviewed. But this, I suspect, is how he operates in business; make people feel special, make them feel unique, but never quite make them feel secure. I don't doubt that he has an agenda going into this interview, a perspective that he wants to get across, and that's fine. He gets to tell his side of the story, and I get to put my byline on it.

Melody Harmon passes by and I can't suppress a wave of pleasure at the startled look on her face. She did not expect to see me in here, much less at Ben Schlattman's table, and I smile lightly at her before turning back to Schlattman, who's now distracted in turn. He's craning his neck to look up at somebody at his right shoulder, and I realize with a thrill that it's Clark.

He doesn't immediately acknowledge me, though he clearly sees me. I'm frozen, though of course on some level I knew he might be here. He's doing the rounds.

'You want to join us?' Schlattman asks, raising his voice back to a normal volume. 'This is Jessica, the hack Reel sent to profile me.' He says the word with a crooked smile in my direction, and I smile back.

'We've met before, actually,' Clark says, and stretches out his hand to me. 'Good to see you again.'

'Don't you have your own afterparty to be at?' I ask playfully as I take his hand.

'He likes us better,' Schlattman answers. 'And he knows he fucked up when he chose them over me. Could've been you tonight, Clark.'

'What do you mean?'

'Careful,' Clark says lightly. 'You better be sure this is off the record.'

'It is,' I say quickly, but Schlattman waves a dismissive hand.

'Hell, this is already out there for anyone who cares. Clark was my first choice for *Idyllwilde*, I said that from the start. Wined and dined him, thought I had him, and then he turned me down for the space movie.'

Clark shrugs in a mea culpa way. 'It was the role of a lifetime, I'm not sure I'll ever read a better script.'

'I can send you ten better scripts from my slush pile,' Schlattman snaps back. It's all in jest, no true venom; this is just how the business works, and we all know it. Still, there's always a grain of truth in the joke. After the pair of them have gone back and forth on this for a while, Schlattman gets called away by another acquaintance, leaving me alone with Clark. And though I'm braced for him to bail, for his eyes to fix on a point somewhere over my shoulder and excuse himself with a painfully polite smile, he stays.

'Can I tell you something?' I say quietly, so that he has to lean in to hear me.

'That's a loaded question.'

'You made the right choice. *Armstrong* is a way better script than *Idyllwilde*, and there's no comparison between the roles.'

He nods.

'Agreed. But who's sitting here tonight with a Golden Globe in his hand? Not me.'

I watch him stare vacantly into his glass and wonder if he's joking, startled that he cares this much about what is objectively the least important award of the bunch. But this might not have mattered so much to him a month ago, or even two weeks ago, before Skye drew a bloody divide between one era of his life and the next.

'I still think you're going to get the Oscar.'

'You must like to go against conventional wisdom.'

'I think a lot of the conventional wisdom around awards season is bullshit. You're not going to stop campaigning, are you?'

84

'I haven't been doing a lot of that, under the circumstances.' His tone pointed, as though I could possibly have forgotten. I was there. And I feel something in me shift, the alcohol and the giddy rush of this evening powering me towards a reckless thing, an idea that will either draw me closer to him, or ensure that I never see him again.

'That's exactly what I'm saying,' I tell him, looking hard into his eyes. 'The Globes voting closed at the start of the year, too early for... those circumstances to be reflected. But the Academy is voting right up until January 30. That's nearly two weeks away."

He regards me steadily.

'The sympathy vote. That's what you're saying?'

'I'm saying you deserve the Oscar because your performance is the best I saw all year. But it's rarely just about that. Right? It's about who campaigned the hardest, who's in favour, who's really earned it? Who reflects the values the industry wants to be seen as upholding? Who do we like the most? Not just their performance, but them as a person.'

'I assume you're going somewhere with this.'

'Everybody likes you. You're one of the nicest guys in the business – I've heard about seven variations on that sentiment this week alone. No one's heard from you since what happened, and that's good because you don't want to seem opportunistic. But I've been thinking a lot about what you said during our interview, before. About wanting to be more present in your daughter's life, and how admirable that is.'

He shakes his head with a bitter chuckle.

'You have a low bar for admirable. Clearly.'

'Maybe. And I would never pretend to know what your family is going through, or how you're feeling after what happened. But there are more absent fathers in this world than not.' Clark frowns, as if prompting me to expand on this, and I don't hesitate. 'My dad went out for groceries one afternoon when I was seven, and never came home. We thought something had happened to him, until the police came to search the house and discovered that he'd taken a suitcase with him, and clothes, and his passport. Money. He ghosted us.'

I haven't told this story in a very long time, and not to anyone since I moved to LA. I tell people that my father is dead, now, because it's so much more straightforward, and if I had the power I would rewrite my own memory to make myself believe it too.

He stares at me, and I dig my nails deep into my palms to steady myself. I had no idea I would be revealing any of this tonight, but it's coming out so easily now, so naturally, and he understands me.

'So believe me when I tell you that trying to be more present as a father is admirable to me. It's not small. It's not nothing.'

He reaches out and holds on to not my hand, but my wrist, a tap of pressure near my pulse point.

'Thank you,' he says quietly, 'for your honesty. It's generous of you to share that with me.'

'It's a little bit self-serving, too.'

'Oh, I know.'

'So you know where I'm going with this. Everybody likes

you, but at least as far as the public is concerned, no one really knows you. I'm willing to bet a lot of voters feel the same way. So. If you ever decide you want to speak to the press, and open up about… anything, maybe before January 30, I hope I'll be your first call.'

He looks at me, unblinking, impassive, and maybe it's the alcohol or maybe it's not but his silence is not unnerving. It feels like understanding, a shining invisible thread between us now, a thread that's been woven ever since that Friday by the pool.

'What makes you think I would say yes to this?' he asks, calmly, curious.

'What made you say yes to the Nest interview? That was a pretty big surprise, from someone who grants so few interviews. A lot of publications were fuming.' This is true. Justin had told me gleefully that a longtime rival had given him the dirtiest look when they'd crossed paths at an event, the kind of look reserved for pure envy. Clark Conrad is a unicorn, now more than ever. 'The fact you said yes, even to a fluffy interview about your house, suggests you're amenable to a little more exposure than usual.'

He stares at me.

'Why am I so fascinating to you?'

'You're fascinating to a lot of people.'

'That's not what I asked. I mean, you're not some hysterical fangirl.'

'Actually—' I hesitate, but to hell with it. 'I am. Or I was. I used to be one of those girls outside on the red carpet, waiting for hours.'

'For an autograph?' he asks, incredulous.

'No.' How can he not understand this, after so many years at the eye of the storm? 'It's not about the autograph, it's about the interaction. I waited outside the Odeon in Leicester Square from five in the morning, before the *Reckless* premiere, hoping to get a glimpse of you.'

'Jesus. That was— what, '07?'

'And you arrived late. It was pouring with rain, the premiere was due to start, but still you spent half an hour signing autographs for fans. You skipped all the press—'

'—And went straight to the fans.'

It seemed impossible, this gesture, in the moment. I can still feel it, the sensation of being soaked through to the point of forgetting what it is to be dry, shivering in the endless January grey, and after fourteen hours on my feet it seemed impossible that this could end in anything but disappointment. I was not going to see Clark Conrad, and the autograph I'd half-heartedly solicited from the movie's director was no consolation prize. I remember bracing myself for it, the soggy walk back to the tube station, the bleak ride home to the very end of the Central Line, the farthest possible place from anywhere Clark Conrad has ever touched. When he'd bounded down the red carpet in his three-piece tux and dress shoes and woollen coat, a frantic umbrella-wielding assistant struggling to keep up with him, he'd seemed like a mirage. He made his way down the entire vast pen of screaming fans, holding his Sharpie pen high to meet the notebooks and DVDs and bare palms that were being desperately thrust towards him, and when he got to me I was so cold and numb and disbelieving that I didn't say a word, only stared as he signed my *Loner* DVD in a twisted scribble. Gone in a blink, and it would take me days before I came back down to earth enough to regret my silence.

'So we have met before,' he says. 'Before you came to the house.'

'I'm not sure it qualifies as a meeting. There's no way you'd remember me from that.'

'Don't be so sure.'

Soaked to the bone, hood pulled tight around my face, a disposable plastic raincoat on top of that, handed out to the crowd en masse by sympathetic red carpet runners. There's no way.

'You still haven't told me,' he says. 'What's so fascinating about me that would have made teenage Jessica sleep on the streets of London?'

'I didn't camp overnight.' But only because my mother absolutely would not let me. One of the worst fights we've ever had, to this day. 'Honestly, I'd spent so much time watching *Loner* that I probably believed on some very deep level that I was meeting Richard Loner, and not you. No offence.'

'None taken. Richard Loner is a much better man than me.'

'But a lot of people's fandom fades away after their show ends. Yours just kept growing. The people out there tonight were here for you, not Loner.' I pause, then adopt a low, dramatic trailer voice. 'The star power of Clark Conrad – what is the secret to his enduring appeal? How did he make the near-impossible leap from small-screen favourite to movie star?' I'm pitching too much, I know, but something about him feels small and diminished and in need of pushing.

'What's happening with that interview, since you bring it up?'

'Nothing. I mean... My editor wouldn't let us publish it, under the circumstances. Do you mind if I ask—' I start, then remember one of the only direct pieces of advice I've ever received. Never apologize for a question. If you feel the need to apologize, you need to either change the question or change your attitude. 'How is she?'

'Alive. I'm not sure what to say beyond that.'

I look down at my hands, trying to remember what I had scripted in my head to say next, but everything is blank.

'I didn't know what to do,' I whisper. 'When I saw her. I froze.'

'So did I.' Then, barely missing a beat, he asks, 'So your editor got cold feet?'

'She just thought we'd risk looking tasteless.'

'Well. That seems like a waste. I think I said at least three pretty coherent things in there.'

'You did,' I say, holding my breath. 'And I'd love to be able to use it.'

'Maybe we can figure something out.'

I hand him my card, the one I've had pressed against my palm for the last half-hour, and just as he takes it an explosion of blonde separates us, and a wave of perfume hits me so powerfully I almost choke. Of course Amabella is wearing her own signature fragrance, as she drapes herself around Clark's neck and kisses him ostentatiously, her perfect ringlets obscuring him from my view.

When she finally lets him up for air, he introduces me as a reporter and Amabella looks right through me.

'Get any scoop?' she asks sharply.

'I'm not sure yet.' I smile back. I'm waiting for him to explain that I'm not just a reporter, but *the* reporter, the one who was there on the day it all happened. The one who found Skye. But he doesn't say anything.

'My feet are killing me,' Amabella complains, folding herself into Clark's lap and letting her skyscraper heels clatter to the ground. There's a headache building behind my eyes, watching them, a haze of something red and painful. I watch his face as closely as I always do, and it's lit up, rapt, gazing at her like she's a wonder.

I mutter a goodbye under my breath as I leave, my words barely registering in their glow.

8

The next morning dawns cold and bright, the sky an impossible vivid blue during my run around the lake, as I try hard to sweat out all eight rounds of alcohol from last night.

Nine o'clock, Schlattman told me to meet him for breakfast, and I'm spending the prep time going over his biography and his filmography in my head, trying to ensure that the details are as solid as possible so that he can't trip me up. If this interview goes awry, it won't be because I was unprepared. Born in Trenton, New Jersey, the eldest of three brothers, father an ex-military pilot, mother a nurse, fell in love with cinema the first time he ever went to the movies, to see *Planet of the Apes* in the spring of 1968. Thought the apes were real and never quite stopped believing it. Co-founded the earliest iteration of Scion in the early eighties, working alongside his younger brother Bill to acquire and distribute arthouse movies, and gradually their savvy selections built up critical acclaim and some modest commercial success, and then, finally, Oscars. A lot of Oscars.

I'm memorizing all of this biographical detail in part because I know Reel does not want a dry recounting of the facts everyone knows about Ben Schlattman, and autobiography is one of the easiest traps to fall into when you're writing a profile. You ask questions about their life, they respond in dry ways that seem interesting at the time because you're starstruck by their presence, and you come away with a page full of nothing.

I'm not concerned about being starstruck in this instance. Schlattman has been unusually, unexpectedly accommodating to me, probably because he's eager to get his side of the story out there before Bill does. There's an ugly rumour that the real reason Scion broke down is that Ben had an affair with Bill's recently estranged wife. I'm saving my questions about this until the very end of the interview, as is advisable with potentially provocative questions. If he walks out, at least I already have my material.

The Hilton is fully accessible once again, my driver able to pull all the way in to the driveway and drop me off at the lobby. Since I'm early, I take a walk around back to where the arrivals area was last night, to survey the glamour deconstructed. The red carpet rolled away, the marquees and lighting rigs still being taken down, metal barriers pulled apart and piled up on the ground.

I'm more nervous than I expected as I'm led over to a table in the window where Schlattman is already waiting, dressed down in a sweatshirt and slacks. He greets me with a brusque handshake, not getting up. After small talk and menus and coffee, I begin recording and ask him a few background questions – the name of the new company, when the official announcement will happen, where they're setting up shop, how many projects per year he's looking at.

'What do you think of the name?' he asks me. 'It's a work-in-progress, may still change.'

'Panorama Pictures? It's fine. People might get it confused with Paramount though.'

'That's what I said.'

'I thought you might just use your name, to be honest.'

'Schlattman Pictures? You want my brother to murder me in my sleep?' He points at my recorder. 'Don't print that. Don't give him ideas.'

'We'll call that off the record. Speaking of which, before we go any further, can I confirm that you're not speaking to any other journalists right now? This is an exclusive?'

'Exclusive access.' He nods with a smirk. 'One journalist at a time is about all I can handle.'

'And you don't have plans to speak to anyone else—'

'You want me to give you a promise ring? It's you, Jessica, just you, only you, now and for ever. All right?' And I say yes, with a laugh, the ice now feeling truly broken.

'Do you live on your own?' he asks me later, abruptly, midway through a conversation about the pros and cons of going into business alone.

'Yeah.'

'No boyfriend? Or girlfriend?'

'Neither, but I appreciate the open-mindedness.'

'Unexpected from a man of my generation, right?'

'Not really. Not here.'

'You'd be surprised. Lot more bigots in Hollywood than you think, but they know how to keep it on the down-low. Why else you think there's still so many closet cases in this business?'

'Just to be clear, you're saying this on the record?'

'Why not? It's not breaking news. Even I can't get a movie financed with an openly gay leading man. Can't do it.'

'Why can't you?' I challenge him. 'If people like you won't buck the trend and take a risk, how is anything ever going to change?'

'You have to take calculated risks. No matter how big you get, you're only as good as your last success, right, and all it takes is maybe three flops to bury even the biggest fish. I'm not out to change this business, I'm out to make money in it.'

I must not be hiding my feelings well, because he lets out a low whistle and murmurs, 'This is going great so far, huh?'

'I'm just surprised that someone of your stature, someone who's known for donating generously to causes like the ACLU and GLAAD, wouldn't want to do more to fight inequality in his own industry. I'm thinking specifically about the lack of female directors on Scion's roster.'

He sighs, audibly. He knew this was coming. It's been discussed enough, online and probably offline, that he can't possibly be unaware that his company came out as one of the worst in a recent audit of gender equality behind the camera.

'Well, I'm leaving Scion. We covered this.'

'Sure, but you had a hand in creating that roster before you made that decision, right? Probably a big hand. Probably at least fifty per cent of the decision-making power. Is that fair to say?'

'A big part of why I'm leaving is in order to have more say over the kinds of projects that get made. And to take more calculated chances than—' He pauses, as though second-guessing whether to continue this thought. 'My brother is a very smart guy, and a great businessman, and in many ways a great producer. But he is risk-averse, and over the years he's rubbed off on me. Is *Idyllwilde* the most daring choice we could've made this year? No. Probably not. Neither is that Armstrong thing, by the way.'

'So now that you're starting your own company, and you'll pretty much have one hundred per cent of the say in what gets backed, do you plan on righting the wrongs that many have identified at Scion?'

'If you're asking whether I want to hire more female directors, the answer is yes. Frankly, I prefer working with women. They're smarter, they're more rational, they're less driven by ego bullshit. They know how to compromise, which is everything. And they're cunning.'

'Cunning?'

'When they need to be. Men aren't subtle. We see something we want, we try to grab it, try to bulldoze our way over everything to get it, and if that doesn't work we start yelling. Maybe breaking things. Women don't make it obvious what they want. They don't play their hand right away.' He's watching me closely as he says this. 'That seem fair to you?'

'Mostly. It's not a great thing, though. Women not being direct in asking for what they want is a big part of the reason the gender pay gap exists.'

Our food has arrived, and Schlattman now seems distracted by the task of trying to cover every square inch of his pancake stack in syrup. The yoghurt parfait I ordered seems insurmountably large, served in a sundae glass and drizzled with something which defeats the purpose of serving actual fruit, and even the granola looks glazed with sugar. So I nibble, and watch him eat, and finally he speaks again.

'So, I take it you're a feminist?' he asks.

'Is that a question? Of course.' At some point, I have abandoned tact, because on some level I can sense that Schlattman respects me more for not being afraid of him. 'I'm so sick of that word being treated like it's controversial. Do I think men and women deserve equal rights? Because that's all feminism means.'

'In my generation, that word has a different meaning.'

'Well, your generation needs to update its dictionary.'

He laughs.

'Maybe so. But like it or not, you're writing about a business that was built by men. I'm not saying that means it should always be run by men, but that's the reality of it.'

I'm imagining the pull-quotes in this profile already, imagining the outrage it will generate, the opinion essays decrying Schlattman as a dinosaur soon to be extinct.

'I agree,' I say. 'And that's why I always hope to see men like you – men who matter – doing their part to change things.'

I back off him a little at this point, because there's a delicate balance at work and I don't want to alienate him. As it turns out, I didn't need to worry.

'You know, I wasn't going to do this, but I want to tell you about the first project I'm developing under the new banner.'

'Go on.'

'You're gonna like it.' He smiles, and I wait expectantly. 'But unfortunately, we're out of time right now.'

'Oh!' I glance at my phone, but we've been here for barely forty minutes. We never agreed to any particular length of time, which was my mistake. 'That went fast.'

'Yeah, listen, sorry to cut you short. Do you want to come back later, maybe this evening or tomorrow night? I'm staying over at the Montage until Wednesday, five minutes down Wilshire. You know it?'

'Sure, tomorrow night is great. Can we do another forty-five minutes? I just want to make sure I get everything I need.'

'Sounds fine. Come at eight.'

And then he's on his way out, heading back towards the lobby where a young, sleek assistant is waiting to hand him his jacket and an iPad. It's the same assistant who awaits me in the Montage lobby when I arrive the next evening, greeting me by name.

'Mr Schlattman's upstairs, if you want to join him up there. He has a business suite on the seventh floor – he's finishing up another meeting which went a little long, so it'll be faster this way.'

I nod reassuringly, because I can tell that she thinks I don't understand.

'I get it, I've done a lot of junkets in hotel suites before.'

'Right.' She smiles. 'So you know the drill. You can just go right up, room 748.'

Schlattman answers the door in a sweatshirt and jeans and socks, his normally slicked-back hair mussed. I had expected to meet him in the hotel's sleek, wood-panelled lobby bar and dressed accordingly. Having seen the Montage only from a distance it has always reminded me of an enchanted castle, the one from the Walt Disney logo, sweeping white arches and a golden-lit fountain, nothing like anywhere I belong. Cocktailwear seemed appropriate, but now in my lacy black dress and lipstick I am overdressed for this room, throwing off the dynamic as though I'm ostentatiously putting in effort.

'Take your shoes off, if you want,' Schlattman offers, waving me vaguely towards the lounge area of this expansive suite where dark leather couches sit at right angles. I take him up on the offer if only to take the edge off my outfit, leaving my heels beside my bag at the door. He offers me champagne from an already-open bottle, and when I ask what he's celebrating, he just smiles and shakes his head and hands me a fizzing glassful.

'Can I start recording?'

'Whatever you want.'

I can hear him breathing though he's several feet from me, his exhales heavy. In suits, there's a heft to Schlattman, a power, but now in his socks he seems older and fatter and sadder, somehow. That champagne bottle may have been opened for him, but he was drinking alone, I'm almost positive.

The first project on Panorama's slate, it transpires, is a female-directed, female-produced, female-written drama about a woman forced to reluctantly become guardian to her dead sister's children. The script is by a playwright whose work I love, and I tell Schlattman with sincere enthusiasm that I can't wait to see the finished film. My excitement is genuine, and not only because this project makes a perfect hook for his earlier quotes about gender equality.

'Now it's just a matter of finding the right lead,' he says, as though to himself. 'We're already out to a couple of people, and now we've got Debra on board to direct they'd be insane to say no.'

He asks me for advice, then, explaining that as a young woman I'm probably more in touch with who the exciting young actresses are. When I give him a few names, he asks, 'Did you ever want to be an actress?'

'Very briefly.' Even this is a stretch – I wanted to be an actress in the most abstract sense of wanting to be in Hollywood at any cost, and when I was young and didn't know better I thought acting was the only way to do it. Never mind that few things make me feel sicker than being looked at by a crowd.

'You still could. You've got the bone structure for it.' He considers me, actually walking around me in a semi-circle. 'You remind me of a young Lauren Bacall. Darker hair, but other than that.'

'Unfortunately I'm a terrible actress,' I say lightly, with a laugh. 'Too self-conscious. I could maybe do voice work. Put me in a small, poorly lit booth and I'm happy.'

'Talent matters a lot less than you'd think. And your voice isn't your best asset.'

The energy shifts. Or else I'm becoming aware of what the energy has been all along.

'So, are there any other projects you're able to discuss at this stage?' I ask, walking away from him towards the window in what I hope is a casual way. 'You know there's this spec for a dark, modern *Little Women* remake, it's been knocking around the Black List for years. I heard a rumour that you might be optioning it.'

'Might be. Might not be.'

'How about the Nina Simone biopic?'

'We gonna go through the entire Black List, script by script?'

I smile, indulgently.

'Fair enough. If you can't discuss any more specifics, is there anything else about your vision for Panorama that you think is important for me to highlight?'

'I think we covered our bases. You?'

I can't shake the feeling that I've forgotten to ask some questions, several questions, and after Clark I can't let this interview end early. I can't let this one slip.

'Do you mind if I check my notes? It'll just take a second.'

Schlattman picks up my digital recorder from the coffee table, regards it for a beat, looks from it to me as though daring me to protest. With a long beep, he presses the Off switch, ending the recording.

'Now that you've got what you need,' he murmurs, handing the recorder to me, 'let's talk about what I need.' Dialogue worthy of a Scion production. His fingers trace along my jaw and my cheek and down to my collarbone, and then he is cupping my breast, and I imagine it. Saying yes to him, letting him close the final inches between us and kiss me with dry, desperate lips, pull me against his fleshy stomach and slip a hand beneath the hem of my dress. I imagine giving in, for just long enough to be repelled.

'I'm going to leave,' I tell him quietly, but he's already moving towards the door and it takes me a long beat to realize what is happening here. What may be about to happen here. He reaches the exit and stands between me and it, his expression nonchalant, and as I stare at my bag and shoes behind him I try to weigh my options, try not to let my thoughts race.

'You should stay,' he says, casually, as though it's a suggestion.

'I should leave.' The bathroom is back behind me, maybe ten feet from where I'm standing, and these luxury hotel rooms always have an emergency phone installed in the bathroom. He's out of shape, drunk, but would I have time to run there and lock the door behind me, and if I do that I'm officially turning this into a chase. My heartbeat is in my ears.

'Lot of women in your position would reconsider.'

I force myself to laugh, force the atmosphere in this room to shift back into the familiar, the cordial. 'I guess

I'm not like a lot of women. I really do need to leave, I'm sorry.'

'It's up to you,' he replies. 'Either way, I trust you'll keep this between us.'

I don't reply. Instead, I move slowly towards him, around him, watching him from the corner of my eye as I pick up my bag.

'You're a rising star, Jessica. Even in a dying field, that's something. I'd hate to see your career end prematurely.'

I put my shoes on and scrabble for the door handle blindly, and leave the room without once turning my back on him. The few carpeted yards from door to elevator are a blur, and on the way back down to the lobby, I gradually become aware that my bag is vibrating against my hip.

'Yes?'

'Hi, Jessica?'

'Clark?' My voice is too high and uneven, but I'd know his anywhere. 'Hi. Sorry, I'm just— give me one second.' Everything is moving too fast, the metal walls vaguely unsteady around me, but this call is now the only thing that matters, and everything else can wait.

'Is this a bad time?'

'No! It's fine.' Breathe. And I hold in my next breath for several beats to try to steady it. The marble lobby spreads itself out before me as the elevator doors finally open, everything wide and bright and warm, and I can hear him clearly now. So close. 'Sorry, I was in an elevator. What can I do for you?'

'Well, I've been thinking about what you said the other night. To clarify: what exactly do you want from me?'

'I still want to write up our interview. I can just do it as a Q&A, a short write-around intro, very much still focused on the house. All I need from you is a few follow-up questions, because I was caught off guard that afternoon and didn't get through everything. You can have copy approval. We don't need to go into what happened, if you don't want to. I can turn it around fast, publish it online before the weekend.' I stop short of mentioning the Oscar voting deadline again. Don't oversell.

'I'm happy to do it. Can we do it over lunch tomorrow, El Coyote?'

The sickness in my spine lingers, the ghost of Schlattman's fingers prickling on my skin, and for a moment I want to say no. But there is no comparison between these two men; Clark is not trying to lure me into anything. I'm supposed to be at Nest tomorrow, the beginning of my final week there, but this matters more. If I deliver this interview, no one will remember anything else, certainly not the long Tuesday lunch I took at short notice.

'Sure. I'll be there.'

'Are you sure you're all right? You sound a little distracted.'

'I had a strange night. I'll be fine.'

'Anything I can do?'

His voice a hum in my ear, and I feel unsteady again. What exactly is he asking me? I wonder, if I told him to come here right now and meet me, whether he would do it. Whether I have developed some kind of allure, a new poise that makes powerful men take notice.

'I'll see you tomorrow,' I say instead, murmuring, playful. And he says yes, you will.

Clark Conrad Is Building Himself A Fresh Start

Published January 19, 2016 on Nest.com

By Jessica Harris

There's a room in Clark Conrad's house where he keeps his trophies. It's a modest, cosy library, its walls lined with overflowing bookshelves and family photographs, and inside a cabinet with his Emmys, his Globe, his Oscar. Crucially, this room is tucked away at the very end of a long corridor where few guests would ever have reason to go. This is not a man who needs the world to see his awards.

'I've personally always found a good character to be a fantastic place to hide,' Conrad tells me, as we sit on the deck of his newly renovated Laurel Canyon home. 'Giving a good performance is really the opposite of being seen.' Notoriously press-shy, the forty-five-year-old Conrad is as warm and affable and genuine in person as you've heard. But it was that desire not to be seen that propelled his move to the canyon from Beverly Hills, where he previously lived with his wife of twenty years, Carol. While he ironically calls it 'the ultimate embodiment of ego… the desire to look down and see everything spread out beneath you', it's clear throughout our conversation that Conrad's real priority is privacy, for himself and especially for his younger daughter Skye, who has her own wing of the house.

Oscar-nominated for the third time this year for his mesmerizing performance in the biopic Armstrong, Conrad sat down with Nest.com to look back on his career to date, and look forward to his new chapter in the canyon.

Q: How long did you own the house for prior to starting the renovation?

I bought it back in 2001, right around the time my show [Loner] was wrapping up. I'd just hit my thirties and I knew I wanted something more permanent, something that felt like a home and not a crash pad, but it was a bit of a fixer-upper. I liked the idea of having it as a project, but I never really had the time to put into it, and so I would just lend it out to friends when they were visiting, and stay here sometimes at weekends. For long stretches I would forget I owned the place at all.

When my marriage ended last year, it forced me to re-evaluate. I know that it's become very faddy to talk about mindfulness, and meditation, but I cannot overstate how important it's been to me. Being out here in the canyon, up above the fray of it all, just felt like the right move, and it's made me re-evaluate what my priorities are.

Q: What was your guiding principle as you went through this renovation?

We didn't change much structurally. It was really more about knocking through some walls, turning two small rooms into one big, bright one, like in the living room. Giving it more flow, as [my architect] Jerome says. I tend to get antsy if I don't have enough light, and these canyon houses can be dark if you don't plan them right, so adding the skylights made a huge difference. I hadn't realized it, but I think that was a big part of the reason I never wanted to spend any time here. It was dingy, and now it's open and light-flooded.

Q: The wraparound pool is a very unusual feature of your house. What inspired that?

I wanted to see if it could be done. I thought about just building a little lap pool, which would have got the job done, but I have a strange pet peeve about having to turn around mid-lap. It always feels like slamming on the brakes to me.

Q: You've appeared exclusively in movies for the last seven years. Would you consider going back to television?

Sure, for the right project. The kinds of movies that I made when I was first starting out after Loner, your mid-budget dramas, your romances, those are all pretty much gone. Now if you're not making a blockbuster, you're making an indie, and most actors like to live somewhere in the middle ground. I'm not interested in superheroes, maybe because I feel as though I've already covered a lot of that territory with Loner. I mean, that character wasn't a superhero, but he was this guy who wore his daytime face as a mask, and lived with this secret burden of responsibility.

Q: How about that Loner revival that's been rumoured for a while?

Absolutely not. This industry needs to learn how to let things lie. This constant drive to revive existing properties because there's theoretically a built-in audience, it's so short-sighted and so motivated by fear. We have to keep making new things, because at some point we are going to run out of things to revive.

Q: The biggest addition you made to the house was a separate wing for your daughter, Skye. What inspired that decision?

I don't think any teenage girl should be forced to share space with her parents unless absolutely necessary [laughs]. And she concurs! No, the truth is she asked me whether I would consider it, because she didn't want to move out but she did want to have her own space, and I thought it made sense. I didn't want her moving out either – I wanted her close by, especially given how much space we have here – but I also understood her impulse to fly the nest. This felt like a good compromise, where we could live together without being under each other's feet all the time.

Q: Skye recently injured herself, which led to an extended hospitalization. How's she doing?

First of all, I want to say how grateful I've been for the outpouring of love and support that has followed this awful moment in my family's life. It has been a very, very difficult year, and all I can say is that my daughter Skye is a really extraordinary young woman. She's doing much better, she's taking care of herself, and her future couldn't be brighter.

Q: You experienced a lot of loss early in your life. What impact does that have on you today?

I suppose everything that happens to you, certainly before the age of ten or so, affects the kind of man you grow up to be. My parents' passing certainly unmoored me, to a degree, and ever since then I've lived a pretty rootless existence, as a lot of actors do – nomadic. With this renovation, my goal was to create a house for the first time that really felt like a home, as opposed to a temporary base. I want to give my daughter a better life, a more stable life, than the one I had.

Q: You were married for twenty years. How are you adjusting to the single life?

With difficulty. Carol was my soulmate, in the truest sense of the word, and there will never be a day when I don't miss her, and miss what we had together. But the truth is that I'm not sure human beings are really supposed to be together for life. One of the most valuable things Carol ever taught me was to accept change; that the only real constant is change. So I suppose in my life now, whether it be my work life or my dating life or whatever, I try to embrace that, and try not to worry about being so in control of everything. I'm never going to be perfectly Zen, but I guess you could say I'm cautiously experimenting with Zen.

9

I sleep badly the night after the Montage, and almost every night that follows, something unsettled in my mind that won't let me rest. This despite the fact that things are coming together; my interview with Clark is finally live, including the follow-up quotes I teased out of him over a lunch of Albondigas soup and guacamole, a lunch during which I finally realized I am no longer starstruck. My feelings around him have become something else, something deeper and less nameable.

'There will never be a day I don't miss what we had together?' Faye texts me, alongside a crying emoji. 'This is HEARTBREAKING. I can't believe he said that!' And though the reaction online has been similarly starry-eyed among his fans, though the piece has been picked up by outlets across the globe and won Nest its biggest traffic month ever, I'm nowhere close to satisfied with the final article. Even the scoops – Clark's first real comment on Carol since the divorce, his first comment on Skye since her suicide attempt – feel to me like a failure. I had imagined a written-through profile where I described the winding fairy-tale roads leading up to the house cradled in the canyon, the sheltered deck where Clark shook my hand for the first time, the way his trademark coiffed hair and pressed three-piece suit and humble charm belied the way he spoke about his past, his need for a fresh start. Admittedly, we didn't have as much time as I'd hoped, but with prose you can extrapolate, you can hint at things unsaid in the interview itself, and in doing so shape the way the reader interprets what quotes there are. I had so many plans, most of them not fully formed until it became clear to me that I wouldn't get to execute them. Jackie insisted.

'This was always going to be a Q&A,' she tells me calmly, while I try to keep my breathing even and not say something I'll regret. 'It's as much about the photographs as the copy.' And sure enough, the Q&A runs alongside a very lengthy series of beautiful photographs of the house, each of them captioned by Jerome's breathless descriptions, and I suppose that this is what Nest readers want. This is the compromise I signed up for, but that doesn't make it go down any easier. At least I didn't end up having to incorporate Jerome the architect into the piece; his quotes ran wholesale in captions underneath the relevant pictures. And in any case, I've now stopped believing that this article is the last chance I'll have to dig into Clark Conrad.

'Skye's coming home tomorrow,' he tells me after we're finished with our follow-up interview.

'That's great!'

'It is. It's a relief.' His tone implies the opposite, and I stay silent, waiting.

'Her mom and her sister are out of the picture, her circle of friends is… not thrilling to me, to say the least, and I'm her clueless dad who's the last person she wants to talk to about anything. I'm concerned she's going to slip back into old patterns unless something changes.'

I close my eyes, picturing her, angelic and frail in a hospital gown, though of course she hasn't been in hospital this past week but at a ritzy rehab facility in Sherman Oaks. Angelic and frail in a rehab-appropriate outfit, then, but alone. Very much alone.

'That makes sense,' I say, and there's an idea forming in me, close to my lips, but I don't want to push too much too soon. 'Does she have any friends that you like? Maybe from before she started modelling, got into that whole world?'

'Unfortunately, once she got into that world, she didn't have much interest in sustaining relationships with anyone who wasn't.'

'I'm not surprised.' I pause. 'This might be a completely insane thing to say – and feel free to tell me if that's the case – but what if I talked to her?'

I watch him as he takes this in, let the silence go on for as long as I can stand.

'You want to talk to Skye?'

'You sound sceptical.'

'You are a reporter.'

'I know, but I don't mean talk to her as a reporter. I know what it's like to be nineteen and lost.'

'I can't imagine you ever being lost.'

If he only knew. I may be overstating the common ground between us – Skye is the kind of sharp-edged girl who would have ignored me at best and targeted me at worst had we been schoolmates, the kind of girl I went out of my way to avoid. But the image in my head of Skye wearing institutional clothes, sitting in a sparse room trying to remember reasons to live, is a scene from my past, not hers. Clark does not need to know this, does not need to know about the seven months during which I ate only steamed vegetables and Special K and one banana a day, until the dizzy spells and heart palpitations become impossible to hide and I was sent away, for a spell, for what my mother called a spa trip whenever anyone asked.

'Believe me, I was,' is all I say. 'I don't know if I'll be able to help Skye, but I do know that back then, the thing I wanted more than anything was to meet someone who made me feel less completely alone and insane. And sometimes it's easier to be honest with a stranger.'

'That's certainly true. You're, what, twenty-five?' He looks at me like he's trying to convince himself. 'You're ambitious, you're smart, you've got your head screwed on. I'd have to ask you to sign an NDA.'

'Of course.'

'And I'll warn you that she doesn't seem interested in talking to anybody right now, so don't take it personally.'

'I'll try.'

'And you should know that a lot of the tabloid fodder about her is just that. She's never been a drug user, she doesn't drink to excess, doesn't party – at least, all of that was true up until about six months ago.'

'When Brett Rickards came into the picture?'

He grimaces.

'So you're familiar.'

'Not personally, but I think everybody's at least a little bit familiar with Brett.'

'If that sentence isn't an indictment of modern society, I'm not sure what is.'

I waver. If he doesn't bring up the leaked pictures of Skye first, I'm certainly not going to do it.

'I take it you're not a fan,' I say lightly.

'He's not without talent. Strong voice, by all accounts he works hard, but as a person? No. Not a fan. Never was, but of course, what nineteen-year-old wants to take dating advice from her father? The less I wanted her to date him, the more appealing he became.'

'So that's when she started partying?'

'I suppose. That's certainly when I stopped ever seeing her earlier than 2 p.m. I try not to ask too many questions about where she spends her time, but...'

I recall the stories from the barman who claimed he used to work at the Chateau, how Clark had to make amends after Skye's meltdown.

'She just had so much potential,' Clark says, before correcting himself. 'Still has. I always felt – probably narcissistically – that she took after me. You can see it in her modelling, she just has this very natural connection to the camera, and she's very intuitive. I think she could be truly great, if she put her mind to it, as an actress. I wanted her to study acting, but she just didn't have the drive. Ended up dropping out of school after her first year.'

'Maybe she could use a break from California,' I suggest. 'The best acting schools are all in New York anyway, right?'

'Them's fighting words.' He smiles. 'But yes, it's hard to argue with Juilliard and Tisch. I don't think she'd ever want to move that far, though.'

'Well, I'll try to slip in some subtle references to how great school is when I see her.'

'I'll let you know where to meet her,' Clark says, signalling a waiter for the check. 'Saturday should work. And by the way, don't be unnerved when she shows up with a security detail. See that bald guy right there, diagonally across?'

I turn and take him in: stocky, six-foot-something, a wall of muscle folded uncomfortably into a booth. He nods at me, and I wave awkwardly.

'That's Lenny. Been with me for twelve years. Mike's my other guy, but he's not here – don't usually need both, except for events where there's a really big crowd.'

'Wow. I really never imagined you having bodyguards.'

'I resisted it for a long time, but *Loner* had – still has – a pretty intense fanbase, and there were a couple of incidents back then.'

'Stalkers?'

'You name it. People showing up at the house, hiding in the bushes, leaving gift boxes on the front porch with God knows what inside. Most of it was harmless, and I could handle it, but it got to a point of not being safe for my family. Some of the letters… it was hard to tell whether they were love letters or death threats.'

'You'd hope that distinction would be clear.'

'One young woman had ninety-nine red roses delivered along with a note that just read "Soon."'

I mime an exaggerated shudder.

'Soon what?'

'I didn't wait to find out. My wife was freaked out by this point, and that was before another fan showed up at our daughter's school.'

'Skye?'

'No, this was my eldest, Sarah. Skye would only have been about four at this point, it was around the time *Loner* was wrapping up. That's when personal protection began to feel more like a necessity and less like some alien luxury.'

Since he brings her up, I have to ask.

'It looks from the news like Sarah hasn't been to see Skye, and neither has her mum. Is that true?'

'They've spoken on the phone,' Clark says with a shrug, disappointment clear in his voice.

'But... your daughter tries to commit suicide. That warrants more than a phone call.'

'Carol and Skye have had a pretty tough relationship for a long time now. I don't think Skye wanted her to come.'

'Still. Isn't it your job as a parent to show up and take the abuse, even when your kid rejects you? Maybe especially then.'

'Well, yeah, that's always been my approach. Especially now. I'm just not convinced of how much good it's doing. She's so...'

'Withdrawn?' I offer. 'Because that's to be expected, probably.'

'Did you ever see the movie *Changeling*? Clint Eastwood picture from a few years ago, based on a real case. A mother gets her kidnapped son back, and this should be the greatest moment of joy, the greatest relief she's ever felt. Except that it's not him. It looks like him, everyone's telling her it's him, but she just knows in her bones it's not.'

He hasn't looked directly at me for several minutes now, his gaze lowered. For a moment, I'm afraid he's about to cry and a chorus of conflicting impulses go through me, but when he looks up his eyes are dry and his smile's back in place.

'Anyway, what I'd really like to do is get her off social media. I know that's like telling the tide to stop coming in, trying to get a teenage girl off Instagram, but she's on the thing 24/7. Every half-hour she's posting some new video, selling some new aspect of her life to the masses, and it's all for Likes, right? That's the point of this stuff?'

'Yeah, Likes and Views. It's a validation farm.'

'Well, I'd like her to be getting her validation from some more wholesome source. Anything you can do to convince her to stay off that stuff, even for a few hours out of the day…'

'I'll try my best.'

Outside, he waits with me until my ride arrives, Lenny hanging back almost out of sight like the pro he is. He opens the car door for me, presses a hand to my shoulder to guide me inside and I can feel the imprint of where he touched me for days to come. Every time we've touched is logged in my mind, catalogued and assigned a sound and a smell and a feeling. Today is traffic, woodsmoke, a prickle like soft lightning.

'He's gonna win the Oscar, right?' my Lyft driver says, not turning around. 'Love that guy.'

I have another text from Faye waiting when I check my phone, and then a series of them, and I have to suppress an actual laugh.

Faye: have you seen Amabella's new website????

Faye: OMG I need you to be seeing what I'm seeing please go to SlayToday.com immediately

Faye: this is a straight quote from the homepage: 'Learn how to SLAY TODAY with world-renowned model, actress, speaker, lifestyle coach and media personality Amabella Bunch!'

Faye: 'I spent years struggling in Hollywood, feeling irrelevant and lame and like my voice didn't matter. I wish I'd known then what I know now – but here's the great news! YOU get to know now what I know now!'

Faye: she says she'll share her secrets to 'a long-lasting Hollywood career' and 'constantly netting more than 10 million press impressions per week'

Me: WOW. How many of those press impressions were from before she started dating Clark tho?

Faye: maybe 3 of them

Me: Also what are press impressions?

Faye: lol you're literally press

Me: And I've never heard of a press impression! Does she mean page views?

Me: My favourite part is 'you get to know now what I know now'. So catchy.

Faye: you have the inside track now are they still together? I give it another month tops, she makes him look trashy and he doesn't want that

Me: No idea tbh

Faye: he wants that oscar BAD

Faye: he should be dating like a Rachel mcadams or kirsten dunst. someone classy who's an actual actress

Faye: tell him for me thx

I'm always the one to let the text chain die. When Faye doesn't have a day job she spends most of her time at the beach or The Grove, and she has unlimited time to text endlessly. Even on the rare occasions when I have the time, I get impatient with any text chain after four or five exchanges, pressed in by the weight of all the other things I could and should be doing instead. I still haven't called Tom.

Four days pass after our lunch, and I have not heard from Clark. It's frightening how fast time disappears when you're in limbo. I have produced no fewer than six slideshow galleries for Nest this week ('25 Rustic Italian Living Rooms To Inspire Your Redecoration', '15 Tiny But Beautiful Coffee Tables For Small Spaces') and now that it's Friday I'm way beyond ready to get out of here at a sprint and never look back.

My phone is face down on the corner of my desk, and I'm typing harder than necessary as though I can dissuade myself from grabbing it by force. Skye came home on Tuesday, but I have heard nothing, and with every moment of silence that passes I'm sure that something I said during our lunch has made him reconsider, made him realize that agreeing to let me talk to Skye was a mistake. Every interaction that we've had – all three of them – feels hazy and fragile in my memory, each one of them tinged with something that distorts their clarity. Every time he disappears, I'm convinced that it's the last time I'll see him.

On my final morning at Nest Jackie beckons me into her office without looking up, waving me towards a seat. It's four full minutes before she finally shuts her laptop, just enough time to make it abundantly clear that I am not her top priority.

'Sorry!' she exclaims brightly. 'What a week.' We don't exchange many more pleasantries before she cuts to the chase, abandoning all pretence that this exit interview is anything but a formality. There was a time when this would have devastated me.

'So, where do you see yourself in five years' time?'

I consider saying that I see myself in her job, just to see what reaction I get.

'I guess ideally I'd like to be a staff writer at a magazine, but I know those jobs are almost extinct. Maybe an editor. I don't think I want to stay freelance for ever.'

'And you're sure that entertainment is where you want to focus?'

'Yes,' I say, so quickly I almost interrupt her. 'That's all I've ever— I don't know how to write about anything else.'

'No interest in going into PR, publicity, that side of things?'

Is she suggesting I'm not a good enough writer to avoid selling out? I try not to visibly bristle, breathing in deep.

'None.'

'Understood. It's a very tough time, as you know, and it's likely only going to get tougher over the next few years. So make sure you're in it for the right reasons.' She looks sharply at me. 'Are you?'

I know that the perfect response to this will come to me an hour from now, but for the moment I'm flummoxed. 'I think so. I just want to write, and to tell people's stories, and feel like I'm a part of the industry in some small way.'

'Hm.'

She's still looking at me strangely, as though nothing I've said has assuaged whatever her scepticism about me is. Or is she hoping to convince me that interior design journalism is where my true passion lies?

'I actually wanted to ask you a favour,' I say eventually, to break the uncomfortable silence.

'Oh?'

'Do you know David Nevins? The new online editor of Reel?'

'Very well. We worked together at the *Tribune* in another life.'

I knew that, of course, and she probably knows that I did.

'I have a story I'd like to pitch to them. Would you consider passing on his email address to me?'

'What's the story?'

'It's an interview with Ben Schlattman, the studio executive. I'm not sure if you're familiar with—' She nods. 'He's leaving the company he co-founded and starting a new one, and I got an exclusive interview with him.'

'Wow.' She raises an eyebrow, in a way that suggests that she has more to say but is choosing not to say it. 'Schlattman?'

'Yep.'

'Interesting.'

She's still looking at me, and I wonder if she knows. Is he known for this? Did I walk directly into a trap that any canny journalist would have seen coming?

'He's an interesting guy,' I reply carefully. 'I don't know whether Reel has anything else in the works with him, but he told me that this was the only interview he'd done.'

'You must have been very persuasive, to get him to agree to speak to you exclusively.'

And now I see what she's suggesting. Of course. Why take me seriously when she could just make the lazy assumption? I wonder whether she's projecting because this is what she used to do to lock in sources, back when she was an actual reporter and not a sellout.

'I didn't have to do much persuading,' I reply with a tight smile. 'Though he is a friend of my friend's uncle, so that's why he gave me the time of day to begin with.'

'I see.' Nepotism: a milder sin than exchanging sex for an interview, but still enough of an infraction that Jackie can believe this of me. 'Sure, I can put you in touch with David. I'll send an email and loop you in.'

'Thank you. I really appreciate it.'

As I pack up the few belongings I've accumulated over my time here, the thought occurs that I will never need her again after this. She will not even be a footnote on my résumé in ten years' time, but the Schlattman piece could be a turning point. It doesn't matter how I feel about him. It doesn't matter what kind of man he is. Put all of that aside, the skin-crawling memory of him, and write a succinct, smart article about his importance to the industry, his groundbreaking track record with Scion that has changed the face of independent film for good, his commitment to ensuring a fairer future for the women of Hollywood.

Most of the office works from home on Fridays, and Jackie offhandedly tells me I can leave after lunch; one final reminder that I am expendable. I take the opportunity to make a long-overdue call to my mother and end up walking more than half the way home as we talk, through the hedge-lined enclave of Hancock Park and the densely packed restaurant rows of Koreatown, taking in every detail of my surroundings to distract from her laundry list of complaints. Her negativity is infectious, and only recently have I built up the mental defences to resist it.

'It's as though he doesn't care at all about my view,' she's saying, in reference to a neighbour who's planning an extension to his house. 'It's going to block out so much daylight from the dining room, but I've told him so and he says he's going ahead with it anyway. Why even ask if you're just going to ignore your neighbours' concerns? I've written a formal complaint to the council, though I'm sure they won't do anything about it.'

'Maybe you should get out of the house more,' I reply, before realizing how this sounds. 'I mean, because then the lack of light probably wouldn't bother you as much.' I have to bite my tongue, but I know she goes days on end without leaving the house, sometimes weeks. Too young to formally retire but too chaotic to hold down a job, my mother also has enough inherited wealth to ensure she never really has to get her act together, and so she rattles around a four-bedroom house alone, stewing in resentments and anxieties that never seem to dissipate or to significantly change. I had to get out. I had to get this far away even to begin to feel human.

It takes me a while to realize that she has changed the subject, to me and my dating life.

'Have you seen Tom?' she asks.

'What?'

'Tom Porter! Don't tell me you've forgotten your beaus from back home now.'

'He's not— How do you know he's in LA?'

'His parents had me over for lunch just last week.'

God. The image of it almost stops me in my tracks.

'We were all agreeing how nice it was that you'd reconnected and ended up back in the same city. And both chasing the Hollywood dream! Have you been seeing much of him?'

He finally seems to have given up on me, after I once again didn't call when I said I would. There never seems to be a moment when I can prioritize him.

'I've been so busy that I haven't seen much of anyone.'

'Tom's not just anyone,' she says, her tone sly, and I want to hang up.

'He and I are just friends. I've told you, we barely went out.'

'Well, I worry about you all on your own over there. You never spend any time with friends, or have anyone special in your life. You always get so twitchy when I even ask.'

She's never got over my decision to move here. Apart from the sheer distance between here and London, she always told me LA was an absurd choice for a recovering anorexic. And though I wouldn't admit it at the time she was right, of course.

'I have plenty of friends, I'm just focusing on my career. Casual dating isn't my thing, and LA's a terrible place to try and meet someone serious.'

'Did he tell you that he got a part? Tom did. Some sort of series on TV, I didn't really take in the details, but—'

'Wait, really?'

And suddenly, prioritizing Tom feels easy.

10

I have to be careful about money. This is one of several anxious thoughts that strike me when I wake up before dawn on Saturday, when it hits me for the first time that I have gone from two jobs to none. Things seem unimportant in one moment and vital the next, and I have to get a better handle on the cold, hard immoveable truths of my life, such as the fact that I need $925 for rent every month no matter what, and now I have no guaranteed way of getting it. I have enough set aside from these past few months of fifteen-hour days to last me a while, but I can't lose sight of the fact that getting published in Reel is not a long-term strategy, not even if I choose to be optimistic about their per-word rate.

In an effort to calm myself, I send out four enquiry emails to editors on my To Contact spreadsheet, along with the formal pitch email to Reel, and with every one I feel my anxiety dissipate a little, though not as much as it does after I've run seventeen loops around the block, watching the dawn gather brighter with every repetition.

Clark's email comes precisely at sunrise, and his view from the deck is so perfect that I doubt this is a coincidence.

> Skye will meet you at midday at the Venice Beach Boardwalk. She wants to be outside and you're less likely to be bothered if you're on the move.
>
> C.C.

Not a question, but a statement of fact. He does not ask whether that time and location works for me, because he knows that I will make it work. Venice is a long way – forty minutes in a cab if I'm lucky, or a full two hours on public transport – and full of aggressively cool, aggressively underemployed people my age who seem to me like another species, their meticulously ragged clothes over tanned skin, their sense of collective belonging. I'm probably being judgemental, but no more so than LA demands.

Lacking any clothes that qualify as grungy or hip, I opt for sportswear, the most expensive pair of running tights I own, a tank top with a denim shirt thrown over it. Athleisure. I have no idea what Skye Conrad will wear for a beach walk with a stranger, but I'd rather dress deliberately down than even try to play the game of competing with her.

On the first of my two bus rides to Venice, I finally call Tom.

'I'd pretty much given up on you,' he says after letting the phone ring five times, joking but not joking.

'I know, I know, I'm really sorry. I always say this, but work's been—'

'Crazy,' he finishes.

'Yeah. But now, role reversal! I'm done at the place I was working, I have nothing lined up, and you're a TV star. Soon you'll be the one who's too busy to take my calls.'

'So you thought you'd better just get in there while you still could,' he says, fully teasing now.

'Look, I am nothing if not a craven opportunist. But seriously, I really do want to see you. You pick a time. And also tell me about this show – is it the hot ghost twins?'

'No, it's about vampires. It takes place in this future world where vampires have taken over and they're basically now most of the world's population, but the problem is that they're running out of humans, and the blood supply's dwindling. So instead of being a post-apocalyptic thing about humans trying to survive, it's actually about the vampire race realizing "shit, all those years of hedonistic bloodshed haven't actually left us with a world we can live in". It becomes kind of bureaucratic: they have to form a government to try and figure out how to deal with the blood shortage, create laws, regulation… This is all just the outline for the first season, but I think it could be a pretty great satire of society. I'm not totally sure the writers have figured out the right balance between comedy and drama, but—'

The ride passes easily with Tom's wry voice in my ear, as he unfurls the long and drily comedic story of his first botched audition for *Undead*, the surprisingly appealing-sounding vampire show. How he'd been running late and had side-swiped another car in the parking lot, still unaccustomed to driving from the left side, and that damaged car was parked in a designated space which turned out to be for the executive producer of the show he was auditioning for, because of course. And rather than confessing in the room and ensuring he'd never get a callback, Tom had walked into the audition and shaken the producer's hand as though nothing had happened, read his lines and done the variations they'd asked for and, two weeks later, had landed the role.

'Are you shocked?' he asks me.

'No, I'd be shocked if you'd done anything else! What kind of lunatic walks into an audition and immediately tells the most powerful person in the room they've just damaged his property? Honesty gets you absolutely nowhere as an actor anyway. Did you lie about your age too?'

'I'm pretty sure only actresses have to do that.'

'Savage and true. Tell me, Man In Hollywood, how does it feel to be just starting out and know you've probably still got seventy bankable years ahead of you?'

'Let's just see how long this thing lasts. The odds that we'll even get picked up aren't that great – everyone keeps telling me not to get too invested, not to take it personally when I don't get a callback, or when my show doesn't go to series, or when an actor I just auditioned with four days ago blanks me at a party.'

'That sounds specific. Who blanked you?'

'I'll tell you when I'm drunk, the memory's still raw. Let's just say it was someone I idolized before, and I could not believe it when the casting director called me back to do a chemistry read with him. He really is a good actor, because he had me convinced we'd bonded in the room.'

If anything will doom Tom's chances at a career here, it is this. He's too quick to believe, too eager to take people at face value and see the best in them, while ignoring all the small tells that should put his guard up. He's never learned to be suspicious, his upbringing giving him no reason not to trust people, and it makes me worry he'll be eaten alive here.

'He probably knew something I didn't, anyway,' Tom continues, as my bus pulls closer and closer to the water, weighed down by the mid-morning traffic. 'Couple of days after that party, I found out I didn't get that part.'

'Well, maybe he just knew you'd probably crash into his car if they cast you, so he encouraged them to go in another direction.' I get off the bus a couple of stops early, opting to walk along the beach from Santa Monica to Venice, since I'm early enough and maybe the salt air will calm my nerves. 'Hey, I've got to go, but when can I see you? Are you insanely busy with pre-production stuff now?'

'Yeah, actually, why don't you just come to the set?'

'You're offering me a set visit? You don't think the publicity department will be pissed off about you inviting some journalist they haven't approved?'

'I don't think there even is a publicity department yet. We don't start shooting until next week, but I've got fittings and training and stuff this week on the lot.'

If I can shadow Tom on the set of *Undead* for a day, maybe observe some stunt training, get friendly with the publicist before the pilot has even begun shooting, I can swing an exclusive to pitch closer to the show's debut, assuming it gets picked up to season. It's a gamble – the vampire craze has been over for several years now, but the premise of *Undead* sounds genuinely promising to me, and the showrunner has a strong track record of well-liked genre shows with deeply engaged fanbases. If this show becomes a success and I have been covering it from day one – interviews, recaps, behind-the-scenes exclusives – it could become a nice earner for me, nothing splashy but a solid source of regular commissions.

Our set visit now scheduled, I hang up and wait for Skye in a bare white-walled coffee shop near the boardwalk, nestled between a tattoo shop and a stall selling goth-inspired T-shirts that my teenage self would have loved. I'm making an effort to sip my drip coffee slowly, conscious of every cent I'm drinking. But that one cup turns into two, and then three, as midday comes and goes and Skye is still nowhere to be seen. I don't have her number, and the idea of emailing Clark to check on her ETA is somehow so depressing, so not reflective of what our relationship should be, that I barely consider it. I should have asked him for her number, but I did not, and so I wait.

It strikes me that Skye probably has no idea what I look like – how could she? – and that she probably blends in perfectly with the effortlessly cool twenty-somethings strolling and rolling past me on the boardwalk, so we could have missed each other. I begin composing and deleting casual check-in emails in my head: *Hey Clark / Hello Clark / Hi,* and then maybe the perfunctory small-talk sentence, *Hope your Saturday's starting out well / Hope all's good with you,* or maybe just straight to the point: *I just wanted to check that I got the time and place right / Do I have the right time and place?*

I'm too wrapped up in my thoughts to notice, for a second, that the seat next to mine is no longer empty. It's her, of course, her cascade of hair pulled back into a messy bun and dark roots showing beneath the gold. She's wearing enough bulky layers of clothing to distract from how tiny she is, and even in her current outfit – sweats and a ragged jumper and a hoodie, an ensemble that would make me look like a transient – she is beautiful, luminously so, the kind of beauty that makes her almost ludicrous. Between the pool and the paparazzi photographs before that, I realize now that I have very rarely seen her face up close, and therefore have not appreciated how much she looks like her father. Even with her eyes hidden behind reflective blue aviator sunglasses, it's clear.

'You have something,' she says, in an unexpectedly deep and sonorous voice. I expected thin, nasal, valley girl.

'What?'

She taps a finger near her left eye, but the shades are so disorienting that I don't immediately understand, and then I do. There's a smudge of mascara below my eye, because that's what I get for experimenting with lower-lash application, and any faint hope that I had of appearing impressive to Skye Conrad dissipates.

'How's it going?' I ask, once the smudge is gone, barrelling ahead. 'I'm Jessica, by the way.'

'It's going well,' she says quietly. Glancing down unconsciously, I see the artificial thickness of her lower arms and wrists, a flash of bandage visible through a hole in her sweater. It was three weeks ago yesterday.

'Thanks for meeting me.'

'My dad wanted me to come.' She shrugs.

'Do you hang out with everyone he tells you to?' I ask this

as a joke, but it comes out accusatory, not that she seems fazed.

'Pretty much. He has good taste in people.'

I ask her if she wants to walk and she says yes; a relief, because long silences and stilted conversations are less unbearable in motion. The January sun is bright and the Pacific sparkling as we set out towards Santa Monica amid the mingling smells of sea salt and marijuana. I keep looking furtively around for lurking paparazzi – Skye has not been pictured since her suicide attempt, and the last I checked online there was still a gaggle of photographers and reporters camped out permanently near the gates of the Laurel Canyon house. But here nobody takes a second glance, Skye's shades and sweats and unimpressive companion seemingly enough of a disguise, and in any case Lenny is following a few paces behind us, keeping watch.

'It's nice to be out,' Skye says, unprompted.

'You haven't been out much, since…?'

'Not really. My dad wanted me to rest, when I got home.'

'That makes sense. How are you feeling?'

'On top of the world.'

It's impossible to tell whether she's being serious or sarcastic.

'Do you know Brett?' she asks, out of nowhere.

'Brett Rickards?'

'Yeah. My boyfriend.'

'I know of him.' Obviously.

'He's a genius,' she murmurs. 'I know everyone thinks he's just hot, and has a good voice, but he's a really amazing writer too. You know, he wrote the entire lyrics for "It's Me" by himself? Nobody talks about that.'

I'm itching to grab my phone and fact-check this on the spot, because even with my limited music knowledge it seems implausible. Brett's last single had five separate producers credited, and I know this because I had to write up the story from a press release.

'So you and Brett are still together?'

She smiles, almost to herself, and says nothing.

'What about, um—'

'About what?' She knows what I want to ask. She has to, and now I have to see it through.

'The nudes,' I say, with an apologetic wince. 'I thought that he—'

'That wasn't him. It was this creep I dated back in high school. The media just loves to blame Brett for everything, because it's a way better story if he did it than some rando who works at The Viper Room. If you look at the pictures you can see they're taken a few years ago, my hair's not even the same.'

'I haven't seen them. I would never.'

'Whatever,' she says. 'I look good in them, so.'

The realization of just how little I understand is overwhelming, now. The question of what on earth I'm doing here, walking next to this impossible girl as though we're friends. We're here because I engineered it, like two children forced into a play date together because their parents are friends, and now I'm finding it hard to remember what I ever thought would come out of this. What we're having is not so much a conversation as a series of almost-conversations, each of them sputtering out within minutes.

'I read your article,' she says, then enunciates every syllable as she adds, 'on Nest dot com.'

'Oh! Great, what did you think?'

'Is that what you do? Write about people's houses?'

'No, I'm—' Now I'm wondering what Clark has told her about me, if anything. 'I'm an entertainment journalist.'

'Isn't journalism dying?' She's softer and quieter than I expected, but she has fangs.

'Yeah.' I laugh. 'Well, kind of. I work mostly online so the whole "death of print" thing doesn't impact me so much. But digital journalism's a mess in a different way. Nobody really knows what the business model's going to be in five years' time, or even a year's time. It's a lot of chasing traffic, trying to get Google to rank you highly, trying to get Facebook's algorithm to favour your content.'

I'm not convinced she's listening any more, and I can't blame her.

'Do you know what you want to do?' I ask, trying not to sound judgemental, just curious. 'You were at USC for a while, right?'

'Yeah. It wasn't a good fit for me. I guess I'm focusing on getting better, and then maybe I'd like to do more acting.' She sounds like she has rehearsed this. 'I don't want to model any more. It's boring.'

'I believe it.' I pause, but this has to get addressed at some point. 'You know I was there, that day. At the house.' I stop short of telling her the whole truth, that I was the one who found her bleeding out in the pool. That I'm still wondering whether she would be dead if I hadn't happened to need some air at that precise moment. 'There were a lot of us there. Me, a photographer, a couple of video producers. You knew we were coming, right?'

'I knew.'

She slit her wrists while her house was swarming with press, because she is that specific kind of famous child who has grown up believing that the world owes her its attention. I thought this meeting would make me feel more sympathetic to her, not less.

'I thought it was dumb,' she continues. 'That a magazine was coming to take pictures of our house, pretending like that's what people care about. When what they really care about is us. Getting the dirt.'

'You'd be surprised. A lot of people really just want to look at pretty pictures of beautiful homes, and read a lot of details about how they were renovated.'

'Not you, though.'

I feel seen.

'No. Not me, so much.' Though I have the high-res photographs from that day at the canyon house saved on my laptop, and at night when I can't sleep I pull them up and imagine myself back there, walking back out onto the deck where he is waiting for me, view spread out behind him and his smile like home.

'Do you live in a nice house?'

'No, I live in a shithole.'

'Makes sense,' she says. It's hard to tell whether she's insulting me, her tone is so placid and unchanging. Clark's

136

Changeling comparison is making more and more sense by the minute.

'So, is that why you did it?' I ask. 'Because you didn't like the fact there was press in your house? You were angry about that?'

'I thought it was dumb, but I wasn't angry. If people want to see our house...' She shrugs. 'Why not? I was just bored that day. When my mind isn't occupied, I have weird thoughts.'

'I get that.'

'I didn't want to kill myself,' she says. 'I would never do that. I didn't even cut that deep.'

'Well, I'm just glad you're doing better now.'

'I am. Thank you. So, are you fucking my dad?'

'What?'

I'm blindsided, but she just stares expectantly at me, knowing that I heard her just fine.

'No. I'm not.' Off her stare, I hear my own voice get louder, higher. 'He has a girlfriend! And I have a boyfriend, too, Tom, he's an actor. He just got cast in a show, actually, he came out here from London for pilot season and he booked a CW pilot about vampires, so.' I'm giving far too many details, padding out the lie with too much truth. I could simply have left it at Amabella.

'So what, then?' she asks, still so gentle, so nonchalant, as though she were asking me for the time. 'What's the deal?'

'I've admired Clark's work for a long time,' I reply, cringing inwardly at how inadequate this seems, how formulaic. 'Getting the assignment to interview him was very exciting. It was a dream, really. And then— I mean, that day ended the way it ended. And now...' I trail off, lamely. There is nothing in any of this to explain why I'm still around, in Clark's life and in hers, except that I asked and he said yes. 'Things got complicated. And I didn't feel like I could just walk away, after what happened.'

'And what did happen?' she asks quietly, her opaque blue bug eyes fixed out towards the ocean, reflecting rolling waves.

'I think that's for you to say. If you want to. If you want to talk about it.'

'Why would I talk to you about that?'

This is a fair question, and I tell her so.

'I'm getting tired,' she says next. I am too, in truth; Venice is too hot and too crowded, and the constant need to dodge cyclists and stoners is draining. We duck into the shade of a graffiti-laden side street, where she offers me a cigarette.

'No, thanks.'

'You don't smoke?'

I shake my head.

'You're pretty skinny, so I figured you did.'

This passes for a compliment from Skye.

'Nope. I used to, but now it's just good genes.' A hilarious lie, but I'm not about to reveal my true past to Skye: a chubby kid, started losing weight at fifteen and then never stopped, spent four months in a treatment centre before finally finding a way to eat without wanting to die, and now I'm just fine. Provided I eat within my limitations.

'Is that why you smoke?' I ask her, wondering if this may be our elusive common ground. 'To keep weight off?'

She shrugs, then gives me a sudden megawatt smile. 'Can't do coke any more, so...' Once again, I can't tell if she's joking. She tells me again that she's tired and wants to head home, and I do my best to hide my disappointment.

'Are you going to the Oscars?' she asks me as we walk a few blocks inland, following Lenny towards where a car is waiting to take Skye who knows where. Maybe back to Laurel Canyon, maybe to some hidden gem in a hip, rapidly gentrifying part of town where she will slip into a booth with a group of her closest Instagram model friends and talk in hushed, hysterical tones about the weirdo she was just forced to spend an hour with.

'I'm not sure.' I don't have an assignment to cover the Oscars yet; I left my enquiry emails too late and now all of my usual editors have already figured out who they're sending, and it's too late now for me to apply for press accreditation. 'I think your dad's going to win, though.'

'Really?' This is the most animated she's looked since we met, her words quicker and sharper. 'He wants it so much. He won't show it, but it's everything to him, especially now.'

I am not the only one who felt Clark was robbed at the Globes, and in the days since then the tide has turned in his favour, according to the pundits who make such predictions.

'He won the SAG, he's won almost every critics' prize going – I just can't see him losing it,' I tell her.

'I hope you're right.'

Once she's in the car, she winds down the window and removes her shades for the first time, fixing me with her piercing grey eyes. I want nothing more than to yank the door open and jump into the car beside her, and be whisked back along the freeway and up into the winding, spiralling hills of the canyon, back to that house that has become a permanent fixture in my dreams. But instead she raises her palm in a kind of frozen wave, and then the car is moving and gone and I'm still here, on the outside, the sun on my face suddenly vicious.

11

I watch Clark win his Oscar from a quote-unquote dive bar in West Hollywood, wedged into a corner trying in vain to hear his speech over the din surrounding me. I did not plan on watching the ceremony with a crowd, but the cockroaches have finally taken the upper hand in our ongoing war, and over the past week I've found multiple dead baby roaches scattered around the apartment, like a harbinger of something.

'Means they're breeding indoors,' the exterminator told me, his face permanently half-twisted in a way that befits his profession. 'When you see the infants.'

'That's bad news, right?'

'It's not good.' Evidently the landlord isn't paying him enough to even try to sugarcoat the truth. 'Gotta bomb the whole place, then put down boric acid.' The upshot is, I had to leave my apartment and can't return until at least four hours have passed, at which point I have to open every window and door for ventilation. Which is how I ended up here, missing most of Clark's words and watching Twitter to try to piece together what he's saying, finally giving up and elbowing my way through the crowd to get right underneath the screen, craning my neck to hear.

'There are so many people who share in this moment, so many people without whom I would never have even gotten to this room, never mind this stage,' Clark is saying now, a little breathless, running through the requisite list of agents, managers, producers, co-stars, executives, Neil Armstrong for his extraordinary spirit and story.

'Most of all, I have to thank my beautiful daughter Skye, my angel, whose courage and humanity is an inspiration to me every day. This one's for you, honey.' He raises the award high above his head as though saluting Skye, and I wonder whether she's watching this from her wing in the canyon, smiling placidly, maybe with tears in her eyes.

Amabella is significantly absent both from his speech and from the ceremony. Rumours began to swirl over the weekend: that she wouldn't be attending the Oscars, that she and Clark were spotted in a heated argument outside Equinox, that she's laying low after plastic surgery that left her with unexpected bruising, that Skye hates Amabella and gave her father an ultimatum, that Clark and Carol are reuniting. All of it and none of it may be true, but I'm choosing to believe that this is the beginning of the end. Six months is far longer than he should have ever have spent with her.

Things are looking up for Clark, and for me as well. After agonizing for an entire day over the wording of my email, I finally pitched my Ben Schlattman profile to Reel, and the editor responded much more quickly than I expected asking for more details, then responded again with a yes, a deadline and a fee. I know I should negotiate the latter, but it's already more money than I've made for a single piece in my life, and David, the editor, signed off his last email with another carrot: 'FYI, we might also want to use some of this in-book for the March 4 edition.' Meaning my profile, or some edited part of it, could be in the print magazine. A first.

As I was transcribing both parts of my interview with Schlattman, I had to focus on forgetting the actual experience of those conversations, and forgetting what happened in that room at the Montage. Nothing happened, in truth, but that's not the way it feels, and so typing up our conversation from breakfast felt like watching myself from afar, about to walk into a trap. There's a niggling sense in me that my first major profile for a Hollywood trade – and potentially my first ever piece in print – will always be sullied now, by something indefinable and dark and beyond my control. Schlattman only agreed to do the interview once he'd met me at the Globes afterparty, when I was a little drunk and eager to impress and wearing that dress, and now it's clear that was an audition of sorts. 'He's been stonewalling us,' David had said in his first email response to me, clearly impressed that I had persuaded Schlattman to talk, but it's not because I made him a pitch he couldn't refuse.

There's been a voice in my head all along telling me hardboiled truisms, things like *nobody ever got ahead in this business by having scruples*, and since I know I did nothing wrong in that hotel room, over the course of this week it's become easier to stop obsessing. Ben Schlattman's appetites do not make him any less compelling as an industry figure, and they don't put a dent in the pay cheque I'm going to get for this piece, nor in the prestige its publication will get me. And dissatisfied though I was with the Nest piece, it's turned out to be a decent calling card purely by virtue of Clark's name and unicorn status. I've sent out a slew of pitch emails cold to editors this week, people I've never met before, and they went less ignored than usual. One of them actually commissioned me, and a second said he'd be back in touch next month. Things are moving, it feels like, finally.

Idyllwilde takes Best Picture, and I slip out of the bar just as Ben Schlattman is emerging onto the stage with his fellow producers, averting my eyes and ordering a Lyft ride home. Even the roach graveyard that awaits me is preferable to watching Schlattman in HD.

But I should have waited, because now my eastward ride home coincides directly with the end of the Oscars, and with the requisite one-mile-radius of traffic hell. A maze of police perimeters and flash bulbs that stretches a full fifteen blocks, or so my driver tells me as he makes a sharp U-turn, trying to circumvent the chaos. 'It's like crossing the border,' he says, 'bomb squads, ID checks, helicopters, everything. I used to drive a limo, I worked the Oscars, the Grammys, the Globes – drove some pretty big people over the years. Jennifer Lopez and Ben Affleck, Cuba Gooding Jr, Christina Aguilera...'

'Really?' I ask, trying to sound impressed. 'Why did you give it up?'

'Big people, bigger problems,' he says with a shrug, and doesn't elaborate. I wonder if he's spent the night longing to cross that border as much as I have, or whether given enough time inside you really can become inured to it.

My phone vibrates in my hand, and I realize with a jolt that Clark has responded to the brief, breezy congratulations email I sent him barely ten minutes ago.

Hi Jessica – thanks, it's been quite a night! Headed to a little shindig in Beverly Hills, love to see you there if you can make it.

C.C.

At the end of his email is an address.

'I'm so sorry,' I say immediately to my driver, 'change of plans. Can we turn around?'

I give him the most generous tip I've ever given, to assuage my guilt about forcing him to make a U-turn back into the mayhem. It was worth it, though, to be here. The address Clark gave me turns out to be a nondescript door on an immaculate street that looks like a loading entrance, but when I ring the bell a suited man answers. There is no line of people, no velvet rope, no bouncers with iPads, but something tells me that I'm in the right place, something about the plush interior that I can see just behind the suit's shoulder, the single silver elevator that promises an ascent. I give him my name, certain that I'm about to be refused entry, already bracing for the rejection as he disappears, but after a moment he reopens the door and smiles and waves me in. Some indefinable string has been pulled, and I am inside.

The elevator whisks me seventeen storeys up to an outdoor rooftop, softly illuminated by gas lamps and furnished like an indoor space, with couches and ottomans and end tables. The crowd is sparse, deliberately so; there are maybe a hundred people here and most of them not recognizable faces, though I'm not paying much attention. There is only one face I'm looking for, and yet when he appears out of the half-darkness and strides towards me I'm still not prepared. All suits look alike to me, but the one Clark is wearing skims his lean silhouette, making him taller and broader and sharper, his hair tousled with flecks of silver visible through the dark, the angles of his face devastating in the firelight.

'I'm so glad you're here,' he says, beaming, and pulls me into a hug, and though his grip is loose suddenly I'm breathless.

'Me too.'

He leads me over to the bar and orders us two Old Fashioneds, because he remembers this is my drink without having to ask.

'Where's Amabella?' I ask innocently, as though I'm unaware of the rumour mill. As though I have no particular interest in his relationship.

'She's not here.'

I suppress a smile.

'Skye couldn't make it either tonight, but she'd love to see you,' he tells me when we're settled at a high table, facing outwards towards the party. 'She really enjoyed the other day.'

'Really?' I ask before I think better of it. 'I mean, that's great – I'm glad. I did too.'

He laughs a little, almost to himself.

'You don't have to be polite. I know she can be… difficult.'

'No, no, she honestly wasn't. I just wasn't sure if I was doing any good, or whether she really wanted to be there.'

'It's often hard to tell whether she wants to be anywhere.'

He looks haunted at this, as though his own words have startled him, and there is nothing in this moment that I wouldn't do to make him feel better.

'I loved your speech. I bet she did, too.' I look around then, realizing that I don't even know what afterparty this is. 'Are the rest of the cast here, the director?'

'No, I made my appearance at the official thing, but it was crawling with press and I just didn't have it in me. No offence.'

'None taken. Journalists are the worst.'

'Actually, it wasn't them that bothered me so much as all the people wanting to congratulate me. Is that strange for me to say?'

'On the night you won an Oscar? Maybe a little bit.'

'I'm sure I'll wake up tomorrow morning and be hungry for attention again – which, as you know, is the natural state of most actors. But somehow tonight it just felt odd to me. All these strangers and near-strangers, being so kind and so gracious and so grateful, as though I'd actually done something for them. When acting is one of the most selfish things you can possibly do with your life.'

'I don't know about that.'

'Convince me otherwise.'

'I'm not here to flatter your ego,' I tell him. 'I think you know acting is valuable. Fiction is valuable. Storytelling – it gives people something to rally around, and believe in, when their own lives are boring or frozen or unbearable. It's not just escapism, it can be community.'

'It's true. I used to get letters a lot on *Loner*, back when my agency still actually sent that stuff through to me, from fans saying things like that. People who were sick, in the hospital, who said that the show got them through. I'll never forget one woman who said that the show gave her a family. Like these characters were real to her.'

There's so much on the tip of my tongue. I was only in the treatment centre for a month, maybe less, and so long ago that I choose to erase it as a part of my personal history. How thin I was then, how stretched, and how close I was to death, or so they claimed. I brought the first three boxsets of *Loner* with me and played them every night after lights out, my clunky Dell laptop whirring and overheating beneath the sheets, and never felt alone. He does not need to know this.

'Right.' I'm trying to stay sharp but it's difficult now, warmed by the whiskey, my senses blurred by the reality of him. 'There you go. So maybe stop with the existential angst and enjoy the fact that you just won an Oscar.'

There are people circling us, trying to be subtle, but even at a party this sparse and secret Clark is a hot commodity, now more than ever. It's miraculous, now I think of it, that we've been left alone for this long. I can see, out of the corner of my eye, someone taking a selfie with Clark clearly positioned in the background, trying to be subtle, and failing.

'Let's talk about something other than me, for the love of

God,' he says, gesturing to a waiter for more drinks. 'How's your life? What's the haps in Echo Park?'

'Wow, I'm only going to tell you if you promise never to say "the haps" ever again.'

I tell him about the roaches, half-expecting his eyes to glaze over from shock because this is so far removed from his reality, but instead he lights up, starts telling me about his past.

'God, when I first moved to Hollywood I was dead broke, sleeping on friends' couches, and for a while I ended up in this place in Koreatown... I mean, you think that area's bad now, you should've seen it in the nineties. Rats, roaches, for a while there was a pigeon problem, something to do with the roof. I woke up once without knowing why, and then realized that a rat had just run right across my pillow. Maybe across my face.'

'How did you ever get to sleep?' I ask. 'The only thing I'll say for my roaches is they've never come near me. They're antisocial and I like them that way.'

'I loved it,' he murmurs. 'It felt like living in the wild. That was appealing to me at the time.'

'That was right after you dropped out of college?'

He raises an eyebrow.

'Yes, '89.'

'Is it weird that I know so much about your life?'

'Only because I know so little about yours.'

'That's how the relationship works.' After a pause, I clarify. 'I mean, between actor and viewer, or actor and adoring public. We see you every week on our TV screens, or at least every few months on a movie screen, and we get to feel like you're a part of our lives, but you're not. The screen doesn't go both ways.'

'Very profound.'

'So, what do you want to know?' I ask him, conscious that I've drunk more than I planned, conscious that I have not eaten enough today, conscious that things are blurring and loosening and I'm letting it happen.

'I want to know why you love this stuff so much.'

'What stuff?'

'Television. Movies. All of it. You don't love it like most people do – as entertainment. It's more, for you.'

'TV is reliable. Most characters on television don't fundamentally change, right? And even when dramatic things happen, they happen in patterns, in narrative arcs. I'd watch the same show over and over again because you can feel things, but in a safe way. Even when someone leaves the show, they get a finale, a payoff, a few goodbye scenes. It's comforting.'

He nods.

'At a certain point when I was growing up, I just needed things that I could control.'

'After your father left.'

I feel shivery, and excuse myself. As I make my way into a cavernous carpeted corridor towards the bathroom I feel eyes on me, though of course there are eyes on me. A nobody with a somebody always attracts attention, even at the discreet kind of party where no one will ask and none of this will end up in the tabloids.

When I return Clark is no longer alone, and I hover awkwardly on the fringes of his circle. A young woman with an impossibly golden blonde bob, two neat, slender men in suits, an older man who I think is Schlattman for one awful second, until he turns.

'Who's this?' he asks, and Clark beckons me over, introducing me by name without explaining my presence. To say I'm a journalist would not behoove me here, and so I stay silent and smile, though I know that from this they can only draw one conclusion. Clark has to know it too.

These are industry people, important people, but for once I can't find the energy to place their faces or to try to remember where I have seen their names in the trades. I want them to leave so that I have him to myself again, and sure enough after a few moments of polite conversation something unspoken passes through the group, and it dispels gently. This is how parties like this work, I think. You have to know the cues.

'*Armstrong* should've got Best Picture, too,' I tell him, sinking gratefully into a sofa beside the warmth of a roaring torch.

'Do you really believe that?'

'No.' I suddenly have no desire to lie to him. *Armstrong* was a solid, workmanlike biopic with a sharper-than-average script and a mesmerizing lead performance from Clark, not to mention a few stunning technical scenes in space, Armstrong's first walk on the moon included. But it's not doing anything particularly groundbreaking, and though it's exactly the kind of movie that gets labelled 'Oscar bait', Best Picture would be a stretch.

'What did you actually think deserved to win?'

'*Obelisk*, but I know it didn't have a chance.'

'Because of the risqué subject matter?'

'That, and the fact it's a tiny Sundance indie – it cost, what, $2 million or something crazy? And it's about a woman, so that was sort of the nail in the coffin.'

'What do you mean?'

'That Best Picture always goes to movies about men. White men, I should add.'

'That's not true.'

'Oh, really? When was the last time a movie with a female lead won Best Picture? I'll wait.'

His brow furrows.

'Yup,' I nod. 'Harder than you think, isn't it?'

'The Clint Eastwood thing,' he exclaims finally, 'the boxing – *Million Dollar Baby*!'

'Twelve years ago? That's your best answer? Also, that movie is more about Clint Eastwood's character and his man pain than Hilary Swank. Her story only matters insofar as it's filtered through his.'

'I can't argue with that,' he says, 'but she's certainly a lead in that movie.'

'Doesn't count. The correct answer would be *Chicago*, in 2002, fourteen full years ago.'

'Which didn't deserve to win.'

'No argument here, but are you seeing my point?'

'I don't think it's as straightforward as that,' he says, 'but you are technically correct about that category.'

'Yeah. So. I knew *Obelisk* didn't stand a chance, but I love to root for the underdog.'

'How do you know so much about Oscar history?'

'It's my job. And I didn't have a lot of friends growing up,' I say with a laugh. 'Gives you time to get really nerdy about Hollywood trivia.'

'I find that hard to believe.'

'Well, I had two friends at uni who also wanted to stay up all night and watch the Oscars with me, and write out our predictions on notecards beforehand. Tom always used to win, he was ridiculously good at working out the technical categories.'

'Who's Tom?'

'Just a friend from back home.' I take a long sip, watching him out of the corner of my eye. 'He just moved here, actually, he's an actor.'

'You don't say! Anything I'd know?'

I fill him in on Tom's history as a stage actor, his bit parts in BBC dramas, and then the pilot, the vampire thriller with an unexpectedly satirical edge. Clark chuckles out loud when I explain the notion of a blood shortage forcing vampires to develop bureaucracy.

'I'm actually going to the set tomorrow, it's their first day of shooting so I'm just going to observe, get some colour, maybe interview a couple of people. I can't really do anything with it until we know if the show's getting picked up, but Tom seems to feel good about the script, so.'

'Well, good for him. He sounds like exactly the kind of actor we need more of over here. Theatre background, some real training, an interest in the work and not the glory that comes after the work.'

'Yeah, he definitely did not get the role on the basis of his social media following.'

He smiles, acknowledging the reference. Our first conversation.

'Did I come off as a completely out-of-touch fool in that rant? Old Man Yells At Cloud?'

'No! I didn't think so. Someone getting passed over for a role because they don't have enough Instagram followers is bleak no matter how old you are. But we didn't really talk for long enough that day for me to form much of a sense of who you are.'

'Well, we have plenty of time.'

My head is spinning, my skin tingling, and I want to move closer and press myself into him, but this is something I can never take back. It can't be me who crosses that gap, not here in public, and not anywhere. This man is not within my reach, even if he's physically inches from me, but the whiskey and the fire and the look in his eyes are making it hard to steady myself.

'How's Skye?' I blurt out. 'Didn't she want to come tonight?'

'She did. But then, uh—' He pauses, clearly struggling with whether to tell me. 'She spoke to her mom, and it seems that call didn't go well.'

'Oh. Sorry.'

'I don't know what's wrong with her. Carol. She's been so... Well, you said it. Your kid tries something like this, I can't imagine wanting to be anywhere other than by their side. But Carol never was very traditional.' There's a bitterness in his tone that I've never heard before, his usual diplomacy about his ex-wife dissipating.

'Maybe she feels guilty for moving away. And instead

of confronting that guilt, she's just doubling down on not showing up,' I suggest.

'She and Sarah were always so enmeshed. From the moment Sarah was born, they were just… they came as one unit. Sarah had terrible nightmares when she was little, so Carol used to go into her bedroom and sleep with her. I got used to sleeping alone. Sarah would sort of cling to Carol, just always be at her side, and by the time Skye came along, there just wasn't any room for her. Probably why she and I have always been close.'

'You and Carol always seemed to have an amazing connection, though.'

But how could I possibly know this? I don't want him to think I'm one of the gullible public who believes everything they see of a star's persona, and yet. Clark and Carol were beloved for so long because they always seemed visibly, genuinely in love whenever they appeared in public together. They were relationship goals, they were flawless, they were the kind of couple that body-language experts were interviewed about in gossip rags, explaining why his hand on the small of her back or her angling her torso towards him demonstrated that they were built to last. I remember seeing coverage like that as recently as last summer, but who ever knows what the truth is behind the show? And it's not as though there weren't whispers. One persistent rumour on the internet's less mainstream, more dubious gossip corners was that Clark and Carol's marriage was a sham, built to cover up Clark's affair with his male co-star in *Loner*. In retrospect, this story probably originated with the show's rabid fans, many of whom wanted to see their antagonistic characters get together on-screen. But I wondered, as a teenager, and I wasn't the only one.

'I've been feeling bad about something,' Clark says, quietly enough that I have to lean in close. 'It's plaguing me, actually. Something I want to tell you, but.'

He finishes there. But. As though this were a sentence.

'You can trust me.'

'Did Skye say anything about her mother, the other day?'

'No.'

'I don't mean Carol. Her real mother.'

My mind is sluggish enough that I don't immediately understand him.

'Skye isn't Carol's. That's what I was hinting at before, just talking around it, but there it is.'

'You—'

'Had an affair. When I was a young asshole who got famous too fast and then married too fast, and I was away from Carol for months on this shoot in New Zealand.'

'With who?'

'A young woman who worked on the set. She was lovely, but not stable, and I didn't treat her very well. Sort of discarded her, after a while.' There's true revulsion in his voice, as though he's speaking directly to the man he was then. 'It was a terrible time. And when she told me she was pregnant, I knew I had to come clean with Carol.'

'But wait…' I'm trying to remember what press coverage there was of Carol's second pregnancy. I was too young at the time to be aware, but in the course of my research for interviewing Clark I went back and looked at archival scans of magazines. Her first pregnancy, with Sarah, was covered extensively, but I can't remember anything about her second.

'You passed the pregnancy off as Carol's? How?'

'You have to remember, this was before the internet became what it is now, and before people could track your every movement. Carol was already laying low at that point, raising Sarah, so when we announced that she'd quietly given birth to a second daughter, nobody really questioned it. Back then, you didn't have to announce everything like you do now.'

'My God.'

I don't know what to do with the image I've always had of the Conrads, now, but I should have known better than to buy in. Nothing is that golden.

'What happened to Skye's mum?'

He shakes his head.

'She dropped off the map, after the adoption. I tried for months to track her down, because I wanted to try and figure something out, some kind of arrangement, but she was gone.'

'And Carol just agreed to raise Skye as her own daughter?'

'Carol is extraordinary. In ways that are hard to describe in words. I have never deserved her.'

I don't know what to say to him.

'Jessica, if this ever got out... Well, you know.'

I want to tell him that I will hold this secret like a treasure and never give it up to anyone, that his confiding in me feels like lightning in my heart. But he looks worn out and I feel unsteady, the skyline and the lamplight pulsing around us, and I should not still be here at this hour. He's saying something, now, and I mumble in response that I just need to close my eyes for a second, sinking back on the couch. I want to sink into him, lean in and see whether he pulls me closer or stiffens, but this is not the moment, and I realize too late that I've said this out loud too, or some version of it.

The last thing I remember is the sprawling backseat of an unfamiliar car, dark wood and darker leather, and Clark saying my name.

12

I see the canyon the minute I'm awake. It takes me several minutes to process anything else: that I'm lying on my side, looking out at the view through two full walls of windows. This is nowhere I've ever woken up before.

I'm dizzy, when I finally raise my head. I'm still wearing my clothes from last night, my shoes and bag lined up neatly on the ground. Someone put me to bed last night, and though I have a dim memory of this, I have no idea who it was. I don't even remember leaving that party. The transition into too drunk came suddenly, and now here I am, unmistakably waking up the morning after in Clark Conrad's house.

A voice in my head that sounds suspiciously like Faye's is telling me to take a selfie in Clark Conrad's bathroom, except that this is not a moment I ever want to relive. Just when I was getting closer, I may have scuppered everything. There is no way he's going to take me seriously as a journalist again after this, if he ever did.

I don't remember seeing this bedroom during our house tour, probably because it's one of so many, all of them equally stunning. This room is quite literally larger than my apartment, and flooded with morning sun, because I've slept in for the first time in weeks. It's almost nine by the time I make it downstairs, showered but still fuzzy-eyed, wishing I had a change of clothes. The kitchen looks exactly the same as in the photographs we ran on Nest, neat and clean and barely lived in, with no sign of the 'bachelor pad reality' Jerome referenced. I can't imagine Clark ever leaving anything out of place.

'Morning, miss,' comes a voice to my left, and I turn to see a woman smiling from behind the breakfast bar. She's middle-aged, Hispanic, dressed in khaki shorts and a polo shirt, and I remember now that Clark has a housekeeper named Lupe. Though a lot of Hollywood stars on his level employ a full staff, Clark keeps it 'low-key' as Jerome put it to me, employing just a housekeeper and a gardener, and occasionally a private chef when he's prepping for a role.

'Morning!' I chirp back, trying too hard to seem casual. After my dad left, for several years my mother hired a cleaner who came once a week, and even though I was young I already felt a deep-rooted kind of discomfort, something close to guilt. I know that given Clark's reputation for largesse, Lupe probably makes more money than I do, and yet I still feel it. I should tip her, probably, but I have no cash.

'Is – um, is Mr Conrad here?'

'No, miss, he's always out by eight. Goes to the water to swim.'

'The ocean?'

She nods, and I understand. He doesn't use the pool any more.

'He said to make sure you eat.'

'Oh.' I laugh, too hard. 'Yeah, I probably— That's a good idea.'

'Any special diet? Vegetarian?'

'No, I eat everything. But I can just pick something up, I don't want to put you out—'

She acts as though I haven't spoken, already cracking eggs into a bowl and halving an avocado and slicing bread, and I'm too hungry to put up any real resistance. It's been a very long time since anyone cooked for me.

'Thank you so much,' I call out lamely as I leave a few minutes later, having washed up my plate and silverware. 'Have a great day!' But she's too far away to hear me, probably outside, and rather than prolong our interaction I leave a thank-you note on the counter, on a pad of thick cream notepaper that I realize too late is embossed with Clark's initials. I put my own name in the corner, for clarity.

Undead is shooting on a studio lot in central LA, less than a half-hour drive from here, and though the rush-hour traffic is close to gridlock I still arrive with time to spare, and pick up my 'guest' security pass from a bored-looking man in the entry booth, who directs me to Stage 17.

I've grown used to these spaces over the years, the jarring fact that the most glamorous industry in the world has its roots in vast, dusty lots full of warehouses and trailers. Visitors are ferried around in golf carts between sound stages – sprawling hangars that house fake worlds, entire city streets and apartment buildings and family homes beloved by audiences who look at them and believe they are real. I've been on sets so large and convincingly lived-in that it's possible to forget yourself, and forget your surroundings, right up until the moment you look through a seemingly sunlit window and see empty space and a lighting rig outside.

Inside the stage it's dark and cool, with stacks of plywood and mechanical equipment lining the walls, and though the sets are still being constructed I can see part of a graveyard from a distance.

'Hello there,' Tom whispers into my ear out of nowhere, and I turn to smile at him.

'Sneaking up on me in a darkened room is very method of you.'

'You could probably get hired to play the undead yourself right now.' He gives me an exaggerated once-over, but apparently the dim lighting here isn't doing much to hide my dark eye-circles and lack of makeup. 'Too much Oscar night revelry?'

'That's only the half of it. Please take a seat while I fill you in on the wall-to-wall horror show that has been my life for the past forty-eight hours.'

I tell him about my extermination saga, carefully omitting everything that took place after ten o'clock last night.

'Wow. From roaches to red carpet.'

'I was nowhere near the carpet, thank God. I watched it from a bar, but only because I had to wait for the roach bomb to clear before I could go home.'

He mimes a dry heave.

'You know, Jess, there are times when I think the unremitting glamour of your life here in Hollywood is going to your head.'

'It was inevitable.'

'So did you come home to a massacre? Bodies strewn as far as the eye can see, one lone roach just screaming for its parents, wandering through the wasteland of its fallen brethren...'

'You're really wasted as an actor, this is beautiful. I almost feel guilty for the roach genocide I committed. Almost.'

'Well, now that we've established your taste for the kill, want a tour of the vampire lair?'

These being modern, urban-dwelling vampires with a satirical edge, their 'lair' is actually a penthouse apartment with Caesarstone countertops and heated floors and sweeping views of an indeterminate skyline. A running comic thread of the series, Tom tells me, will be that the vampire protagonists move into this apartment building for the amenities, only to gradually discover – thanks to the new world order in which vampires now outnumber humans – that all of those amenities are unavailable without humans to run them.

'There's no concierge at the front desk, no staff to clean the pool, nobody to repair the machines in the gym, the rooftop terrace is unfinished, there's nobody to take Amazon Prime deliveries—'

'Do vampires use Amazon Prime? Or gyms?'

'These ones do. They're very entitled.'

He shows me around the apartment set, which so far only consists of the open-plan living room and kitchen, the refrigerator impressively already stocked with vacuum-sealed sachets of fake blood.

'Isn't this living room going to be kind of... sunlight flooded?' I ask, pointing at the huge windows. 'For vampires that are allergic to sunlight?'

'Yeah,' Tom replies slowly. 'To be honest, I'm not sure the writers have entirely got their version of the vampire mythology down. Maybe they'll just explain it away as being sunlight-proof glass. I do know we're doing a hell of a lot of night shoots.'

'Wait, you haven't even told me what your character is.'

'Oh!' he exclaims, then slips seamlessly into a honeyed Southern drawl. 'Why, I'm the eccentric neighbour with a cross nailed to his door who carries holy water in a flask. Which is smart, by the way.'

'So you're not a vampire?'

'You're gonna have to watch the pilot and find out!'

'Oh come on, I'll sign whatever NDA you need me to, just don't leave me in suspense.'

'Basically, it's unclear what his deal is for the first couple of episodes, but he's a vampire hunter who lost his entire family, and now he's kind of unhinged. Not in a single-minded vengeance way – he's kind of lost his edge, and so if we get picked up to series, he's going to end up being turned into a vampire by about midway through the season. Which is his worst nightmare.'

'Sounds dark.'

'Yeah, but then I think he'll probably discover the upsides, reunite with his undead family, or whatever.'

'And they're letting you keep the hair?' It's not as long

now as I've seen it before; cut to just above his shoulders, but it's still an unusual look for a teen-skewing network TV show.

'Oh yeah, they love the hair. I think that's why I got the role, honestly; it's a bit of a Jesus vibe.'

He takes me to another corner of the stage filled with racks of costumes and props designed to be worn by extras and background actors.

'So your boy won his Oscar,' he says quietly as I'm rummaging through a box full of prosthetic fangs.

'Yeah! I missed half his speech because the bar was so loud, but seemed like people online were happy about it.'

'Well yeah, everybody loves him.'

Feeling the need to distract him, I slip on a set of fangs and grin.

'You'd better keep those, and don't tell anyone. Thief.'

'I'm really just here for the free stuff.'

There's something different about Tom. He carries himself differently, a little taller, maybe he's started working out since moving here, or maybe the confidence of having landed a pilot has shifted something in his body. I can't entirely put my finger on it, but when I briefly turn away and then look back at him, there's a moment where he seems new to me.

'If we get picked up, we might end up shooting in Vancouver or maybe Atlanta,' he tells me as we're walking from the stage towards the makeup trailer, where he's due to get fitted for his own customized set of fangs.

'For the tax breaks?'

'Yeah, which sucks.'

'I don't know, I'd rather live in Vancouver than LA.'

'No you wouldn't.'

'Well, okay, I wouldn't. And you wouldn't. But most sane people who aren't trying to get into this industry would. Anyway, a ton of stuff shoots in Vancouver, you could probably just as easily get cast there than here. Here just has the mystique of Tinseltown.'

'I hate that,' he grumbles. 'What is the tinsel part about? It's not like this is a massively Christmassy place. Or is it secretly always Christmas in LA and Tinseltown is like, a code word for those in the know?'

'You've clearly given this a lot of thought,' I say, bumping my shoulder into his. 'Weirdo.'

When we get to the makeup trailer, I excuse myself, leaving Tom to his fitting. Wandering aimlessly around the studio lot disoriented by all the identical-looking sound stages, I run into a chunky brunette who's juggling two cellphones and a clipboard. When I ask, she confirms that she is a publicist, and doesn't seem fazed by the fact that I'm a reporter.

'You're not writing this up for anybody yet, right?' she asks vaguely, eyes down at the larger of her two iPhones.

'No, I wouldn't pitch a piece just on the pilot, but I'm really excited about the show. Just on a hunch, I feel like it has the potential to become something.'

'We're hoping so. Who are you with?'

I tell her that I'm a freelance journalist, and barely contain a laugh as I see her face visibly fall. Not even the news that

I have a piece in the works for Reel seems to help, and so I bring out the big guns.

'You might actually have seen a piece I wrote recently, on Clark Conrad.'

'Oh!' She looks up from her phone. 'The Nest piece. Yeah, that was… Good job getting him to talk!'

'Thanks,' I smile, glossing right over the way she trailed off from describing the actual piece. I know that it was mediocre, a compromised version of what I want it to be. And now having spent real time with Clark, seen glimpses of the insides of him, I know how much better a piece I could write.

'I've gotta run, but take my card,' Gina, the publicist, says, pressing it into my hand. 'Let's stay in touch.'

I smile and tell her yes, great, but my mind is elsewhere now, stewing once again on Clark and the way I could describe him in words, the way I could reintroduce him to the world in the way he deserves.

'I'm glad you came,' Tom tells me later, when we're taking a break from the sun inside the craft service trailer.

'Me too.'

Something about the way he's talking, the way he's been watching me all day, has set a tension in the air. Conversation is never stilted between us, but now I can't think of anything to say, and I don't think it's just because my head is pounding again.

'Jess—' he starts. 'This whole move to LA, uprooting myself, it's got me thinking about everything. About what I want out of this next phase of my life, you know? And whatever happens with the show, it's always going to be a great big question mark. It might get picked up and then cancelled at midseason, or it might become a huge hit and then I'll be tied into a five-year contract and eventually start hating it.' He's talking faster and faster, a tell that he's nervous. 'I have no control over that. But I don't want to be so rootless any more in every aspect of my life, you know?'

'Mm-hmm,' I say, uncertain.

'I don't want to be one of those clichés who just never commits to anything, is what I'm saying. I've always been like that. And I've only been in LA for a couple of months but I already see what it could do to me, how you can just get sucked into this endless cycle of parties and pills and better parties and better pills, and— anyway, what I'm saying is, I've been thinking.'

'Okay.'

'Do you want to have dinner with me?'

There's a moment where I know I could choose to wilfully misunderstand him. I could choose to take this as a casual friend invite, instead of the larger question it clearly is.

'Tom…'

He reaches over the plastic table to take my hand, his thumb pressing into my palm, and I try to remember how I felt for him. But it's impossible now for me to contemplate kissing him.

'Tom, I'm so… I'm flattered. But we've been there, done that. Right? We were great, but we both knew when it ended that it was time. I don't want to ruin what we've got now by—'

'Don't give me the "ruin our friendship" line, Jess.'

'I'm pretty sure you used that exact line on me back in the day.'

'Yeah, because I was pretending to be okay with us ending things.'

'Tom, that's insane, you were the one who broke it off. Don't rewrite history, because there are at least four girls in London I could call up right now to corroborate my memory of how that whole thing ended.'

'I know, I was a dick, but you were never really there with me when we were together. You were always somewhere else, always chasing some fictional world, even when we were – you know – together. And I loved that about you, that you got so absorbed in your work and in movies and in all of it, I still do. But now we're both older and established and—'

'Come on, I'm twenty-five, you're twenty-seven, I'm starting to feel like I might be getting somewhere but even saying that is probably jinxing it. You just got your first pilot. We're not established.'

His face is falling now.

'Okay. That's a no to dinner, then?'

'Tom, do you really want to do this right now? Here? It's your first day, why don't we just— In fact, yeah, let's get dinner, and we can talk this over properly.' I grasp inside my bag for my phone, intending to pull up the calendar to schedule a date. 'Let's just pick a day when I feel less like death.'

The moment I look at my phone, I forget the calendar. My screen is taken up with a series of push alert news notifications, three in a row from different outlets.

Clark Conrad Accused of Domestic Violence – Report

Amabella Bunch Alleges That Clark Conrad Physically Assaulted Her

Clark Conrad, Fresh Off His Oscar Win, Accused of Abusing His Girlfriend

13

I read the words over, three times. Then I get up without saying another word, a hot tingling rising through my body, making me numb. I step out of the trailer, trying to take a deep breath but the air feels too close. Within my immediate line of sight, three separate people are holding their phones, looking nonplussed. I see Gina huddled in conversation with what looks like another publicist, their expressions sombre, and though I can't be sure I know they're talking about this. Clark has nothing to do with *Undead*, but there's no way anyone can be talking about anything but this.

Tom tries to stop me leaving, tries to hold on to me and I shake him off, fully running away until I find a private shaded area behind a row of trailers to the west of the lot. There, I read the headlines over again, and then brace myself to read the full articles. Amabella has filed for a restraining order against Clark, claiming that he's been physically and verbally abusive throughout their relationship. There are photographs of her, no makeup, close-up, looking directly into the camera, with bruises visible on her neck and her left cheek.

I zoom in on each of the photos in turn, squinting as though there's any way I can possibly tell anything from pixels. Even as I'm doing this, I know that it's more a distraction tactic than anything, because I don't need to look this closely to know that the bruises are not real. It's not possible.

I start walking home on instinct, almost unconsciously, because I'm so wrapped up in reading every detail of this story. Amabella's specific claim, as detailed in the restraining order filing, goes as follows: Clark was mentally abusive almost from the very beginning of their six-month relationship. 'He was controlling about what clothes I wore, what kind of work I did, how I spent my spare time,' she's quoted as saying, 'but it was kind of flattering at first. Until it didn't end.' He got physical with her on several occasions, she says: grabbing her by the wrists, the throat, pushing her against walls, throwing things at her. One time, she claims that he locked her in the safe room at his home – a room that should in theory only lock from the inside – for two full hours. And then, most recently, the physical violence, as evidenced by her bruises. The judge granted a temporary restraining order, preventing Clark from coming within one hundred feet of Amabella or her residence.

I feel shaky, almost outside of my body as I run all of this over in my head, letting the images solidify, waiting to see if any part of them feels possible. Could he? The brute in these stories is so remote from the man I've known Clark to be for most of my life, never mind the man I've actually got to know over the last month. Objectively, I don't know him that well, but there's a gut level on which I've known him for a very long time, before we even met. That part of me, coupled with the strange expression on Amabella's face in these photos – the solemn eyes and tiny almost-smirk – confirms my sense that something is off.

When I first moved to LA, in defiant denial of the realities of the city, I walked everywhere. Time and time again I would map out a manageable-looking route on Google Maps – only a forty-minute walk, entirely feasible – and set out with a spring in my step, enjoying the sweetness in the air and the miraculous quiet of manicured streets. These walks would inevitably end with me sweating, sore-footed, on some sun-blistered portion of an endless freeway – or, even worse, on a road where the sidewalk suddenly ended without warning, giving me no choice but to turn back. But today, the bleak walk home gives me exactly the head space I need. Midway through I get a text from Faye, the alert sliding down to partially block the photograph on my screen.

Faye: I'm sorry, but those bruises look fake as fuck.

Jessica: One of her many skills is makeup design, right?

Faye: YUP. And there's a bunch of pics of her on Getty from the day this attack supposedly happened, looking just fine.

Jessica: Wow. She's not even good at this.

Faye: Have you spoken to him??

I don't reply to this.

The route from the studio lot to my apartment is a straight eighty-minute shot along Melrose, and by the time I'm home I'm drenched with sweat and desperate to get out of last night's clothes. But once I'm showered and changed, it becomes very clear to me that there is somewhere else I need to be. And for once, the traffic from Echo Park to Laurel Canyon is close to non-existent, which I would take as a sign if I believed in such things.

When my driver gets halfway up the winding roads into the canyon, it's another story, and of course, I should have counted on this. A small mob of paparazzi has assembled outside the gate of Clark's house, photographers on small ladders, reporters clutching microphones and digital recorders, all of them lying in wait. There is no way for me to get to the intercom, and even if I could, I can't risk having these vultures flood in after me.

But something comes back to me from my interview with Jerome, something that wasn't relevant to the piece but still struck me as interesting. There's a second entrance for deliveries and large vehicles, he said, but with a wink that indicated subtext. What this second entrance is really for is keeping secrets.

And sure enough, when I walk around the sharp downward bend and follow the road down, there's a tiny alleyway leading upwards to a gate with another intercom. When I ring the buzzer, there's no answer, but when I try a second and then a third time, finally a familiar voice answers.

'Hi, Lupe? It's Jessica, from this morning. I just wanted to see if he's here.'

A silence, during which I literally grit my teeth. And then the sound of the buzzer, and I'm inside.

'Hello?'

I move cautiously through the hallway, which feels quieter and more still than ever, and I see him. He's wearing a variation of his usual three-piece suit – fitted jeans, waistcoat and shirt, but no jacket and the shirt is half untucked, and he looks like he did in that newscast I saw after Skye almost died, leaving the hospital under the flash of neon bulbs. Drained.

'Hey,' I say, softly. 'I just wanted to see how you're doing. And I also wanted to thank you, for last night.'

'Quite a night.'

'I don't really know when I went from being pleasantly tipsy to embarrassing, but I'm sorry about that.'

'You weren't embarrassing. Sort of bewilderingly charming, in fact, even when you couldn't quite string a sentence together any more.'

'It's probably the accent. Hides a multitude of sins.'

He shoots me that same crooked smile, a smile like he's ashamed of it, and I follow him to the couch.

'So.'

'So,' he echoes, pausing as his phone begins to vibrate on the coffee table. I glance at the screen: Peyton.

'Been dodging her calls all day,' he says.

'This is probably one of those times when you want to take your publicist's calls.'

'Come on, you met her. She's not really— I mean she's

great, incredible at her job, but it's just not a fit for me. I've never had a personal publicist before, I'm not sure what made me think I could start now.'

The only way I can process this is to not think too hard about it; the fact that Clark Conrad is currently undergoing the biggest crisis of his career, and the only person here to witness it, or to advise him, is me. My mind is racing, but I can't just stay silent.

'If you don't want to deal with Peyton, you might want to look into hiring one of those crisis management people. Just temporarily.'

Head in his hands, he gives no indication that he's heard me.

'You know, like in *Scandal* – they spin a situation, figure out the best way to redirect the narrative, discredit the other side...'

He looks up, sharply.

'You mean hire someone to make Amabella look bad?'

'No, I mean—'

'Because I would never do that. It doesn't matter what she's said or done, I will not stoop to that. That kind of mud-slinging, it's crass.'

Having him glare at me for the first time, snap for the first time, should make me wither. I would have expected it to wreck me, and yet I feel energized. I know how to handle him.

'Okay. You're right. But the fact remains that she's making you look very, very bad, and staying silent is basically an admission of guilt as far as the media is concerned. You don't have to take my advice, but you should take someone's.'

He sighs.

'I don't want to hire anybody to handle this. Apart from anything else, the fact that I've hired someone will be news in itself. Talk about an admission of guilt.'

On this, he has a point. I've seen news stories created from much less.

'It's my own fault,' he murmurs. 'I should've known better than to get involved with her – I knew she was too young, and a little flighty. But I didn't know she had such a temper.'

'Was there any warning? That she was planning something like this?'

'I don't even know what that would look like,' he says, hopelessly. 'She'd certainly been unhappy, but it was an inconstant thing, with us. Kind of volatile. We broke it off for good about a week ago – or I suppose I did, in the end.'

'And she didn't like that.'

'Well, it was mutual, I thought. It's not as if I dumped her out of the blue.'

'Do you know what she's saying? The details of it?'

'That I was a monster. Beat her up, called her terrible things, made her miserable, tried to control her? I mean… my God, anyone who knows Amabella, the one thing they'll say is that nobody could control that girl. She's headstrong. You'd be a fool to even try.'

'Well, I don't know much about the legal side, but from my perspective the restraining order is the part of this that looks worst.'

'It's a temporary restraining order, and they hand those out like candy – there's no hearing, nothing. My lawyers didn't even get the heads up until it had already been filed, it's a total racket.' He doesn't even sound angry, I realize, just truly bewildered. 'I mean, we never even lived together and I think I probably went to her apartment twice? Maybe three times in our entire relationship? The idea that I'm going to show up there, it's just so strange.'

'It's for show. She knew "judge granted a restraining order" would look bad for you.'

'I mean, the truth is most of our relationship was conducted in public to some degree. We spent a lot of our time out – she always liked to be seen, you know, to be in the right places, events and so on. If I'd been the kind of boyfriend she says I was... It just doesn't make sense that nobody else would have witnessed it. It never happened, there is not a single person who will back her up.'

'That's good. If it's just her word against yours, and people start coming out in support of you—'

'What are people saying?' he asks me, with a vulnerability I've never heard in him before.

'Well...'

I open Twitter on my phone, along with the comments sections on the three news stories I read earlier, and skim a selection.

'I met Clark Conrad once and he was the sweetest most lovely man. No way he could do anything like this.'

'I've always found something slightly creepy about Conrad. His Nice Guy thing is too carefully honed not to be an act.'

'why are so many people jumping to conclusions based on one allegation? has he ever been accused of anything like this before? seems like you want him to be guilty.'

'I know for a fact Clark isn't capable of hurting anyone, much less a person he loved. People who read everything they see on the internet are part of the problem.'

'Oh look, another woman coming forward about abuse in Hollywood, another online mob just chomping at the bit to discredit her.'

'Does anyone else find it creepy that his ex-girlfriend looks like a clone of his daughter? I thought this Amabella chick was Skye.'

'This is AWFUL Clark and his family have been through enough! This scheming bitch is taking advantage when he's vulnerable.'

'What exactly do you people think she has to gain by lying about this? How does this help her in any way? She has plenty of her own money, and she's going up against one of the most powerful men in the industry.'

'Pretty convenient she's just coming out with this now her divorce is finalized. She got nothing in that settlement (pre-nup) so she needs to go elsewhere for her next payout. Anyone who doesn't see this for what it is is a moron.'

'It's amazing how much more willing people are to believe

that women are lying than they are to consider the possibility that a man they admire might not be a good person.'

'Those bruises are FAKE, I am a certified nurse and that is not how bruises would present after the kind of attack (and timeframe) she says happened. Can't believe people are buying this, it's full *Gone Girl* shit.'

'It's a mixed bag,' I tell him, honestly. 'But a lot of people are on your side. And this is before you've even said anything, which is why I think you should say something.'

'Peyton and I did talk, briefly. We're issuing a denial, kind of a boilerplate thing, just making it clear that the allegations are untrue.'

'That's not going to be enough. Even if it doesn't look bad to most people, there will be enough media outlets that spin it so that it does. I promise you, there are a huge number of media companies right now on the verge of collapse, just panicking and looking for any way to get traffic so that they can keep themselves afloat, and a story like this is like a lifeline to them. They're not going to let it go. So you might as well try to take some control of the narrative.'

'Why do I need to hire a crisis manager, when I have you?' He says this not sarcastically, but with real admiration.

'Well, maybe you don't. Because I have an idea.'

'I'm sure you do.'

'I want to write a real profile of you. No Q&A, no softball questions about your house, just an in-depth piece about who you really are.'

'After this, and after what I told you last night, *that's* what you want to write about?' He shakes his head incredulously. 'You must be a masochist.'

'Come on.'

'What reputable outlet is going to run a piece like that right now? And risk looking like they're supporting an abuser?'

'It'll be a tougher sell than it would have been two weeks ago, for sure. But people will want to hear your side of the story, and I think a lot of editors will jump at the chance to give you a platform to tell it. I already have an in with Reel.'

'Reel? They're a trade.'

'I know, but have you seen their online stuff? They're doing more and more glossy profiles, junkets, even clickbait galleries. They need traffic just like anyone else, and I think doing this in a trade will look better. We can angle it as a post-Oscar victory lap, what you're doing next and so on, and then work in the personal stuff in a more subtle way. That way it doesn't look like you're trying to get sympathy.'

'What's your in with them?'

'I have an interview with Ben Schlattman about to go live.'

He laughs sharply.

'Really? Well, if I'm following Ben, I guess I do stand a chance of looking good by comparison.'

I smile tightly, sitting on all the things I wish I could say.

'Okay,' he continues, nodding slowly. 'God help me, but your cockamamie plan is actually sounding good.'

'As it should. Amabella doesn't have much of a reputation as it is, so you don't need to badmouth her at all in the profile, just give your perspective on things, say that you're bewildered by the allegations and you wish her only the best, and then we focus on your career, your upcoming projects, and your new life as a single father. Because the thing you want to avoid is—'

'Is what?' He looks expectantly at me, because I cut myself off.

'Is for people to start drawing a connection between Skye and Amabella.' Silence, for a long time, but I hold my nerve.

'Yeah, that had occurred to me as well,' he murmurs at last, his head falling back into his hands. 'God. I just… I hate this. I hate having my family go through this. I hate the chess game of it all.'

'I know.'

'I don't know how any of this happened.'

It's an impulse, to run my hand through his hair, but once I start I don't stop, and he doesn't move. It's less soft than I expected, more like wire, but warm. After a while, he reaches up and takes my hand in his and holds it, our fingers intertwined against the nape of his neck.

14

Just as Clark anticipated, the profile is a tough sell. Reel's editor David calls me back immediately when I email him the pitch, and it's clear that he's confused, trying to figure out how seriously to take my claim of access to Clark.

'Just for my own edification – are you really telling me Clark Conrad has agreed to this?' he asks, and I say yes, trying not to sound too self-satisfied. David is clearly wrestling with his conflicting impulses to snap up this story, and to protect Reel from the inevitable criticism it will face if it runs a fawning profile of Clark in this particular moment.

'But isn't Reel sort of bulletproof in that regard?' I argue. 'That's why I brought this to you, instead of someone in the men's lifestyle space. The profile can be industry-focused, about what's next for him after his Oscar win, but I'll weave in the personal life stuff and you'll still get all the buzz and pickup from those quotes.'

He still says no, though I can hear in his voice that he's tempted. 'Let's stay in touch,' he says, obviously unwilling to let me get off the phone, especially when I make it clear that I'll be taking the pitch elsewhere. But the truth is I won't, at least not for now, because I don't know where to start and I have a sneaking suspicion that David will come around. A new spate of articles has emerged pointing out that there was no record of the police ever having been called, either to Skye's apartment or to Clark's home, with an LAPD statement confirming as much. A model ex-boyfriend of Amabella's posted a Snapchat video in which he seemingly called her a liar, facing into the camera with his shirt off as he talked about 'girls who try to tear you down when they can't get your money'. And Amabella herself was out at a club in West Hollywood last night, 'not exactly keeping a low profile in the wake of her allegations of abuse against ex-boyfriend Clark Conrad', as one tabloid sniffily put it. The comments below the article were even less kind. Clark's fans have started a hashtag campaign across social media, #WeBelieveInClarkConrad, which has gained support from a lot of industry power players. Already, the narrative is shifting.

The real clincher comes the next morning, two days after Amabella's accusations broke, when Skye posts to Instagram for the first time since her suicide attempt. The picture was a black-and-white shot from her childhood: in a forest, a young, shaggy-haired Clark grinning at the camera with tiny Skye in his arms.

When I was five, my parents took me to the Big Basin Redwoods State Park on a road trip. I wanted to climb this tree so badly, but of course it was too dangerous and I'd never have made it up there on my own. So my father carried me up on his back, then let me sit on his shoulders to see the view. Just like he's been doing for me my entire life. He's always been my rock. There will always be people who try to take advantage of his kindness and his strength, but the truth will always win out.

Skye's post explodes, of course, prompting media coverage just as feverish as the accusations did, and puncturing any possibility that she and Amabella may be linked as abused women in Clark's life. It's less than half an hour before David calls me back.

'Can you get this done for Friday?' he asks. 'We're on the line with his publicist right now trying to organize a quick shoot – we want to blow this out, maybe even get it into the print edition if we can.'

'Wait, you're speaking to Peyton?' I ask quickly. 'I'm not going through her on this. I'm dealing with him directly. You can organize the shoot through her if you want, but just make it clear that her purview begins and ends with the photos.'

David clearly doesn't know quite what to do with this, but when we speak again a couple of hours later, he drily asks me if I'm psychic.

'As it turns out, Peyton is no longer working with Clark. I guess he fired her this morning.'

'Yeah, that doesn't surprise me.'

'So I have to ask, can you talk to him and figure out when to get this shoot done?'

'Sure.'

I can hear the smile in Clark's voice when I call. He wants to do the shoot not at the house, but at the office he's just leased to house his new production company.

'Your production company? When did this happen?'

'Well, you know, I saw your interview with Schlattman and I just thought: that could be me!' he jokes.

'God, perish the thought.' I'd actually forgotten the Ben Schlattman piece was going live today, and ironically it's been more or less buried by all the Clark news.

'In all seriousness, you did a great job. Ben's never sounded better, and I know that can't have been an easy one to wrangle.'

'Thank you. He's definitely a character.'

'I only hope you can do half as good a polish job on me.'

'Oh, I'm not too worried about making you look good.'

The shoot is arranged, and I tell the photographer where and when to meet Clark at the offices. As for me, Clark suggests that we do the interview over dinner.

'Back in the day when I actually did one or two of these things, that seemed to be the norm. Do an activity during, make it seem less like an interrogation. One guy wanted to take me paragliding while he interviewed me.'

'Hard pass. But dinner sounds good, assuming you know somewhere discreet.'

And of course, he does.

Clark Conrad Is Not Without His Insecurities

Published March 3, 2016 on Reel.com

By Jessica Harris

I'm sitting across from Clark Conrad on a sun-dappled patio in Silver Lake, trying to figure out why he's so reluctant to talk about himself. 'It's always seemed strange to me that so many actors are such narcissists,' he tells me, the corners of his eyes crinkling in bewilderment. 'Because acting is the opposite of talking about yourself. It's disappearing into someone else's skin.' The decision to speak with me this evening, then, is a conflicted one. But Conrad has had what he drily describes as 'an interesting year' thus far, and the forty-five-year-old actor is nothing if not proactive. 'I started to realize that if you just say nothing, people end up saying things on your behalf. Nature abhors a vacuum, and this business abhors a silence. I figured it was time to say something.'

Conrad has a lot of things to say. He is articulate and measured and immensely witty, his trademark coiffed hair becoming increasingly tousled over the course of the evening as he runs his hands through it. It's a gesture he goes to when he's in search of the right phrase; in conversation as in work, he is a perfectionist. We are speaking just three days after the Oscars, where he won the Best Actor prize for his meticulous, nuanced performance in the biopic *Armstrong*.

'What do you want from me, here?' Clark asks, as our waiter refills our glasses of Sancerre. 'What do people say about these things?'

'I don't know – I haven't profiled a lot of Oscar winners before. Say something winning, yet modest.'

'What did you call it, a victory lap?' He shudders. 'Can't you just make up something the internet will like and pretend I said it?'

'That would be unethical.'

I clink my glass against his, and turn my recorder back on.

After a string of acknowledged box office failures including the much-anticipated adaptation of bestseller *The Silver Circle*, Conrad admits he had a lot riding on this performance.

'I was at a moment where I was no longer sure of my choices,' he admits with a wry smile. 'And *Armstrong* was the first time I had felt really strongly about something in a while. I knew how great the material was, I knew how great the people involved were, but I was not sure I was the right guy for the role. So that validation meant a lot. What a surreal evening.'

Insecurity might seem a surprising word for someone at Conrad's height of fame to use, but he uses the word more than once during our conversation. A lack of security marked his early life, too; Conrad was orphaned by the age of ten. His father, the photographer Philip Conrad, and his mother, a part-time teacher, were both killed in a car accident in 1980, after which he was raised by his paternal grandparents. 'The first ten years of my life, I would describe as idyllic,' he admits, recalling his upbringing in the suburbs of San Diego. 'My parents were as good as it gets, and everything I've ever done right as a father, I learned from them.' But though he has never gone into details, and declines to do so this evening, his teenage years with his grandparents were less sunny, with 'wrongdoing on both sides. I was chomping at the bit to get out of there once I was eighteen.'

And so, to Hollywood, where Conrad couch-surfed for the better part of a year before landing his first speaking role on *All My Children*. The pace of daytime did not agree with him, he says, though he credits the show with developing several of the muscles he still uses in his work today. 'Memorizing twenty, thirty pages of dialogue a day, and regurgitating it all in one take? That's one hell of a bootcamp, particularly if you never had the opportunity to do theatre.'

It was a full seven years before Conrad landed the role that would become his against-the-odds breakout – the title part in a midseason replacement NBC drama called *Loner*, about a seemingly cynical and ruthless lawyer moonlighting as a heroic vigilante. 'It didn't feel like anyone really had high hopes for the show,' he recalls. 'We were coming in at midseason, and it seemed they only gave us the order out of sheer desperation, because they didn't have anything else to fill the gap. The ratings were rough for that first season, but NBC, God bless them, took a chance on us.' As many, including Conrad, have noted before, *Loner* was ahead of its time in many respects, a superhero show before they were a dime a dozen, inspired more by *Batman* than by other legal dramas. While there are a lot of things about the show that should be laughable – not least of them the lead character's actual name, Richard Loner – it was consistently so much richer and deeper and smarter than anyone anticipated that it developed a dedicated audience, and a viewership large enough to keep it on the air for five beloved seasons.

Much like George Clooney had done on *ER* a few years prior, Conrad found an unlikely route into movie stardom by way of network television. His heartthrob status among teenagers and their moms alike translated into a global fan base that propelled him to blockbuster success – the *Reckless* trilogy has grossed more than $1 billion worldwide – and critical acclaim. And for twenty years, he was one half of Hollywood's most beloved golden couple, ever since he and Carol Conrad (née Marsh) first stepped out together at the 1995 Emmy Awards, she in a green silk Dior gown that became instantly iconic. 'Carol and I had no idea what we were getting into that night,' he laughs now. 'She was wearing this dress – which, my God, I knew it was a spectacular dress, but I don't really understand fashion or anything about that world. Her dress became a story, and my winning became a story, and the two of us together became a story.'

'Something wrong?' I ask him, because he's stopped.

'I just don't know how to approach this – I mean, I've already told you more about my marriage than I should have.'

'You know your secret is safe with me. That wasn't an interview, it has nothing to do with this. Tell me whatever version you want, just something wistful and reflective about your marriage.'

'Keep that glorious myth of Clark and Carol alive a little longer, huh?'

I look at him in surprise, his tone suddenly abrupt and cynical.

'The thing is, what people loved about us, it was all surface. Not that we were unhappy, but nobody could possibly live up to this thing people wanted us to be. It doesn't exist.' He sighs, taking a long gulp of wine. 'Sorry. That's not what readers want, is it? Look, I'm giving you permission here – put some words in my mouth. Something moving. Make it about her.'

Humble though he is about his own stardom, Conrad admits he was never surprised by the public's fascination with his marriage. 'It's because we were truly, genuinely in love. And I think people could tell. I credit Carol with most of that – she's a much braver person than I am emotionally. All that warmth, that chemistry people saw in us, it was all her.'

The Conrad marriage is a story in which America has remained invested for two full decades. But last summer the couple confirmed their divorce, which was finalized in November and heralded the beginning of that aforementioned interesting year. Early in January, Conrad's nineteen-year-old daughter Skye injured herself, prompting a stay at an inpatient treatment facility; she has since recovered, and has vigorously denied rumours that she was attempting suicide. And earlier this week, mere hours after his Oscar win, Conrad's former girlfriend Amabella Bunch publicly accused him of domestic abuse, a charge that Conrad has vigorously denied in a statement issued February 28.

'I'm bewildered by the whole thing,' he tells me now, still visibly shaken. 'Though we were only together for a short time, I feel immensely grateful for my time with Amabella – she's a great spirit, really one of a kind.' Though he can't speak to any of her specific allegations, a court hearing still pending, Conrad 'wishes her only the best'.

'For this part, do you think Skye will be okay with me saying that it wasn't a suicide attempt? I don't want to draw attention to the rumours by mentioning it, but so many publications are still calling it that. I'd like to be as specific as possible.'

He looks confused.

'I mean, this is a way she could deny it without having to make a statement or go through any more scrutiny.'

'Two denials for the price of one.'

'Are you okay?'

His eyes are bright, and he looks away from me as he asks, 'Did she tell you that? That she didn't want to die?'

'Yes. She did.'

And I realize she told me more than she told him. Because this, of course, is a far easier conversation to have with a stranger than with the person you love most, and Clark probably couldn't bring himself to ask. How could he?

'Sorry,' I say quietly. 'I assumed she'd told you.'

'I've never been sure. I just hoped.'

He shakes his head, his relief tangible and overwhelming, and I reach across the table to squeeze his hand.

The morning after our dinner, I meet Conrad in his corner office at his new production company, an eclectic cave filled with movie prints and rock 'n' roll memorabilia. He's drinking a green juice 'reluctantly', he says, at the behest of Skye. 'At nineteen, she's a far more responsible adult than I'll ever be, and she's got me on this healthy living regime with her.' After an admittedly rocky start to his days as a single father, Conrad says he now cherishes his close relationship with his daughter, who since her injury has been focusing on self-care and reading; the pair are often seen hiking together in Griffith Park, and enjoying bonding time at neighbourhood haunts like Pace. 'She's my best friend, in many ways, and it's taken us a while to get there. She's the best thing in my life.'

Conrad's goal with High Six Productions is to have more control over the projects he acts in, and to give opportunities to filmmakers from a variety of backgrounds. 'I didn't grow up wealthy, or connected,' he says, 'and if anything it seems to me that it's become harder over the years, not easier, to get a foot in the door if you don't know people. One of our priorities is going to be seeking out new talent, maybe the folks who don't necessarily have an agent yet, or their agent isn't the highest on the totem pole.'

But the company will balance out that risky agenda with some safe bets, including one that's sure to make legions of fans very happy. Conrad reveals to me exclusively that Loner is getting a ten-episode revival series, a co-production between NBC and High Six. 'I've been very resistant to the idea of rebooting Loner,' he admits, acknowledging that he dismissed the possibility of bringing the show back as recently as last month. 'But Richard [Davis, the show creator] came to me with, if you'll forgive me this reference, an offer I couldn't refuse. And a script I really couldn't refuse.'

The Loner reboot is due to begin production in May, with a tentative release scheduled for next winter. But that project aside, Conrad is planning to take some time off from acting, in order to prioritize his relationship with Skye. The production company is appealing, he says, in part because it will ensure he can spend more time in Los Angeles and less time living the travelling life of an actor.

'If there's one thing I've really learned from this last year, it's that none of this matters,' he tells me, gesturing around at the walls of his production office. 'I'm being glib, of course – I take my work seriously, I always have. But in the end, none of it matters unless your family is secure. I've lost sight of that at times in the past. The business is very seductive, and it can warp your priorities and make you believe things are important that aren't. I know what's important now.'

'Do you always go through two bottles of wine when you're conducting interviews?'

'Listen, sir, you're the one who suggested we move on to red. We should have just got two bottles of that to begin with.'

I reach for the check when the waiter brings it, and Clark snatches it out from under my hand.

'You've got to be kidding.'

'No!' I protest. 'I can expense this, it's a business dinner.'

'You'd still have to charge it on your card in the meantime, right? Until their accounts department got around to deciding to process your receipt and send you a cheque in the mail? Forget it.'

'Clark—'

'Jessica.'

It's the first time I've called him by his first name and I find myself saying it again, my mouth lingering on the sound.

15

I've thought about waking up in Clark Conrad's bed more times than I can count. I have never once thought about him waking up in mine.

'Your place is close, right?' he murmured into my ear as we left the restaurant, the length of his body pressed against mine. Though I was conscious of the interview throughout dinner, half-writing an opening paragraph in my head, I couldn't stop staring at him. His broad shoulders, the thick wire of his hair, the hollow of his neck visible behind the open collar of his shirt, every detail of him that I had gone from knowing on-screen to knowing in the flesh. By the time he finally kissed me my entire body felt electric, dizziness so overwhelming that I had to hold on to him and look hard into his eyes until I was steady again.

He arrived at dinner looking flustered and shaken, spitting about the mob of paparazzi that has once again set up camp outside the gate of his house, causing chaos on the already narrow and winding street outside. He drove himself here on his motorbike, stubbornly resistant as ever to being ferried around even when it would make life infinitely easier, and it means there is no discreet way for him to bring me back home with him. Laurel Canyon is not an option. And maybe he picked this neighbourhood because he knew it would be only a short ride to my apartment afterwards.

So I climb onto Clark's motorbike behind him, my arms tight around his waist and my face pressed against the soft leather of his jacket, and remind myself to breathe. There is only one helmet, which he gives to me, despite my protests, and I spend the ten-minute ride home imagining how if we were flung off the bike I would hold on and wrap myself around his head and his neck, protecting everything that he is at all costs.

When I comprehend what is happening, that Clark is coming home with me, there's a part of me flooded with panic, imagining what his reaction will be to the cramped space, the strange smell, the bugs that still appear reliably once or twice a day, crawling out of the walls to die out in the open. I imagine a hundred variations of Clark's reaction, what dry words he'll come out with upon seeing where I live. But in the end when we reach my apartment, his lips on my neck as I struggle with the keys and get the door open and pull him inside by his shirt, there is no time for talking. Neither of us would have noticed if the room was flooding.

But now, in the morning light, Clark is awake and thumbing through my hair and looking around with a mixture of concern and confusion.

'This place is—' He searches for words. 'It's really something.'

I stifle a laugh at how horrified he's trying not to look.

'Something?'

'It's— it has a lot of charm.'

'"Full of character" is I think the real-estate term.'

'"Quirky old-word charm".'

'It's also a great deal – my landlord's never raised the rent.'

'I would hope not. I'd forgotten what it's like to live in a place without walls.'

'Yeah, I'm sure it's been a while since you could see your kitchen from your bed.'

He's walking around the apartment, examining surfaces, fittings, the layer of dust that's accumulated on my dresser.

'So where do you do your writing?'

'Usually just in bed, if I don't go out to a coffee shop. Sometimes I'll stand at the kitchen counter. I dream of an actual desk, but you know. One day.'

He looks down at something beside his foot and of course it's a cockroach, dead on its back. I wince.

'Be careful where you walk. I hate those things.'

'I'm not wild about them either.'

'I can't believe you lived in an apartment with pigeons. I've never even heard of that.'

'I wouldn't be surprised if there's a few pigeons lurking in the roof of this place.' He looks upwards, dubiously.

'There's three more floors above mine, so unless they're living in the floorboards I think we're safe. Anyway, I thought you said you loved that place. Felt like living in the wild?'

'Well, yeah, but then I discovered camping.' He slides back under the sheets and holds on to my waist, pulls me on top of him.

'I've actually never been camping,' I say, my voice unsteady.

'We should go sometime. There's a great place I like to hike up to on the West Fork Trail, pretty secluded, especially this time of year.'

I nod, leaning down to kiss him with a shiver. He's already talking in the future tense, as though our ongoing present is a certainty.

'You know what's incredible?' he asks, when we come up for air. 'I slept better in this terrible apartment, with you, than I have in weeks. Maybe months. And honestly, this is the longest I've gone without thinking about— everything.'

Stroking a thumb over his jaw, I'm struck by the fact that I, too, haven't checked Twitter or the news, not since before dinner last night. He and I are in a kind of suspended animation together, and I'd stay here, except that I only have until the end of tomorrow to file my profile of the man currently in my bed. A tight turnaround, but I told David I would get it done and I will get it done.

While Clark's in the shower, I break the spell and check the news, but nothing much has changed. My fear was that the story would now be entering the think-piece stage of its life cycle, with writers filing essays on what Amabella's accusations against Clark mean in a broader sense – about abuse in Hollywood, about domestic violence in America, about sexism – despite the fact that she is lying. But it seems as though everyone is still holding their breath on the story before committing to a narrative, perhaps because the evidence against Clark is looking increasingly flimsy. Several prominent people in the business have spoken out in support of him, though; among them Ben Schlattman, who's quoted as saying, 'I've known Clark for a couple of decades now, through most of his career, and I've never seen him so much as raise his voice. The man's a labrador. A lot of people say a lot of things, but the truth always sticks.'

Clark emerges from the bathroom with a towel slung around his waist, steam billowing, and I quickly put my phone away like I'm guilty of something. I doubt he wants to be reminded of all this when he's finally succeeded in distracting himself.

'So I was thinking, seriously, we've got to get you into a better place than this,' he says, the muscles in his chest and stomach visible as he towel-dries his hair. 'Will you let me make that happen?'

'Absolutely not.'

'It doesn't have to be anything extravagant. Just something that doesn't violate any housing codes, maybe with an outdoor space of some kind. And a real desk. I hate to think of you locked up in here trying to write at the kitchen sink.'

'Clark, there's no way I'm letting you pay my rent for me.' It's bad enough that I'm sleeping with you, I almost say, but the truth is there's no part of me that really considers this a bad thing. I'm still on fire from last night, and I know the moment he leaves I will disbelieve that any of this really happened.

'Wait,' I say on impulse, 'just stay right there,' and I snap a picture of him with my phone, then another, preserving the memory of him standing in my kitchen half-dressed. He raises an eyebrow at the lens.

'Blackmail material?'

'Yeah, I'm planning an exposé on your morning hair.'

He wants to show me something, he tells me, as we're drinking hemp milk lattes from the vegan place on the corner. A deliberately ridiculous order, because Clark asked what I wanted and I replied, 'Surprise me,' and he did.

'So where are we going?'

'That's another surprise. Put your helmet on.'

I spend forty full minutes holding on to Clark tighter than I need to as the freeway whips past us, somehow unafraid. He pulls in to the parking lot of a sleek, glass-fronted apartment building in Studio City, and leads me into its chic lobby where a suited man at reception greets Clark by name, and directs us towards a private elevator to the twelfth floor.

'Do you want me to write another feature for Nest about your new bachelor pad?' I joke as we step into an immaculate open-plan apartment, all marble and metal and light oak, with a view of the Hollywood Hills beyond sliding glass doors onto a generous terrace. It looks as though nobody has ever lived here, and in fact it's hard to imagine anybody living here.

'I think I mentioned that I own a few properties around the city,' Clark says, guiding me over to look at the kitchen, with its gleaming island and built-in appliances. 'Right now I have a couple in Beverly Hills, a beach house in Malibu, a place in Calabasas, and this apartment. I flip a lot of them, or rent them out through my property guy, and this one's just sitting empty.'

'Wait—' I suddenly realize what he's suggesting as we're walking towards the master bedroom, and turn to stop him on the threshold.

'I know you need to be near green space for your running, and it's less than a ten-minute walk from here to Fryman Canyon. Some of the best views in the city, and a great, hilly trail. You can walk to most everything you need in this neighbourhood, just like your current place. There's a second bedroom, which is a nice perk if you ever have family or friends visit from back home, and a nook off the living area that you could use as a study.'

He's really thought this through.

'Plus, doesn't your friend's show shoot at the CBS lot?'

'Yeah,' I say in surprise, '*Undead*? How did you know?'

'A buddy of mine's one of the producers. They're right in this neighbourhood, as I'm sure you know, so you'll have easy access for visits.'

I imagine how Tom would react if he knew Clark Conrad wants to install me in an apartment down the street from his workplace. We haven't spoken since that day on set.

'Clark, this place is amazing, but I can't just—'

'It's just sitting empty. Look, in all honesty I could use someone to be here, deal with any maintenance things that come up, maybe take packages, dress the place up a little. You'd be doing me a favour.'

This makes no sense, of course; this is the kind of building where maintenance issues are dealt with by staff and packages are accepted by a doorman, but Clark's not-so-smooth desperation to convince me is endearing. What's also going unspoken here is that Studio City couldn't be much closer to Clark's house, a ten-minute drive north of Laurel Canyon. He wants me nearby, and it's the warmth of this realization that makes me give in to the temptation that was already keen.

'When is your lease up?' he pushes.

'It's month to month,' I admit.

'All the more reason to get out. Listen, I understand trying to be sensible with money, and I applaud you for not getting over your head in debt like a lot of young people in big cities do. But you're a professional. You're entering a new phase of your career, and you need a place to work. And a place to rest.' He lowers his voice, speaking urgently. 'That place you're in right now is going to crush you, so slowly and subtly that you won't even know it's happening until it's too late, and you are too talented to let that happen.'

I stare at him, unnerved because I believe him, and finally nod yes.

'But I'm paying you rent, to be clear.'

'Fine, fine, but not market. We'll come to a compromise.'

He pushes me gently down into the bed, both my hands in his hair as he straddles me, takes off my dress, begins a path with his mouth downwards from my neck.

Things move quickly, after that day.

'So how does it feel to go viral?' Faye texts me the morning after my profile with Clark goes live. She's exaggerating, sort of, but the article has been trending all day across social media, with quotes picked up and aggregated everywhere from tabloids to blogs to the *LA Times*. I deleted Twitter from my phone, overwhelmed by the blend of delirious gratitude and just-as-delirious rage, but I still periodically check in on a browser.

Overwhelmingly, the reaction seems positive towards Clark, who comes off as his charismatic, generous self, bewildered by a bad year. Most of the attention is not on me, but some of it is: 'It's pretty depressing that a female writer is behind this,' goes one representative comment, while others openly accuse me of trying to silence another woman. I'm not trying to silence Amabella. After the slew of unflattering coverage that's come her way lately, I didn't need to.

I also have a handful of enquiries from editors in my inbox, two of them offering me work upfront, and more LinkedIn notifications than I've ever seen in my life. A magazine wants to profile me, most surreally of all – an online-only women's brand that claims to be spotlighting powerful young women in the media. 'We'd love to hear your story,' the reporter tells me over the phone, her tone breathless and earnest. 'A kind of day-in-the-life thing about how you spend your hours, how you get it done, and then if you're comfortable talking about it, some specifics on the Clark Conrad story. How you got him to talk, how you navigated the various scandals during your interview, whether a publicist was involved. I'm kind of dying to know how you pulled it off, honestly.'

I politely turn down all of the requests, explaining that I don't want to complicate things for Clark by talking publicly about the story. When *Access Hollywood* calls, also wanting to interview me about the piece, I tell them the same. I don't want to give anyone a reason to focus on my relationship with him. I am not the story, flattering though it was for a moment when this reporter made me feel as though I could be.

Because the truth is that the work is not front and centre in my mind any more, and hasn't been for some time. I've never slipped easily into relationships, never understood how people around me could go from being single to having their existence permanently blurred into another person's, coupling and uncoupling as naturally as moving between jobs. The idea of seeing someone every day, of going to bed with them and waking up with them and living with them, has always felt like a trap to me, until now. Every minute I don't spend with him feels like a waste.

Tonight Clark is due to make his first post-Oscars, post-scandal appearance at a charity gala in Santa Monica. The press coverage will call him newly single, because he will arrive at the event alone, and he will leave alone.

'I wish I could walk that carpet with you on my arm,' he whispers into my ear, seconds before we leave in our separate cars. There was a reckless moment when I wanted to risk it, a moment when I even considered wearing a wig or dyeing my hair or otherwise disguising myself enough that I could be by his side. I am not famous, but anyone who attends any event with Clark Conrad will be instant tabloid fodder, and it takes only a quick Google search to connect my face with my byline. It would be the end of my career. And so, separate cars.

Though I'm supposed to go directly inside the event, I pause on the far end of the carpet to watch him. He's in his element, signing autographs and taking pictures with elated fans, many of whom are holding up signs declaring 'WE BELIEVE IN CLARK CONRAD'. The scandal already feels so distant, somehow, that the signs seem redundant to me, but it's a sweet gesture nonetheless and I know it'll mean a lot to him. I imagine he's telling the fans as much at this very moment.

He looks up from the autograph pad he's signing suddenly, looks right over the heads of everyone in the crowd, and locks eyes with me. As though nobody else exists.

16

Time passes differently when I'm with Clark. In our first clandestine month he has taken me all over California; on a private tour of five vineyards in Sonoma and Napa Valley, where I learned the term 'volatizing the esters' and tasted the tannins on his tongue as we kissed beside endless rows of vines. He took me to dinner in a private dining room at Spago, a restaurant I've never imagined setting foot in, where everything tastes like a more vivid and perfect version of itself. He took me whale-watching in Monterey and hiking in the Point Lobos State Reserve. He took me to see the rugged, impossible coastline of Big Sur, where we drove up the 1 overnight on his motorbike and arrived in time to see the sun rising over the Bixby Creek Bridge, red dawn sky gradually receding as the daylight turned the waves aquamarine. 'Let's go to Big Sur,' he said to me shortly after midnight, as we lay together in the Studio City apartment that only feels like home when he's there. 'Right now.' And I thought he was joking, of course, but Clark is never joking when it comes to these things.

Only when he suggested the Maldives did I finally have to remember how to say no. I am finally getting work now, a lot of it, and tempting though it is to let Clark consume my world and replace it with his own, I know that opportunity knocks rarely in this business. So we stay in-state, and I spend my days conducting junket interviews and attending press conferences and press screenings of new movies, networking with editors and with other journalists and pretending to be one of them, filing articles that talk about the industry as though I'm not living a double life. As though I'm still on the outside of Hollywood looking in, instead of spending my nights with Clark Conrad.

'You are extraordinary,' he tells me. 'I was a dead man before I met you, and I didn't even realize it. You brought me back to life.' And though in a critical mood I'd have to call his dialogue a little corny, it feels true. Clark was on a kind of brink before we met and I have pulled him back, and Skye along with him. She's doing immeasurably better, he tells me, newly committed to the self-care lifestyle he referenced in my Reel profile. 'Healthy living is its own kind of addiction, I guess,' he acknowledges, 'but I'll take it over the alternative.'

There is nothing he and I don't talk about now. In a moment of nauseous recollection I tell him about Schlattman, and how small and gutless I'd felt in that hotel room, how stupid for thinking he was interested in my opinions on the industry. After I finish, there's an expression on Clark's face I've never seen before, real rage, and on my behalf. 'I'm going to make sure that son of a bitch never works again,' he mutters through gritted teeth, and my heart swells.

Amabella is the only subject we avoid. I find out from an article that he has settled with her out of court, and that she has therefore withdrawn her application for a permanent restraining order. 'She got her payday,' he tells me at last. 'Which is what she wanted all along, I think.' And that's the end of Amabella, between us, which is fine by me.

What he can't do is take me anywhere public, though there are ways around even this. One of our first tentative attempts to test this boundary comes midway through April, when Clark and his business partner throw a small gathering to celebrate the official launch of High Six Productions. It's a crowd of around a hundred people at Soho House, spectacular views sprawled out in 360 degrees around us. One of the biggest perks is that there are no paparazzi here, because everyone enters and leaves the club through a basement parking lot, and once inside there's an unspoken guarantee of discretion that gives us a little more leeway. And so I am here with Clark, but not overtly with him.

'Let me do a loop, and then come find me,' he'd told me as we emerged out of the elevator into the bar with its dark leather and indoor trees and endless skylines. I keep wondering when I'll become inured to the beauty of sights like this, particularly now that I live in an apartment with its own panoramic view, but it doesn't feel imminent. And so I wait, letting Clark make his initial impression at the party alone, because it's in the entrances and the exits that most rumours get started.

Skye is here too, looking languidly elegant in a floor-length peacock blue maxi-dress, made of some silky material that floats around her as she walks, and falls into perfect layers when she sits down beside me on a barstool. I'm watching Clark and pretending not to, and Skye stares as though she's caught me in a lie.

She knows, of course, about Clark and me, and I can't imagine how to tell her that I was telling the truth in Venice, that I wasn't *fucking* her dad at the point when she asked. It's not particularly clear to me that she cares. She has her phone in her hand but she's not using it, and I don't understand why she's here beside me instead of anywhere else in the room. Instagram royalty, socialite, It Girl, she should be with her squad, and yet every time I see her she's alone. If she were a character in a movie, this is the point where I'd begin wondering if she were a ghost, because I've never seen her interact with anyone or make any impact on the world around her. But that's not entirely true – as cool a crowd as this is, there are a few people who do a poor job hiding their stares as they realize who she is. She's drinking a bottle of Fiji water with a straw built into the lid, a new accessory I've seen springing up on red carpets lately, and I feel suddenly conscious of my own cocktail.

'You went to school, right?' she asks me, without preamble.

'As in college? Yeah, I studied English.'

'Very English of you,' she says quietly, like she's trying to make a joke, but I'm not sure enough to laugh.

'I thought about doing a master's in journalism,' I continue, barrelling onwards as I tend to do in uncomfortable moments with Skye. 'But it was a lot of money, and I decided everything they could teach me I could learn better actually doing the work, so.'

'I maybe want to go back to school.'

'Really?' I'm not sure why I'm surprised. Skye has never seemed stupid to me, if maybe lacking in curiosity. 'That's great. At USC?'

She nods, fidgeting with the ring on her finger, slowly spinning it around and around. It strikes me, not for the first time, that she must be on some kind of tranquilliser. The soft, slow voice and unshakeable calm that I've witnessed in her don't mesh with the glimpses of the girl I saw from afar prior to our ever meeting; that girl was gutsy and loud and walked into every room secure in the knowledge of her elevated place within it. The Skye I know is hesitant, quiet, and gives you the impulse to shield her from things.

'Just depends on my dad.'

'What do you mean?'

'He was never wild about me going to school for anything but acting.'

I frown, looking instinctively towards Clark who's deep in conversation with two suits.

'Why not?'

She shrugs.

'He always says I take after him. That I'm a natural in front of the camera, and it'd be a waste not to use that.'

'It doesn't really matter what he wants, though. Right? I mean, I think he just wants you to do whatever's going to make you happy. He was probably encouraging you with the modelling and acting because that's what he thought you wanted.'

She nods, vaguely.

'But if you want to go back to school, you should. Maybe somewhere out of state, even, somewhere you wouldn't draw so much attention.' I can only imagine the paparazzi pile-on at the USC campus if Skye were to return now.

'I'd never want to move away from him. He's like my lifeboat.'

She means lifeline, I think, but I'm not going to correct her. Nor am I going to tell her that I know why she sees Clark as her only real family, that I know this is more than metaphorical. He comes over to join us then, bending down to kiss Skye on the head and ruffle her hair, which slips effortlessly back into place afterwards as though it was never touched. I take his hand as it's offered and let him pull me into a loose hug, exactly the kind of gesture that will appear normal for casual work acquaintances. It's so studied, the way he performs in public, that later at my apartment I have to ask.

'Have you ever been involved with a journalist before?'

He looks up.

'Well, for over two decades I was only involved with one woman – with one exception, as you know. Then Amabella. Then you. There's not a huge pool of dating history to pull from.'

'What about before you met Carol?'

'No,' he says with a frown, clearly stymied by my sudden curiosity. 'I dated a lot of women, but to my recollection none of them were in your field. Why?'

'I just wanted to know. Sleeping with a source is unmapped territory for me.'

'Come on.' He half-scoffs. 'A source?'

I stare at him.

'Yeah. Why, you wouldn't call yourself that?'

'I just always think of that word as applying more to hard news journalism. You're not exactly breaking Watergate here.'

'Are you saying you don't see me as a real journalist?'

'No, that's not what I'm saying at all.'

'I think that's exactly what you're saying.'

Though I'm stung, I'm also having fun. Playing the part of the angry girlfriend, to see how he will make this up to me, because he's the kind of man that will.

'Jessica…' He puts his hands on either side of my face, pulling me gently towards him. 'That wasn't about you. It was about me, and how trivial my life and career seem when you put them in the context of sources and reporting and— You know I've never been comfortable with all this. The Reel thing was good, and now it's done, and I'm excited to get back to making movies and being a father. And being with my girl.'

I lean into him as he kisses me, warmed by the realization that I'm the one he's calling his girl, and the nagging voice in my head gets quieter. And he's not done yet making it up to me.

The next day, I get a call from Clark when I'm midway through running in the canyon, and my reception is so bad that I have to wait and call him back when I'm at the base. He tells me to meet him at an address in

Burbank that evening, offering no explanation beyond 'trust me'.

'What should I wear?' I ask, but he's already gone.

The address turns out to be an unmarked warehouse in a lot that does not seem to belong to a studio. When I knock hesitantly on the metal door there's no answer, and so I go in, half-expecting a sound stage, but this looks more like a storage locker.

'Hello?'

'This way,' I hear Clark say from somewhere to my left, and follow the sound of his voice until I round a corner and almost gasp out loud.

Richard Loner's office was the most iconic set on the show, and not only for its unique design: an L-shaped room with an ornate bed tucked into the nook. By virtue both of being a workaholic and living a double life, Loner spent a lot of time in his office, often sleeping overnight there and holding clandestine meetings with unsavoury associates from his vigilante duties (his law firm, always bustling with activity by day, was reliably and mysteriously empty by night). In retrospect, this set was clearly a cost-cutting measure devised early in the show's run, before it became a hit, but by the time the producers had money available it had become too integral to ditch.

And now I'm walking into that office, where Clark is waiting for me dressed in a black polo neck and leather trousers, an outfit that he would never wear but Loner would.

'Oh my God,' I hear myself say, and I know I'm trembling a little. Fiction colliding with reality has a kind of impact, a physical weight, and Clark takes my hands in his to steady me.

'Surprise.'

'What— How does this exist?'

'You're the first person to see it in advance of the revival.'

'They've rebuilt the set already?' I ask, looking around at the white carpet, the dark wood panelling, the artwork in exactly the places I remember from the show.

'They never demolished it. The rest of them got torn down, but I refused to let them take this. I paid to have it shipped over here, preserved in plastic and just kept in storage. Sometimes I'd just come here and walk around, you know, get back into character.'

'That's… incredibly weird. And amazing. I love that you did that. I love that you kept this.'

'I know you're a fan,' he murmurs against my hair as he lifts me into his arms, lowers me down onto the desk, and moments later on the bed I have to bite my tongue to avoid calling him by his character's name.

'I have something to ask you,' he says afterwards, and I look up at him, trying to steady myself in the rush of *this man, in this room.* 'I'm going to Cannes next month. It'll be a lot of meetings, networking with distributors, drumming up finances for our first couple of projects, all of which I'm sure sounds fascinating to you. But there'll be screenings, and parties. And beaches. And the flat-out best hotel I've ever stayed at in my life, bar none – it's in this beautiful cape, tucked into the side of the ocean, twenty minutes from Nice.'

'The Hotel du Cap?'

'Of course you know it.'

'I just know *of* it. I've written about Cannes before.' I lean back a little on my arms, trying to work out if he's really asking what I think he is.

'It's beautiful. And I'd like you to come with me.'

But when he tells me the dates, my heart sinks.

'I have something that week. For the first three weeks of May, I'm freelancing in the office for Reel. Their associate editor's having surgery, so they asked me to come in and help with reporting, copy-editing... and with Cannes coverage, actually.'

'Well, wouldn't you be of more use to them if you were actually in Cannes?'

'They have people there already. They need me on this end.'

When David called, he made it clear without explicitly saying it that if this goes well, I could be in line for an actual job. Two high-profile interviews is good, but I need to prove myself in the office, prove that I can report on day-to-day stories and edit copy and play well with other journalists. This is not the kind of opening that comes up often.

'I need you too,' Clark tells me, tracing shapes I can't see against my shoulder blade. 'More than they do.'

'Ha.'

'I'm serious. Pitch it to them. Can you do whatever work you were going to do for them in a cubicle here, but from a suite overlooking the ocean on the French Riviera?'

'I'm sure that'll really endear me to these overworked, underpaid editors,' I say. 'Also, nobody has cubicles any more. I know it's been a while since you saw an office, but—'

'Stop joking.'

His tone is calm, but firm, and I sit up to look properly at him.

'Jessica... Look, you've been present for a pretty huge, transitional chapter in my life. I know we've only known each other a couple of months, but it feels like longer to me, which I guess is what happens when you're trying to process a lot of change. Time moves differently. Or maybe it's you. Maybe it's the two of us together.'

So he's felt it too, the time distortion. The creeping sense that you could wake up tomorrow and have lost a month, two months, three months, and not even care because this thing we have eclipses everything else, and so it should.

'The truth is, I don't want to do this without you.'

He looks at me, and lets me see him, and there is no way I can say no.

17

Cannes is a dream come true, I keep telling myself.

Back in London I knew people who regularly attended, and always fantasized about being one of them. And though I know Clark is here not for glamour but for the Marché du Film, the marketplace where filmmakers in need of funding network with financiers, distributors and publicists, he's promised we will have time for both.

But the reality is that it rains solidly for the first several days after we arrive, turning the view from our palatial hotel room from idyllic to rugged, the cape a sickly shadow of the images I had in my head. And Clark is gone all day, disappearing to meetings after our daily breakfast out on the terrace, leaving me with the daily festival trade magazines which list all of the screenings I can't go to and the news I'm not breaking. Reel turned down my offer to work remotely from Cannes; they have more people on the ground here than they need and are short-staffed back at the office, which is why they offered me the gig to begin with.

In anticipation of my work in the office, I had been given access to Reel's content management system, the back-end website that reporters use to upload and publish their stories remotely, and my login credentials have not been revoked. So in my grimmest moments I log in and just look at the queue of pending articles, the news breaks and the reviews and the interviews that I'm not writing.

Here, I don't have press credentials, and without them the process of actually seeing films is labyrinthine, too overwhelming for me to tackle. I do have a badge for the festival, the best Clark could arrange at the last moment, but it's the very lowest of Cannes' many, many tiers of access, a badge that gives you a tantalizing taste of the festival but never lets you take a full bite. A surly employee at the festival office tries to explain it to me in French, and then in broken English, and though I smile at him and nod I leave feeling more confused than ever, understanding nothing except that I'm screwed.

The hotel is far enough from the centre of Cannes – half an hour in good traffic – that it's impractical to return there during the day. So I wander alone up and down the Promenade de la Croisette, the town's main oceanfront drag which during the festival transforms into a buzzing, chaotic thoroughfare for movie stars, industry elites and the press, the pavements becoming packed with throngs hoping for a glimpse of the stars. Lined on one side by the ocean, and private yachts on which exclusive parties are held, and on the other by a procession of grand hotels, each with their own outdoor patio bar out front, La Croisette serves as a reminder of all the places to which you are not invited. And without Clark, the list of places to which I am not invited is long.

Tom is here at Cannes too. We're finally in touch again, tentatively, small talk only, and though we made vague plans to meet up while we were both here, neither of us has followed through. He's here only briefly – *Undead* has been picked up for a full season, and though the show won't air until autumn it's already getting some significant buzz, thanks to the pilot leaking early online.

'Guess we're both moving up in the world,' he said when we last spoke on the phone, in a tone that made me wonder just how much he knew. Right before he asked, sarcastically, if the pickup news made me more interested in seeing him.

'That's not fair,' I said, but in fact it's very fair. I'd put him out of my head with barely a second thought once things with Clark accelerated, with an ease that's breathtaking to me when I look back on it. And so I don't push when he says that his Cannes schedule is packed. I deserve this.

I stand for a long time outside the Grand Palais, the convention centre that serves as a hub for press attending the festival, and watch all the bedraggled, sleep-deprived journalists come and go with their credential badges in different colours, each spelling out a different level of access. I try to overhear their conversations, some loud, some muted; what's the frontrunner for the Palme d'Or, whether that new Von Trier really deserved to get booed, why this year's festival just feels more muted than last. I start eating things that I never eat – crusty brie-stuffed baguettes from a boulangerie at the far eastern end of La Croisette, Nutella and banana crepes from a vendor near the beach – during my walks up and down, anything to distract me from the overwhelming anticlimax of this reality.

My text missives to Faye betray none of this – I'm having the time of my life, I tell her, with the emojis to match. She has no idea that I'm here with Clark, or that we're involved, and I'm going to keep it that way, because there is nobody more guaranteed to leak your secrets than Faye. And when I see Clark in the evenings, I betray none of this to him either, though he does know that I wasn't able to get press credentials at short notice, and promises me he is 'working on' a solution.

'So what have you been doing with yourself all day?' he asks me, slipping in behind me as I'm lining my eyes in black pencil, his arms around my waist.

'Oh, you know. Keeping busy,' I tell him, flashing a charming and mysterious smile, because I do not want him to know just how unconnected, how helpless, how out of my depth I truly am. The power imbalance in our relationship is heavy enough already. He takes me with him to a party that night, an informal affair in the front garden of one of La Croisette's hotels, where magnums of rosé are served beneath a marquee and the rain continues to pour. Rosé is a drink that only appeals in the sunshine.

Finally, on my fifth day of sad Croisette wandering, I make a breakthrough. I'm sitting on the nearest bench to the Palais feeling particularly dejected, when I realize a young woman nearby is looking at me. She's petite and neat and polished, blonde hair in a sleek bob, immaculate trench coat tied at her waist. Her slim legs are crossed, her right ankle tucked behind her left calf in a way I find bewildering.

'I know you,' she says, so quietly that at first I think she's talking to someone else. Her accent is German, I think, but subtle.

'Oh, right!' I say automatically, once I realize she means me. I don't recognize this person at all, but I'm so bad at remembering faces that I'm functionally face-blind, and have found that pretending to remember everyone is the best way to avoid awkwardness. 'We met at—'

'Bâoli Beach.'

Our first night in Cannes, when I was feeling giddy and jet-lagged enough to risk attending the opening night premiere party with Clark, albeit in our usual separate cars. Held in a white marquee overlooking the beach, with white-gloved waiters handing out pink champagne flutes and ramekins of truffled mac and cheese, bona fide movie stars everywhere I turned, the afterparty felt like a dream.

We reintroduce ourselves and slip into conversation about the film, a bloated and self-indulgent biopic of Vincent Van Gogh which I'd had to force myself to stay awake through. Though it drew a seemingly endless standing ovation at the premiere screening we attended, the atmosphere seemed tense as the cast and director made brief appearances onstage – reports of jeering and booing had emerged from the first press screening that morning, followed swiftly by scathing reviews.

'I thought it wasn't so bad,' Lina, the German, says with a shrug. 'Everything at Cannes is always genius or trash, there's no middle in the reactions.'

'Yeah, I've always heard that. Didn't expect to see it in action so quickly.'

'What else have you seen?'

'I actually don't have a badge. I decided to come here kind of last minute, so.'

'Still, there are ways.'

I scoot a little closer to her on the bench, leaning towards her like she's about to spill state secrets.

'You notice how there are these crowds of well-dressed people waiting beside the red carpet at premieres here? At the Lumière, the Debussy even. They're in dresses, tuxedos, dressed up, but they don't have tickets. That's because they're waiting to see if someone gives them a spare. You get penalized if you have a ticket and you don't use it, so badge-holders will just give them away sometimes if you're dressed well.'

'That actually works?'

'Oh, yes,' she says. 'My friend and I, we used to do it all the time – it's easy if you're a woman. They always come to you first. I got in to see *Foxcatcher* this way, and *Blue is the Warmest Color* the year before. You just must pass the fashion test. Those guys, they won't let you in unless you wear heels, a dress, nice jewellery. They love to turn people away.'

This sounds nightmarish, but I'm already mentally scanning the wardrobe options I brought. The premiere of the film I most want to see here is this evening.

'You don't do it any more?' I ask her.

'I don't need to now. My boyfriend, he works in the industry, so I'm in for real. And you too, I think? The other night, you were with...' She trails off, in the way people sometimes do in lieu of saying a very famous name.

'Oh, Clark and I aren't— We're just friends.'

She smiles at me, knowingly, non-judgementally, and I realize she doesn't know the backstory, probably does not keep up with American celebrity profiles, so I tell her. I'm a journalist, I just wrote a profile on him a few weeks ago, and we happened to run into each other at the party last night, it's a small world after all. None of this is making her knowing smile go away.

'It's okay,' she says, laughing a little, and I can feel that I'm not lying well, that my face is betraying me. 'I don't care, I'm not going to expose you.'

I'm not panicking. I feel strangely calm, even detached from the fact that I'm having a conversation with a stranger about my relationship with Clark, because on a gut level I can tell that Lina truly doesn't care. She's not an *Us Weekly* source undercover, or at least she probably isn't.

'It's very new,' I say quietly.

'You know that you can't be public with him. It's something without a future. Which makes it appealing, no?'

'I don't see it that way. We can go public, we're just taking it slow, waiting until the buzz around the profile dies down.'

She doesn't press the issue, but the truth is she's put a bug in my ear that I won't be able to shake. Because when, exactly, will it be possible for me to go public as Clark's girlfriend and not immediately torpedo my career? No matter how long we wait or how many more professional wins I can rack up, that profile will always be one of the first things people know about me; in all likelihood it will be the first Google result under my name for some time. What bothers me more than this fact is the question of whether Clark knows it, too. Whether he knows that there's no future in this. Whether that knowledge is the real reason he's interested in me.

There is no way for me to ask him without ruining my facade of breezy casual, and I know I need to play it cool; this is what you must do for at least the first three months of any relationship, no matter how hard you're being swept off your feet. But the idea of going public, of being known as Clark Conrad's girlfriend, has taken hold of something in my chest and won't let go. The idea of everyone I've ever known reading about me, seeing me pictured climbing out of a car with Clark, eyes demurely downturned against the camera flashes. Heather Lamford, the girl who bullied me in such subtly vicious ways throughout year nine that I faked illness for a month; Harry Cromwell, the boy who took my virginity and then ghosted me. My mother, who has never made me feel secure in anything I do. My father, who walked out of my life without a second thought. I want all of them to know who I've become, and who I'm beside. I want him to lay claim to me.

All of this is still churning in my head later that evening when Lina and I are standing in formalwear at the side of the Grand Théâtre Lumière trying to look hopeful, but not desperate. We are both holding signs bearing the name of tonight's film, which Lina assured me was the customary way of marking yourself out as a ticket beggar, and sure enough there are little clusters of people nearby doing the same.

'You really don't have to do this,' I told Lina, conscious of the fact that she has a boyfriend who can get her in without this humiliation.

'Oh no, this is fun. I like going back to a time when I had to try for things,' she replies cheerfully.

We do not get in to the premiere, but the experience of trying is strangely enjoyable, less soul-destroying in a pair than I imagine it would be solo, and over the next few days I accompany Lina to a series of random events, some of them smaller screenings, some branded parties for companies with sponsorship deals at Cannes. We don't have much to say to each other beyond small talk, nor much in common besides acquaintances, but for this kind of transitory travel friendship, it doesn't matter.

One afternoon I catch sight of Skye across the hotel bar terrace, and for a second I'm sure I'm mistaken. Lina offhandedly asked me if I wanted to come with her to this L'Oréal party but immediately abandoned me once we were inside, anchoring herself to a group of similarly shiny young women who looked at me with vague bewilderment, their body language collectively telling me to excuse myself. I've spent the time since making notes on my phone about the decorations and the famous attendees I spot, half-heartedly thinking maybe I'll pitch a writeup to Reel's party diary.

'Jess!' Skye cries out, her stilettos making a dramatic clip-clop against the polished floor as she bounds towards me and hugs me. I give her a quick squeeze in return, jarred by this unfamiliar nickname from her.

'We have to stop meeting like this,' I joke, and she looks blankly at me. 'Because I keep running into you at parties. What are you doing here?'

'I've been here a long time,' she tells me in an exaggerated whisper, leaning back in, her breath hot against my ear, 'but it's a secret. I'm keeping a low profile. The good news is I'm a total fucking nobody in Europe so it's actually easy. What are you drinking?'

She takes the gin and tonic right out of my hand and sips it, then pulls a face and shoves it back towards me so hard it spills.

'So are you loving Cannes?' she asks, saying it like *cans*. 'I just come to party but I think it's boring after a few days, like the ocean back home is better and bluer and I get seasick on boats even when they're not moving so I can't go to yacht parties, which sucks because that's where my friends all are right now, but now I get to be here with you instead so lucky us, right?'

There is something wrong with her, her pupils dilated, her skin flushed, her gaze unfocused, and she's talking so fast I can barely keep up. She must be on something, and whatever it is it's not the same something she was taking back in California. I insist on getting her water from the bar, and she drinks it like it's the first water she's had in days.

'Does Clark know you're here?' I ask, and she laughs and says nothing, but I know the answer. There is no way he would have signed off on her coming here, to a place known as much for its parties as its prestige.

'Wait,' she gasps then. 'You have to meet my boyfriend, come on.'

She drags me by the arm over to the outdoor portion of the terrace where a short, slim figure in ripped black skinny jeans and an oversized hoodie turns around to meet us, and I recognize Brett Rickards. Skye makes her singsong introduction – Jessica, Brett, Brett, Jessica – and he says,

'Hey,' with a bored glance up and down at me, barely feigning interest. Only someone this famous could get away with being this underdressed.

'Love the new single,' I tell him, which is a lie, since I don't even remember the name of it, but it's been playing in every other bar and ice cream shop I've visited here.

'You and everybody else, I guess,' Brett says solemnly, as though the burden of his music's success weighs heavily on him.

'It's so fucking good, right?' Skye yaps, and grabs two champagne flutes from a passing waiter, downing the first immediately like it's just more water.

'Are you sure it's a good idea for you to drink?' I ask quietly, while Brett appears distracted by his phone. It's never been entirely clear to me how sobriety played into Skye's rehab programme, but every time I've seen her up until now she has been markedly drinking mineral water.

'It's a great idea,' she replies.

'Yeah,' I agree quickly, not wanting to rile her. 'So... so you guys are...?'

'Still going strong,' Brett says lazily, an arm snaked around Skye's waist.

'That's great.' Everything I say rings hollow and false, like I'm a stand-in for this role of Cannes Partygoer With Celebrity Friends. But there's also a part of me that knows whatever I can get out of them will make a good story, even though whatever they say now can only be used on background. 'I know I should know this, but how did you guys first meet?'

'Through her dad,' Brett says, and gives a kind of half-laugh, as though acknowledging an in-joke.

'Oh, Clark introduced you? That's funny,' I say, too heartily, because it's not that funny unless you know that Clark hates Brett.

'Yeah. Her dadager,' Brett replies in his drawl, and I try to understand what he just said.

'What do you mean?'

'You know, like a momager, only he's her dad.'

Skye glares at him, but Brett's already looking elsewhere. 'Carl!' he yells, and bounds across the room right into a bro-handshake with a bearded hipster type, who's only slightly less underdressed than Brett.

'Guess he found a friend,' I say to Skye, trying for jokey, but she is not in the mood. 'So what did he mean by that?'

Skye murmurs something in response that I can't hear, her body coiled like a spring.

'What?'

'How did you pull this off?' she says then, her tone completely changed. Now she's furious. 'You just appeared in our lives like you've always been a reality, but the thing is you have not. Groupies don't usually hang around for this long.'

'I don't—'

'You inserted yourself at some point and I want to know how you did it, and how I can un-insert you.'

This whiplash turn leaves me stunned. I have no idea what to say, which is not a new experience when it comes to Skye, and yet nothing about her is familiar. For the first time, the girl in front of me resembles the girl I always imagined her to be.

'I don't even know who the hell you are, but you're in every room,' she goes on, more quietly. 'It's a little creepy, to be honest. You just happened to show up on the worst day of my life, and then you just hung around like a curse. Hey – maybe that's it. Are you a curse, Jessica? Because things have been increasingly fucked up lately, and now that I think about it the common thread is you.'

'Things were fucked up long before I came in to the picture,' I tell her. 'If I didn't know better, I'd say you were jealous that he brought me here, and not you.'

There's regret, somewhere deep in me, as soon as I say it.

'Skye, wait—' I try to hold on to her but she's gone, floating away through the crowd, and drawing attention to myself with her is not an option. So I keep an eye on her from afar, watch her fold herself into Brett's arms so tight it's like she's trying to hide inside him, all while he's looking away across the room, barely acknowledging her. I watch her almost lose her footing as she leaves the bar, half-supported by Brett, and try to shake off dread.

18

Los Angeles feels strange to me after we return from France, and it takes me longer than it should to admit that the problem is Studio City. Though it's technically better located for the places I need to be, it feels more remote than my old neighbourhood ever did. Running in Fryman Canyon is nothing like the greenery of the lake; it's bone-dry up there, the trail steep and dusty and fully exposed to the elements. Now that it's spring, the sun beating down makes it hellish to run at any time of day other than the crack of dawn, or soon before sunset. Both of which are times I spend with Clark, or at least hope to.

He spends every other night at my apartment, sometimes more, but I never know in advance. One night I was out for a sunset run and missed him; when I got back to the trailhead I had a text from him telling me as much, and though I had no idea he was coming I still felt guilty, as though I'd let him down.

'You have to give me some notice,' I told him later. 'I

have a life too, you can't just expect me to sit around here in the hopes that you'll show up. I never know what your schedule is.'

Hearing myself, it's unnerving how fast I've already settled into the role of the nag, when I should be the fun, footloose young girlfriend. But Clark agrees with me, apologizing sincerely for being so unpredictable. 'Things are just all over the place right now with the company,' he says ruefully, and of course, this makes sense. His name is now fully out of the headlines, with only the odd trade writeup about his plans for High Six, and this new lease of life has only galvanized him to work harder than ever.

For me, though, work is no longer going well. My two-week absence in Cannes feels like it has cost me; I let things slide while I was there; leaving emails unanswered, pushing deadlines back. Editors who were pitching me a month ago are now not responding to my emails, while those that do respond no longer seem to want copy in the traditional sense; one asks if I have any experience writing quizzes. Another wants me to write scripts for videos.

And so when David from Reel calls me, I scramble to answer so fast that I almost drop my phone.

'Listen, have you heard any of the scuttlebutt that's out there about an *LA Times* exposé?' he asks.

'What?'

'Lot of people are saying there's more to come on the Conrad story, more accusations, and that the *Times* has a big piece in the works.'

I take a heavy breath.

'He certainly knows about it,' David continues offhandedly. 'His lawyers have been going back and forth with them for a while, so we're already late to this game, but we need to start digging into this. Especially in light of the profile we published – if it turns out that this guy is bad news, we really need to get out ahead of it.'

'He's not. Whatever this is, it's just more Amabellas who see an opportunity for a payday.' Hearing myself, I add, 'At least, that's my hunch.'

'Look, this is a courtesy call. I just wanted you to know that this might be coming, since you've really been owning the Conrad beat lately.'

Am I imagining the implication in his tone?

'We have a reporter on this. Amanda Heston, she's a real pro and she's been digging into Conrad's past, trying to get these women to go on the record—'

'Wait, you're trying to build a story about these allegations against him? A takedown?'

'We're trying to report the truth. Which is what we do. I know you're a fan of this guy, and who isn't, but some of what's being said is… rough.'

'Like what?'

'I'm not really at liberty to—'

'Just in broad strokes. Is it recent stuff? Or further back?'

'Nobody knows exactly how many sources the *Times* has, but it is multiple women, at least two of them are claiming to have had extramarital affairs with him that turned nasty, and there may have been sexual misconduct on set.'

'On set? That's insane, Clark is a complete professional, he's known for it. He's the guy who learns everybody's name on the crew, pays for catering trucks, mentors younger actors...'

'Who are you trying to convince?'

He's right to ask.

'Well, if you want Clark to give you a comment on this, he's not going to speak to anyone but me.'

'We'll get a statement from his lawyers if that's the case. This is not just about him any more, it's not a profile, it's actual journalism.'

'I know.' I try to keep my voice steady, try not to immediately snap back. I don't deal well with being patronized. 'I just think I can bring something to this story, if you'll let me co-report it.'

'What's your plan? You're gonna go and talk to ten sources about how great he is? How he's never done anything to them? We can't run that – what we *can* run are specific allegations, and corroborations of those allegations or denials of those allegations. General character stuff is meaningless.'

'If you tell me exactly what the allegations are, then I guarantee you I will get you something you can use. I have access to more than just him.'

'Look, you're not his defence counsel: you're not going in trying to clear his name. Assigning a feature writer to something like this, it's unorthodox, it's not how we usually work. Never would have happened five years ago, but all the lines are blurred now, nobody's got a clear job description any more.'

David's prone to do this, I've learned, veering off into tangents about the state of the business, and in this case I think it's in my favour.

'I'm not biased. I know it seems that way, but honestly I'm just fascinated by this guy, whatever the truth turns out to be. Like I said, my hunch based on the time I've spent with him is that this doesn't add up, but I haven't read the allegations. If you'll send me the details, I can start working. And if there are any people Amanda hasn't had time to contact yet, or anyone who's refused to talk to her, it can't hurt for me to try. Right? I mean, she's an amazing reporter, but I've heard her style can be a little aggressive.'

This is true, and I give silent thanks to the loose-lipped freelancer I sat next to for two months in a co-working space, who loved nothing more than to talk shit about other media people. She was from New York, where she clearly had more of a circle, and having moved west she was in search of a crew to gossip with. Amanda Heston's pushy, take-no-shit style was of limited interest to me back then, but for some reason that piece of information hunkered down in my brain until now, when it's become useful.

I hear David sigh, and say 'Yeah' in a drawn-out, deliberate way.

'So… is there anyone?'

'Do you remember Shelly Brook?'

Her face instantly comes to mind fully formed; feathered blonde hair, delicate pixie features, a regular for the first three seasons of *Loner* as Clark's morally principled love interest Alexis. She left the show midway through season three, in a plot turn that never made much sense – having finally declared her love for Loner after two seasons of star-crossed back and forth, the character abruptly had a change of heart and moved away for a new job. I'd never much cared about their romance, but a lot of fans were furious. Though the official line was that it was a 'mutual creative decision' between Shelly and the producers, the whispered truth was that she was impossible to work with, had demanded equal billing with Clark, regularly showed up late to set and did not know her lines.

'Yeah, I remember her. Can't remember the last thing I actually saw her in.'

'Right, she dropped off the map. I'm hearing that she has allegations – that the real reason she left the show was Conrad. I don't know the details, but it was all hushed up at the time, and she's completely stonewalling Amanda.'

'I can try, if you give me her details.'

Now I'm intrigued. I want to know why Shelly Brook – who at one point had all the makings of a rising star – disappeared, and I want to know what she has to gain from telling a story like this about Clark. Maybe she would open up to me if I approach her as a fan of the show first, not a reporter; someone who always wondered what happened to her.

'Who else do you think you can get?'

I pause. The thing is that I'm fairly certain I know where Carol lives. This information is not available by Googling, but Clark said something offhand that has stuck in my mind, when I asked him what Carol does now in New York. She has not taken any new acting roles in more than a year, which has been noted in press coverage.

'Lives the good life, as far as I can tell,' he'd replied, his casual tone barely masking bitterness. 'Got herself a great Manhattan apartment in the centre of everything, luxury building, a Whole Foods on the ground floor.' He'd stopped short of saying that she's paying for it with his money, but the implication was clear.

There are not that many Manhattan apartment buildings with a branch of Whole Foods on the ground floor. It takes less than five minutes of Googling for me to narrow it down to one.

'I think I can speak to Carol Conrad,' I tell David, who does a poor job of hiding his scepticism. 'I know that the allegations aren't about her, but if people are claiming there were affairs, she can address that directly. And I don't think you can be married to someone for two decades and not know if they're abusive.'

'You're overselling. It's fine, you can go after this, but strictly on spec. It's still Amanda's story first, and if you don't get anything of value, we won't use it.'

Within minutes of hanging up, David sends me an encrypted email with three names – the women accusing Clark: Shelly Brook, plus a costume assistant, and a woman whose profession is almost impossible for me to find online, until deep in the bowels of IMDB Pro I find her name listed as an intern on the second *Reckless* movie. While I'm assembling a quick Google collage of these women's lives, in another tab I'm booking a flight to New York. Carol, Shelly Brook and the intern, Karen Daniels, are all based there from what I can tell online, and flying there makes more sense than anything else, not just because I'm restless.

What I told David doesn't really make sense, and we both know it. A statement from Carol in support of Clark

– 'During the years of our marriage, he was never once violent towards me' – would be a valuable addition to the story, but it won't be enough to turn things in his favour if the other allegations pan out. But I imagine it. Finding enough information to kill this story once and for all, clear Clark's name, expose the accusations as lies. I imagine forever being the woman to whom Clark Conrad owes his reputation.

'I'm going to New York,' I tell him over dinner, 'for work.' Daring him to ask what for, why now, can he come with me. Something has shifted since Cannes, there's a new lack of urgency in our dance, and though I tell myself that this is normal and the honeymoon phase of any relationship can't last for ever, it feels abrupt and deadening. When he invited me to dinner this evening I expected him to follow up with a venue, a time, some kind of surprise, but instead he just emailed: 'You pick a place, whatever works'.

If he wonders about my New York trip at all, he doesn't show it.

'Sounds good,' is all he says, frowning down at the leather-bound wine menu. 'I've got to get back there myself sometime soon, always love a Manhattan break.'

'I've never been before.' This is not technically true; when I was seven, before my parents' marriage became an incident spoken of only in hushed tones, we took a family holiday to New York. I remember seeing the Twin Towers stretching up endlessly into the sky, standing at their base and looking up at them vanishing into the morning fog, trying in vain to imagine the mechanics of even beginning to build something like this. I remember asking my father how it was possible, how anything could be so tall without toppling, and though I don't recall his response I know that it was terse and impatient. Then again, this may all be a false memory; when I once asked my mother if we had any pictures from that day, she insisted that she and I had visited the Towers alone, that my father was elsewhere that day, maybe in a bar, maybe in a stranger's bed. She likes to write him out of our history, just like she cut him out of every picture in our house, save for one single photo I managed to save before she got to it. I don't even know where that photo is, now.

'Let me know if you want any recommendations,' Clark says. 'I can live vicariously through you.'

'Or you could just come with me,' I say casually, as though the thought has just occurred to me.

'I wish,' he sighs, taking my hand without looking me in the eye. 'As it turns out, this whole starting-your-own-company business is actually... well, business. You should see my calendar, it's just a nightmare of different coloured blocks, each one of them spelling out some other thing I don't want to do. They're fast-tracking the *Loner* reboot, so that's going into production a lot sooner than I anticipated. Also – you'll like this. They're making me get on Twitter.'

'*What?* For the reboot?'

He grimaces, and I laugh and just let him talk, because the more he talks in that earnest, faintly bemused way I've come to love, the easier it is for me to avoid thinking about the other shadow looming in my mind. These new allegations, whatever they may be, are nothing more than a problem to be solved. When I'm away from Clark for too long a kind of sickly instability begins to creep in, but when I'm with him I have never been more certain of anything.

'You're a good man, Clark Conrad.'

It comes out of nowhere, this misquoting of a famous phrase, and I laugh at myself right before he does, and then he kisses me, and we melt into the evening like nothing was ever wrong. Because nothing was.

I wake up in his arms the next morning and lie perfectly still for as long as I can stand, committing to memory the feeling of his body pressed against mine, his arm slung over my waist, his hands on me. This memory is what will sustain me through whatever comes next, and whatever I have to dig through in New York. He can't know what I'm doing for him, not yet, but once it's done there will be no more room for distance between us.

19

The city looks strange on the day I leave, as though I'm seeing it through a filter, the sky a sickly orange-grey. It takes me a while to comprehend after opening my curtains, overcome by a surreal feeling as though I might not have woken up at all, might still be in a dream where the world is bathed in this nightmare lighting. As it turns out, it's smoke.

There have been wildfires further north in California, but now the blazes have moved close enough that a layer of smoke has been unfurled over the city, choking the air with a burned wood smell and raining a light smattering of ash onto cars. This frightens me, the notion that such a thing is even possible, but the newscasters seem calm, the experts earnestly explaining that this has been an unusually dry winter and an even drier spring, and as a result grass and foliage have become like kindling, ripe for ignition. The air quality is not dangerous, they say, but those with asthma or other lung conditions should stay indoors, which sounds like an admission of at least some danger.

I go to the airport much earlier than I need to, eager to seal myself into a hermetic cube away from this airborne toxic event. The security line at LAX is chaotic, three distinct lines with no clear labelling leaving everyone to ask each other what they're in line for. Children whining, couples passive-aggressively muttering to each other, people frantically choking down the beverages they forgot they couldn't take through security. An airport employee yells something incomprehensible at the line miles ahead of us, and I close my eyes and mentally run through the order in which I'll put my things onto the security belt – roller bag first; jacket, shoes, bag of liquids in one bin; laptop in another bin; handbag in a third bin, or do shoes go directly onto the conveyor? I can never remember this, and it feels important that I get this right, because I'm not sure I can handle a security employee yelling at me this evening.

While I'm waiting at the gate, I pace back and forth and make a call to the number David gave me for Shelly Brook. I get an assistant's voicemail and leave a message, already feeling discouraged. I send the intern, Karen Daniels, a LinkedIn message. None of this feels promising.

I try to sleep on the red-eye flight, but my mind won't slow down for long enough, jolting me back every time I begin to drift. When the wheels hit the tarmac, the first blush of sunrise is creeping onto the horizon, and by the time I make it into Manhattan it's fully light, too overwhelmingly so for sleep to be an option. No matter how tired I am, daytime naps always leave me feeling worse. So, a quick shower, an obscenely tall black coffee with two extra espresso shots, and I'm back out, feeling blurry but newly determined, walking New York streets while I make calls because the pace of the city feels fitting, spurring me along.

And I need to be spurred, because things are not starting well. Shelly Brook's assistant answers the phone this time, and before I've even got through my third sentence she snaps, 'Do not call here again,' and hangs up. I briefly think I've found a website for Bridget Meriweather, the costume assistant, but when I click the link from Google it's a dead end: *This website has expired or the hosting has been removed.*

Later, Karen Daniels responds to my LinkedIn message: 'I'm not able to talk about anything relating to my time on *Reckless 2*. Sorry that I can't help.' The stiffness of her language, the implication of some external force preventing her from speaking, unnerves me. But I'm just tired and wired and reading too much into a polite, formal, two-line response.

By now, I have walked all the way from my hotel near Times Square down to the general vicinity of Carol's building. Chelsea is a strange neighbourhood, at once moneyed and almost completely without character, or at least that's my impression from an hour spent walking its streets. The building itself is a nondescript beige block, a converted fabric factory that, since the nineties, has become known as one of Manhattan's most exclusive addresses. Having run out of leads on my actual story, I spent much of the plane ride reading up on the history of the building, because being armed with useless knowledge is better than no knowledge.

But now that I'm here, I realize that I don't have anything like a plan. I had a vague mental image of going up to the reception desk and asking them if they could call up to Carol Conrad's apartment, tell her a guest was waiting downstairs, but this is clearly insane. This is not the kind of building where a random person can walk in off the street and ask to speak to a tenant, not unless they want to be escorted out and permanently barred. I do know that Carol is in the city; candid photographs of her leaving a Soul Cycle class in this neighbourhood emerged just yesterday, and she is also on the guest list for an exhibition opening at the Met tomorrow evening, the press release for which landed in my inbox by chance. But there is no chance I'll be able to get near her at that event, and so for now I've resorted to my best bad option: lurking in the coffee shop opposite her apartment building, hoping to spot her coming or going through the revolving doors at the front of the grand marble lobby. Hoping, too, that the doorman waiting just inside can't tell that I'm staring.

With one eye on the doorway across the street, I scroll through Shelly Brook's social media accounts, which are surprisingly active for a forty-something woman whose acting career is intermittent at best. Her Instagram is full of food pictures, inspirational quotes written out in pretty fonts, and group shots of her with a rotating cast of women, three of whom I identify as close friends by the regularity of their appearances. Two of them, Susan and Mel, have work email addresses that are easy to find online, and so I send a message to both.

Bridget Meriweather does not have a social media presence of any kind, and so at this point she's a dead end. I make a list of crew members from the productions that Shelly, Bridget and Karen worked on, and Google all of them for contact information. Many of them have websites listing their credits and skills, so it's easy enough to find email addresses, and by the end of the day I've sent out probably seventy-five cold emails asking them to contact me if they want to talk. I tell myself that I'm not wasting my time; I am casting a wide net.

That night, I dream about Bridget, her features vague and indistinct based on the single low-quality photograph I was able to find online. She is striking, though, and stands on a vast and verdant mountaintop looking out at the sky, on a precipice but in no clear danger. It's only when I wake up that I realize this is my subconscious brain's rendering of New Zealand, based entirely on the *Lord of the Rings* movies.

This is the connection I was too tired to make yesterday, the link that I missed. Bridget's expired personal website had a New Zealand domain. The production on which she overlapped with Clark was filmed just outside of Wellington. Bridget is the woman Clark was talking about when he confessed his secret to me; she is Skye's real mother. She has to be.

While I'm brewing subpar coffee out of a pod, my phone rings, and I feel a pulse of adrenalin as I see it's an unknown number.

'Is this Jessica?'

'Yes.'

'It's Susan Watson.'

'Hi!' I try not to sound too eager. 'Thank you for calling me back.'

'Yeah, I've got a few things to say.'

'Does Shelly know you're talking to me? Can you get her to call me?'

'No, she can't talk to you. And this has to be anonymous, I don't want my name anywhere near this.'

'Okay.'

'Something bad happened, with her and him. They had a fling, and then it got ugly.'

She's just jumping right in, while I'm still scrambling to find my notebook and also putting her on speakerphone so that I can record this.

'Ugly how?'

'I think you can fill in the gaps.'

'I really can't.'

'I mean, he's Clark Conrad. He can do whatever he wants. He came on strong, she said, like a lightning storm, and when someone that handsome and powerful and wanted wants you, you don't say no. But she knew he was married, she felt bad, and she knew her reputation would suffer way more than his if people found out, because people love to scream home-wrecker at the woman and forgive the man for everything. So she ended it, told him she couldn't do it any more.'

'Okay,' I say, 'but—'

'He wouldn't let it go. Harassed her, humiliated her on set, threatened her future on the show. He had an exec producer credit by then, so he was in the writers' room whispering in their ear, getting them to cut down her screen time, planting the seed that she was difficult.'

'Right. I remember the stories about her being a diva.'

'It's so insulting. Shelly was always such a hard worker, took her character seriously, had nothing but respect for everybody on that set. But he wanted her off the show. Didn't want her around as a reminder of something he'd failed to control, is how she put it.'

I feel a chill.

'But he wasn't abusive to her? I mean, he wasn't violent? Not that I'm diminishing what actually happened, but—'

'Not that she ever told me,' Susan replies. 'But he is not a good guy.'

'So he forced her off the show?'

'By this time, she wanted out of there just as badly as he wanted her gone. She didn't want to be anywhere near him, so they agreed to let her out of her contract, but they were worried about what she'd say afterwards. They tried to pay her off to keep her quiet, offered a lump sum in exchange for signing an NDA, which didn't work.'

'But she never did talk about it, did she? I remember all these fans trying to figure out what had happened, reading all the interviews she ever did, but she just never mentioned it.'

'Nope. They found a way to muzzle her. And honestly, this was a dumb move on her part – I could have told her so. She did need money, is the thing. Clark had badmouthed her so much that I guess word had spread, and people did not want to work with her now that she was known as difficult. So she sold her story to *The Daily Reporter*. They promised her this big exposé, spent hours interviewing her, and then they stuck the story in a drawer and never returned any more of her calls, because Conrad is buddies with the publisher. There's some name for it, apparently it's a thing tabloids do when they want to protect someone. They buy your story just to bury it, make it impossible for you to ever talk about it in public.'

'Is that even possible, to sell away the exclusive rights to your own story?'

'It sure is. And if you violate that exclusivity deal, you'll be sued for millions of dollars by a company that has lawyers on retainer just waiting for an opportunity like this. That poor Amabella girl who's gone radio silent? I wouldn't be surprised if they did the same thing to her.'

'What about Bridget Meriweather? Do you know anything about her?'

She pauses, for long enough that I fear the line has gone dead.

'Hello? Susan?'

'I'm here.'

'Do you know anything about Bridget?'

'I have to go,' she says abruptly, and though I persuade her to let me call back, I have a sinking feeling she won't answer. This was lightning in a bottle, I just happened to catch her at the right moment, and so I write down everything I can and force myself not to consider the implications yet. It's just information. That's all.

When I pick my phone back up, I'm jolted to see that there's a message from Clark waiting on the screen, which must have arrived while I was talking to Susan: 'I miss you.'

I don't reply.

What I do is Google Bridget Meriweather again, and this time I go deep, searching only for articles published before 2005. Bridget's last credited job is from 1998, as costume assistant on a straight-to-video movie I've never heard of, and after that there is nothing. Somewhere in between Skye's birth in 1997 and that final credit, Bridget vanished.

And finally, down in page 8 of the results, I find the obituary. There's no picture alongside it, but the moment I read the details – twenty-three years old, aspiring costume designer, based in Wellington, New Zealand – everything falls into place. She died in February 1998, less than a year after giving birth to Skye, and all that remains of her now is this single, sad, two-paragraph article. No cause of death listed.

Anxiety is making me nauseous, my pulse too loud in my ears, and not even a hard six-mile run up to Central Park and back is enough to restore my calm.

The rest of the morning is a wash; no more calls, no replies to my emails, and coming all the way to New York for this is beginning to feel insane. But I'm back at the coffee shop opposite Carol's, watching the doorway closely, and when I see her coming out of the entrance I have to strain my eyes to be sure I'm not hallucinating. Then I throw myself out of the door and sprint across the street so fast I don't notice the red hand sign, and a truck horn blares as the driver narrowly avoids running me down.

'Excuse me, Carol?' I say, ignoring the driver yelling abuse at me. She's already looking at me, startled, having seen me almost get pulverized. 'I'm sorry to bother you, I'm—'

'I know who you are,' she says, not angry and not surprised. 'Trying to get yourself killed?'

'Yeah. I mean, no,' I say, breathless, laughing. I can't believe it's really her. 'Sorry, I don't mean to intrude, I just didn't have any better way of getting hold of you, and I need to speak to you. If you'd be willing.'

'Depends on what you mean by speaking.' Her voice sounds different to her on-screen roles, twangier, the vowel sounds more pronounced, and then I remember that she's from the South originally. Her accent flattened out over the years, as tends to happen when your job is to be a chameleon. 'Speak to you as a reporter? No. Have a cup of coffee? Sure.'

I didn't expect this, and my face must show it.

'Let's get out of this area, though.' Her eyes dart around, searching, and then she nods westward. 'Walk with me this way, we'll go to the water.'

The Hudson is glittering in the early summer sun, a taste of ocean salt in the air, and I wish I were able to enjoy this as we walk. I'm too conscious of my heartbeat, pounding in my ears, flooding me.

'How did you know who I was?' I ask her.

'When someone writes a puff piece about my ex-husband – never mind two of them – I make a point of knowing who they are.'

I busy myself with taking out my notebook, trying to act unaffected.

'That's not what I agreed to,' Carol says sharply.

'If I can just take a few notes—'

'Do you take notes during most of your regular conversations?' She's immensely polite, smiling, but steely.

'I meant what I said. I don't speak to the press, I don't give interviews, so let's just cut the illusion that that's what this is.'

'What is this?'

'You're not really here as a journalist. You're telling yourself that, but the truth is you're here as a fan.' Before I can open my mouth to respond, she adds, 'and as someone in love.'

'I'm here to get the truth.'

She looks at me, her impossibly blue eyes piercing, and I hold her gaze defiantly.

'If you want the truth from me, you're going to have to return the favour,' she says. And I think that there's nothing to gain from lying to her.

'Okay. Yeah, we're involved. It's all been pretty sudden.'

'It always is with him. Ice and fire and nothing in between.'

'But there are these stories. Rumours about more allegations, the *LA Times* supposedly has a piece, and I just— I'm trying to figure out what to believe.'

'You're trying to absolve him.'

I don't answer, and she sighs.

'Look, I signed an NDA as part of our divorce agreement. I don't talk about our marriage, and he gave up his visitation rights to Sarah, agreed to stay away from us. But he's not holding up his side of the deal.'

'In what way?'

'We've had to move twice, because he was having us followed. Our emails were hacked, there were strange black cars parked across the street 24/7, he'd have flowers sent to the apartment on a regular basis. No card, no reason, just a reminder that he knew where we were. It's always about control with him.'

I wonder if she knows that Clark moved me into an apartment he owned.

'He still knows where you are,' I tell her. 'I got the building description from him.'

'I know. We're not exactly off the map here. We were renting a brownstone before, because I thought it'd be more anonymous, and he found us within days. So did the paparazzi. The building where I live now, it's not low-key, but they have a twenty-four-hour security staff. That's better.'

'What are you worried he'll do?'

I expect her to laugh this off, say that she's not worried so much as irritated by Clark's persistence, his refusal to respect her boundaries. I expect her to reassure me that Clark does not pose a threat, that the suspicion laced through my dream is nothing but paranoia.

'I don't know,' she says instead, and for the first time she sounds hopeless.

'He told me the truth about Skye. That you're— that she has a different mother.'

She looks intently at me.

'What exactly did he tell you?'

'That he had an affair, while he was on location in New Zealand, and that she got pregnant, and that you agreed to pass off the baby as your own.'

'That's all he said?'

I'm nonplussed. 'That's not enough?'

Carol pauses in her tracks, her mouth twisted over to one side like she's trying to hold something in.

'At the time, all I knew was she was young, troubled, came on to him, and he couldn't resist. He said she got herself pregnant deliberately, because she couldn't bear it when he ended the relationship. He said he offered to pay for an abortion, and she refused. He said he was worried she'd hurt the baby, and so we had to adopt her. He said, he said, he said.'

'What about her? What did she say?'

'She said that Clark raped her.'

I feel weak, my limbs suddenly heavy.

'I dismissed it. It was so absurd, and so far away from anything I'd ever seen in him, and she was on another continent. I wanted to forget that she had ever existed. And that's exactly what we all did. Pretended that I'd been quietly pregnant and then quietly given birth – people bought it, back then.'

'She's dead now. Bridget.' My voice sounds strange, even to me. 'Did you know that?'

She shakes her head.

'She was twenty-three when she died.'

Again, a tiny head shake.

'Does Skye know the truth?' I ask. 'I mean, that she's not your daughter?'

'Clark told her when she was thirteen, I think to spite me. She wanted nothing to do with me after that, and he loved it. She'd always felt like a little bit of a misfit in our family, I think, and just kept it to herself. But once she had solid evidence that she actually didn't belong...' She trails off.

'Skye was always his girl. Crafted in his image. He wanted her to be as famous as he was, got her an agent when she was barely out of diapers.'

'He arranged for her to date Brett Rickards.'

'Oh yeah, he was particularly proud of that one. He saw Brett's star rising before most people did – he likes to play dumb about millennials and social media, but he has this intuitive understanding of what sells. And he wanted Skye to sell.'

And a crack in Clark makes itself clear to me, suddenly. The way he hates influencers, but started dating one the minute he got divorced. The way he wants to protect Skye, but pressures her to act instead of going to college. The way he claims to be fame-weary and press-shy, but has courted both relentlessly in the time that I've known him, all the while letting me think I'm the one steering him.

'But Brett has such a terrible reputation. I can't believe Clark would set his daughter up with him, even for publicity.'

'Like I said. He knows what sells. I hope you know it's not a coincidence that he picked a journalist to get involved with at this particular moment.'

Nausea twitches in my gut, but I hold steady, keep my expression neutral.

'Someone told me that Shelly Brook sold her story to a tabloid, exclusively, and they buried it. Instead of publishing it, they did the opposite. Is that possible?'

'Honey,' Carol says, the twang even more pronounced now. 'Of course. Happens all the time – catch and kill, that's the term. And if it's done well, you never hear a word about it. There are so many ways to keep women silent in this business. Including good folks like yourself waiting hungrily in the wings to write an adoring profile about how sweet he is.'

I bite my tongue.

'People always say "there's no smoke without fire", right?' she asks. 'But what they actually believe is that there's no fire without smoke.'

'I don't understand.'

'People think that if they haven't heard about something – at least in whispers, at least in the comments section of a gossip blog – then it can't be happening. They think that what they see is the totality of what exists. When in Hollywood, nothing could be further from the truth. You see what people want you to see. Manufactured gossip makes people feel like they're getting the inside scoop, but it's just more product.'

I nod.

'Listen – we made it work. You'd be surprised what you can make work. Clark is a truly phenomenal husband, a wonderful man, until he isn't. The ways he could twist reality, make you doubt yourself, because he was so fabulous ninety per cent of the time, that when the other ten per cent came around, you'd think "well, I must be the problem here". I'm the reason he's so furious. I'm the reason he'd rather be at work than here with us. I'm the reason he needs to go elsewhere to get his needs met. So I stopped existing for myself. It got to the point where I would not leave the house unless I had his permission.'

Carol stops then, pursing her lips as though physically preventing herself from saying more.

'Do you believe what Bridget said?' I ask her. 'Now, in retrospect?'

She looks up to the sky, and doesn't answer me. I ask again, and she does not answer, and this is the kind of silence that's an answer in itself.

'You know what's funny?' she says as we're crossing the intersection back towards her building. 'Our best times were always when his career was in a downturn, when he'd had an off year, when something had bombed. The better things were going for him at work, the more controlling he got at home.'

The silence is mine now; my throat feels frozen, no words coming.

'Be careful,' Carol says under her breath as we part ways, right before the sssssssh of the revolving door whisks her inside and I can't know for sure whether I heard her right.

I walk too far east and end up lost on my way back, and instead of looking at my phone for directions I just keep walking, in a daze. When I finally get back to my hotel, I realize that I've forgotten my room number.

'Room 307,' the clerk tells me, 'and actually, there was a delivery for you. Give me one sec.'

He disappears, and re-emerges with a bouquet of flowers so vast that it obscures his entire head. Red roses and tulips and white Alstroemeria arranged into a breathtaking explosion, and alongside it a card bearing my name. Up in my room I open it with unsteady hands.

To Jessica, my favourite fan. My translator. My saviour.
Always,
C.C.

That night, I lie awake for hours, staring at the silhouette of flowers in the dark. Because I never told Clark where I was staying.

20

My unsettled mood doesn't last. When I arrive at my gate at LAX, my neck and legs stiff from five hours crammed into a middle seat, a text message lands on my phone from Clark. 'Go to Passenger Pickup D.' He has come to meet me at the airport, and when the blacked-out door opens and he is waiting inside, I feel a physical pull towards him that's stronger than all my misgivings.

'I missed you,' he tells me in a murmur, pulling me onto his lap and I fall into him, let Carol and Susan and Bridget Meriweather become memories from another time, another planet, another reality. That night in my bed, I wait until his breathing has evened out into sleep and then press myself hard into him, my face against his neck, one of my legs between his like I'm trying to climb into him. I can't get close enough, or cling hard enough, and still I can't sleep.

'How's the work going?' he asks me the next day, after he's brought me coffee in bed.

'Good. It's going great.'

It is not. I missed a deadline, for the first time in my life. Fully forgot that it existed, days ago, and remembered far too late to do anything but send a frantic email to the editor, who did not respond. It would have been easy money, a gallery list of '25 Fall TV Shows You Need To Watch' based on early buzz, and it would probably have led to better things, but now I'm likely dead to that editor. I have to get my shit together. But I don't know precisely what it is that I'm striving for any more.

I avoid David's call the first time I see his number on-screen, then regret it and call him back. I have nothing to show for my time in New York, nothing usable, and I'm no longer even sure that I want anything to do with the story. I want to go back to a time before I knew the story existed.

'Well, don't feel bad,' David says when I tell him I have nothing. 'The *Times* is killing their piece too. Couldn't get enough people to go on the record.'

'There are a lot of NDAs involved. I don't think most of these women are able to talk.'

'Right.'

I want desperately to discuss this with him, and wonder if he would agree to meet me in person, somewhere private, somewhere there's no chance we could be recorded. Carol has got in my head, and I want someone objective to lay this all out for. Someone more anchored than me.

'There's something else,' he says, hesitating with every word. 'You shouldn't pitch to us any more. I'm not going to be able to commission you.'

'What?' Everything around me becomes very still. 'Is that a budget thing, or...?'

His silence is endless.

'No.'

'Then what?'

'Are you seeing anybody?'

'I'm sorry?' I laugh a little, thinking maybe he's making a weird joke. 'Is this— What?'

'I'll be more specific. Are you seeing anybody that you have also profiled for us?'

My stomach feels leaden. I run through tens of possible responses in my head, ways to deny it, but we have been sloppy so many times now. Restaurants, hikes, parties, even the airport last night. The door was open only briefly, but photographers are always at LAX, and all they need is to be in the right place for the right second.

'How many other people know?' I ask, at last.

Another endless silence.

'I wish you all the best, Jessica,' David says heavily, as he hangs up.

I stare at the phone for what must be ten full minutes after that, trying to think straight, trying to stave off a full panic attack. The room around me feels inconstant, as though its walls could shift and fall away like in a dream where things are fluid, and I don't think twice about where to go. The radio said that the wildfires had receded, that the air quality was improving, but to me the smog still feels heavy enough to choke on. The sky is not its right colour, and on the ride to Laurel Canyon it's hard not to feel as though the world is ending.

Skye answers the door, and I barely recognize her. Her hair pulled back in a tight ponytail, she's wearing a neat dress and subtle makeup, and her eyes are clear. It's enough to make me wonder if her appearance at Cannes, manic and wide-eyed and unsteady, was some kind of mirage. She is a different girl every time I see her.

'I have an audition,' she tells me, seeing my surprise at her outfit. 'My dad arranged it. My character's supposed to be kind of uptight, so.'

'Speaking as someone who's kind of uptight, I think you're nailing it,' I say, doing a fine impression of someone having a normal day. And though Skye never really laughs, there's the shadow of a smile. 'So you're not going back to school after all?'

She shakes her head.

'That was dumb.'

'Jessica?'

I spin at Clark's voice, and let him pull me close. From the corner of my eye I see him make a sharp gesture to Skye, dismissing her, and on cue she turns and drifts back towards her wing of the house. It strikes me that I've almost never seen them share the same space, not for more than a snatch of time.

'What's wrong?' he asks me. I want to feel consoled by his presence, taken in. I've worked hard to put Carol's words out of my head, but my body remembers.

'What happened?'

'Someone found out about us.'

'Who?'

'I don't know, but the editor of Reel knows, and I'm done there. If he knows, then the media gossip circle knows.'

'So?'

'So?' I stare at him. 'So, my career is over.'

'Don't be dramatic. There's no law against a journalist dating an actor – one of my best friends is married to an editor.'

'I know you never saw me as a real journalist, but the fact that I'm sleeping with the interview subject who basically made my career makes me a joke. It's the worst stereotype about female reporters.'

He takes my hand and pulls me over towards the deck, as if to whisk me away from this subject altogether.

'Listen,' he tells me when we're outside, steering me towards the edge to look at the view. 'Take some deep breaths. I can make a call any time and get this straightened out. If Reel don't want you, there will be people who do. I've got a buddy at the *The Daily Reporter* I can connect you with.'

His arms are tight around my waist, and I look out at the canopy of trees and try to feel held, not clutched.

'I don't know,' I tell him. 'I don't think it's going to be that easy.'

'You went to New York for that assignment, didn't you? Sounded promising.'

'Yeah. It didn't pan out. By the way, can I ask you something?'

'Anything.'

'Did you know that Skye was at Cannes, when we were both there?'

I feel him go still.

'Yes,' he says, after a long silence. 'With Brett. I didn't like it much, but she was desperate to go, and she'd been cooped up for so long that I felt terrible saying no.'

'Right. I just wondered, because Brett said that you were the one who introduced them. Like a setup. And that you sort of managed Skye's career.'

Silence, again.

'I mean, it's Brett,' I say, already giving him an out. 'It's not like I take his word as gospel, but I just wondered—'

'Why were you at my ex-wife's apartment?'

I stop breathing.

'Huh?'

'Since we're asking each other things. Why were you at Carol's apartment?' He asks it calmly, enunciating the words fully.

'Why did you send those flowers to my hotel? Were you watching me?'

'You didn't answer my question,' he says lightly, his breath a featherweight on the nape of my neck.

'I wanted to talk to her. I was told that there was a story coming about you, the *LA Times* one, and Reel had a reporter pursuing their own version. I was hoping she would tell me something that made it clear the story wasn't true.'

'And did she?'

I shake my head, still gazing directly outward into the trees. I'm afraid to turn around now, like Orpheus, afraid that if I look properly at him it will be the end of something.

'Do you believe her?'

'I don't know.'

'Carol always had a pretty active imagination. It's why she was such a compelling scene partner. But also why it was difficult to sustain trust in our marriage.'

'Oh. I assumed that was difficult because you cheated on her.'

His eyes flick towards me, and I know I'm playing with fire. I want to bring up Bridget, but something holds me back.

'So, what? You're on the anti-Clark train now?' His tone is still light, but I know better. 'Your next piece is going to be a takedown?'

'No, of course not. I'm just trying to make sense of what's smoke and what's fire.'

'That'll make a nice intro.'

He's not touching me any more, gripping the wooden railing in both hands like he's wringing it out. I picture him suddenly, holding Bridget down, tearing into her, smothering the life and the power out of her, and the world starts to turn grey at the edges, my ears ringing, my palms sweating. When I used to faint these were always the warning signs, the world growing insubstantial.

'I am wildly imperfect,' Clark is saying, but I realize he's been talking for some time and I haven't heard him. 'I've always been open about that with you. I'm human.'

'You're not supposed to be human. You're supposed to be better.'

His superiority is not a matter for discussion; it's soaked into every fibre of his being, his existence. He has star power, that indefinable magnetic pull that draws every eye in a room, and he makes the world around him feel bigger and brighter and more full of possibility. This, maybe, is the meaning of being a movie star. I've been so close to him in these past months, closer than I ever dreamed, but looking at him now, I'm not sure that I've truly been anywhere near him.

'I have to go,' I say quietly, already backing away into the house as he asks, 'Are you sure?' The ringing is gone, my palms are dry, and I have somewhere to be. Weeks ago, I confirmed my attendance at a publicity firm's summer party, and I will go, to prove to myself that I can still exist in this industry. A few gossipy hacks may care about my personal life, but Hollywood at large does not. A sprawling party full of executives and actors who don't know or care who I am is exactly what I need.

That logic crumbles as soon as I arrive at the venue. It's much smaller and more intimate than I expected, a courtyard within a hotel shrouded by vine-laden trellises, a jazz band playing instrumental versions of Frank Sinatra classics. There are eyes on me everywhere, following me, but my face is not recognizable and so I am being paranoid. I must be. I'm sure of nothing now, from one moment to the next, and I sip Bourbon until that ceases to matter.

And that's when I see Ben Schlattman, holding court in a corner, and an idea comes to me as naturally as my next breath. I need a new story, again. Something that has nothing to do with Clark, and ideally something that has nothing to do with me, but this would at least be halfway there. That hotel room, the blend of adrenalin and bewilderment and instantly suppressed rage as I realized what Schlattman really wanted from me, all of it's now flooding back.

This could be my next story.

And so I duck into the bathroom, freshen up my lipstick, turn on the recording app on my iPhone and slip it into the front pocket of my bag. And walk up to Schlattman with a coy smile on my face, letting my hips sway a little more as I walk, letting my fringe fall just slightly over my eyes as I look up at him.

'I've Got You Under My Skin,' he says by way of greeting.

'Yep. I know the song.' I see him trying to unsettle me, but I smile, trying to be charming. 'I'm holding out for "My Way".'

'Regrets, I've had a few,' he smiles. 'You're probably too young for those.'

'You sure about that?'

I glance at him, searching for an indication that he knows, and there it is. So it really is all over town.

'You're not the first, and you won't be the last,' Schlattman tells me, in a conspiratorial tone, and I want to smack his fleshy face until he looks as hollowed-out as I feel.

'I'm not sure what you mean,' I say. 'But I have been thinking, lately, about how we left things. I guess I feel a little bad about that.'

'About storming out on me?'

'I don't think I stormed. I wasn't sure how to take what you were doing.'

'I was thinking you wanted to talk about our mutual friend.'

'Clark?'

'I love the guy, but I wouldn't trust him further than I could throw him. Do I want to put him in a picture? Any time. Do business with him? All day long. Do I want him dating my daughter?' He gives a meaningful shrug.

'It's good that you're aware I'm young enough to be your daughter.'

'Funny.'

'How much longer do you think you can get away with this?' I ask him. 'It was pretty clear this wasn't a first-time thing for you. You had a routine.'

'How many movies you think you've seen in your lifetime? Ballpark figure.'

'I'm not playing whatever game this is.'

'Come on, humour me. How many?'

'Probably a thousand.'

'A thousand, sure. Shoot for the stars. Out of those thousand movies, how many do you think had my fingerprints on them?'

'You really are a narcissist. You're not that powerful, Scion was not the only production company in Hollywood.'

'That's not what I asked. I'm talking about the invisible hand, the forces that actually make things happen, which you'd know if you ever bothered to get to know this business. A call I put in for someone. A writer whose script I put at the top of the pile. That tentpole director who got his first break with Scion. You think you love Hollywood? Hollywood was built by men like me. Men like me are the world.'

'Men like you are a dying breed.'

'I don't know why you're getting testy. I'm the one telling you the truth. Look, I'm not a perfect guy, but I've always tried to be honest. I'm just trying to look out for you when I say Clark is not a saint.'

'And you are?'

'You know what it is?' he says, completely ignoring me. 'I figured this out a while back – actually, when he bailed on my movie to go do that astronaut thing. The thing with Conrad is he's the most fun guy in the room, you'll have the best time with him, and then you'll leave and think… I have no idea who that guy is. That's all actors, in a way, they're shapeshifters. But him? All the time I've known him, I've just never sensed a genuine person inside of him.'

'It's interesting that you've changed your tune since he cut ties with you.'

'Cut ties? Who do you think's putting up half the capital for High Six's first feature, sweetheart?'

I falter. Trying to remember, now, exactly what Clark told me about the financing deals he'd made at Cannes.

'He would never take your money. Not after what you did to me.'

'You want to see the documents?'

He still hasn't admitted to anything, and I know I'm going about this wrong. I was supposed to get him to say something damning about himself, not Clark.

'Look…' I say more softly, moving closer to him, 'I don't want to talk about Clark. I just want to know whether the only reason you agreed to an interview with me is because you wanted to sleep with me.'

'Sleep with you?' He frowns. 'Where did you get that idea?'

'Are you joking?'

'California's a two-party consent state.'

'Excuse me?'

'That recorder in your bag. What is it, your iPhone? One of those old-school tape recorders? Whatever it is, it's useless, because I do not consent to this recording.'

He doesn't grab for my bag, doesn't even bother looking down to confirm whether he's right. He knows he is.

'I hope you see the irony in your giving me a lecture about consent laws,' I say. For the second time in as many minutes, trying to appear unfazed.

'I'm not sure what you mean,' he says blandly. 'But I'm sorry Conrad did such a number on you. He's a tough man to say no to.'

I'm so angry it's making me close to dizzy, fists clenched hard enough to leave nail marks in my palms, probably. But what was I really thinking, coming here hoping to score a desperate last-ditch scoop? This is not how stories come together. This is not what journalists do.

I turn away from Schlattman, resisting the urge to smash my glass into his face, and head for the door. But it's blocked by a crowd of partygoers with eyes locked on their phones, oblivious to the fact that they're in my way.

'Excuse me,' I snap, trying to force my way through, but finally I realize this is the kind of gaggle that forms around one specific piece of information, something so shocking that people instinctively band together. I pull out my phone, and the push alerts are already stacked up high.

Amabella Bunch Dead At 27 – Report

Amabella Bunch has died at twenty-seven years old.

Police were called to Bunch's Valley Village apartment Tuesday afternoon, after she failed to appear for work on a sponsored content shoot. The LA County Coroner's office has confirmed that Bunch was pronounced dead on the scene at 2.30 p.m. A cause of death has not yet been determined.

A source close to Bunch said that friends had been growing concerned about her for weeks, in the wake of her breakup from actor Clark Conrad, and her allegations of domestic violence against him.

'She was really getting desperate,' the source claimed. 'Certain people had made it impossible for her to get work, just blackballed her all over town to the point where she couldn't make rent.'

Bunch worked regularly as an actress, model and social media spokesperson, and recently launched SlayToday, an online lifestyle coaching brand.

More to come…

21

I feel raw, my chest hollow and my limbs unsteady. My fists are clenched hard, as though without holding on to myself I will scatter and evaporate, and all I can think about is that afternoon I sat with Clark in his living room, strategizing over how to spin Amabella's accusations, how to minimize the damage. How to minimize her.

I have a text from Faye that just reads 'omg'. Uncharacteristically brief, and I can sense in her three letters the same creeping, hot kind of shame that's paralysing me. I read every single near-identical article one after another, as if in a trance, re-reading until the words grow fuzzy.

A representative for Conrad denied that the actor had played any role in blacklisting Bunch, and released the following statement: 'Clark Conrad is deeply shocked and saddened by the news of Amabella's passing. While their relationship was brief, it was sparked by deep respect and fondness on both sides. It is Clark's greatest hope that Amabella has finally found some respite from her troubles, albeit under the most tragic of circumstances. He sends his deepest condolences to Amabella's family and friends.'

'I didn't expect her to live in the Valley.'

This is the first thing that comes to me when Faye and I talk on the phone. As soon as I say it, it sounds absurd, but it's true. 'I thought she'd have more expensive tastes.'

'She was kind of a hustler, I think. She came from nothing, parents were super-poor, she basically got on a bus to Hollywood when she was seventeen from farm country. They were saying that on the radio.'

I don't say anything. I don't want to hear this, and yet I know I deserve to be confronted with Amabella's backstory now, to have to reckon with her as a human being.

'Where are you?' she asks me. 'Do you want to come over?'

'I'm just walking home,' I lie. I'm actually at the lake in Echo Park, trying to find the calm it used to bring me. It's on the verge of getting dark, the last laps of orange sunset fading behind palm trees, but there are still people around, children playing on the grass banks of the lake, a few boats on the water. I can surround myself with life here, for a while.

'You think what they're saying is true? About Clark blackballing her?'

Faye does not know about Clark and me; there's no way she could hide it this well if she did.

'I think it might be.'

'I still just don't buy her whole story. I'm sorry, I know that's garbage-y of me to say now, but I don't! It kind of seems like she tried this ploy to get money out of him, it didn't work, it totally backfired on her and she spiralled. Is that terrible?'

Maybe I was wrong. Faye isn't shellshocked in the same way I am, she's just wondering how long she has to be tactful before going back to the same old schtick.

'I have to go,' I tell her flatly, and hang up though I know that I'm being unfair. Faye doesn't know what I know; she has not spoken to Carol or Susan or Skye. She has not heard Ben Schlattman talk about the lack of 'a genuine person' inside of Clark. She has not seen Clark's whole demeanour change, like something in him has disintegrated, like the mask has slipped. No one in the general public has heard or seen any of this. And so, within days, the general public will do the same as Faye; they will revert to remembering Amabella as a dumb blonde, a trophy girlfriend with easy-to-mock ambition, a joke with an unexpectedly brutal punchline.

Trying to sleep is absurd. I lie in bed, close my eyes, reopen them seized by the urge to check Twitter again for new reactions, to Google Amabella's life story now that Faye has opened that floodgate, or to look at Clark's number on my dial screen for minutes at a time and not call. He has not called or texted me, either, and the significance of this is unmistakable. I want to see him, desperately, and yet I don't dial.

When I finally fall into twitchy sleep, I dream of the hotel courtyard from this evening, but larger and more industrial like a studio lot, vines growing over warehouses and trailers instead of trellises. There's a swimming pool in the courtyard's centre, and in its cerulean-blue water floats a female body, blonde hair haloed in the water. I try to move over towards her, but my legs are leaden and I'm blocked by the party crowd, all of them oblivious though I'm trying to warn them that there's a girl and she's not breathing, I've seen this before and she needs help. She's already dead.

My phone is ringing, jolting me wide awake with my heart pounding so hard I can feel it move. It takes me a minute to remember how to work my phone.

'Hello?'

Silence. I glance at the number – an unfamiliar one, 323 area code – but some bleed-over from my dream makes me sure.

'Skye?'

I hear her inhale, and know for sure.

'Are you okay?'

'I cut her out,' Skye whispers, hoarse with tears.

'What? You mean Amabella?' Of course she does. Amabella was with Clark in every single photograph taken at the hospital, and I never considered the possibility that she was actually there for Skye, not for exposure.

'I stopped taking her calls, her messages. Unfollowed her on everything. And I did that fucking Instagram post calling her a liar…'

She doesn't say *because he told me to*. She doesn't need to.

'It's not your fault. Where are you right now?'

Silence.

'I'm thinking of leaving town for a few days, just to get away for a while,' I tell her. 'Get some space. You should come with me, we could take a train somewhere—'

She's gone, the dial tone confirms, and when I try calling back there's no answer.

I see myself as if from above, inside this glass box of his. Lying in the bed that he owns, looking up at the ceiling he owns, behaving just like something else that he owns. And then I start packing. Half my things are still in storage; it felt wrong to bring too much with me when Clark moved me in here, as though clutter would kill the fairy tale. But maybe I knew I wouldn't be staying long. Fairy tales are short, and the authentic ones end badly.

I keep trying Skye every ten minutes as I fill laundry bags with clothes, unable to stop thinking of how she chose to call me, how she must have seen me at least fleetingly as someone who could help her, how she may finally be ready to get away from him.

At the sound of movement, I freeze, my arms full of dresses. I see him outlined in the doorway, a silhouette, his features in shadow.

'I didn't know you had a key.'

He's always rung the bell every time he's come to see me, maintaining the illusion that this place is actually mine.

'Of course I have a key. What are you doing?' he asks, eyes on the laundry bags.

'I'm moving out.'

'Why?'

'This arrangement was a bad idea. I should never have let you give me an apartment – although I really appreciate it. I've loved being here.' I hear myself placating him. How early do girls learn to do this? How early did Skye learn it?

'I don't want you to go.'

'You didn't answer my calls earlier. I wanted to check if you were okay, after the news.'

'I'm fine.' He's moved forward enough for me to see him now, his face a mask, as though nothing of consequence has happened.

'Are you? Really?' I ask. 'Because I'm not, to be honest. I feel awful for her.'

'Me too. She was always a little bit unsteady, you know, and she told me that she'd struggled in the past, but she really seemed to be doing great while we were together. I just hope she's found some peace now.'

A modified version of his press statement. How fitting.

'It just must be a lot to deal with, after Skye. Even for me, the two things in combination feel overwhelming, so I can't imagine how you feel.'

He doesn't say anything.

'Have they confirmed the cause of death yet? The report that I read said it was an overdose, but...'

Nothing, still. The more silent he is, the more I want to needle him.

'Did she really commit suicide?'

'What are you asking?' He keeps walking towards me, and my back is at the wall now. 'If I had her killed?'

I laugh, a nervous involuntary reflex, and he laughs too, but this is not a moment we're sharing.

'No. Of course not. You just had her career killed.'

'Her career?' he spits. 'What career? You of all people never missed an opportunity to laugh at that.'

And it's true. I never missed an opportunity. Once Amabella's allegations were far enough in the past that I felt bold enough to joke, I was positively elated by it. I showed Clark clips of her terrible YouTube original series, and her SlayToday website, neither of which he had seen before, and we were in hysterics. It was so easy to laugh at her.

'You're right. But I feel horrible, and you feel nothing. Her being dead makes things a lot easier for you. Did you get your friend at the *The Daily Reporter* to buy exclusive rights to her story, and then bury it?'

'What are you babbling about?'

'Shelly Brook.'

He flinches, his face actually flickering like an old movie projector switching between film reels.

'I know about her, and Karen Daniels, and Bridget Meriweather.'

'Are these names supposed to mean something to me?'

'Just tell the truth for once.'

'You're naming people who've had their knives out for me for years. When you've been in this business as long as I have, it happens. People want a piece of you, and they'll tear it off if they can't get it otherwise.'

'It was you who leaked the truth about our relationship to my editor. Right? Once you decided I wasn't on your side any more, you wanted to discredit me. I'd served my purpose.'

'You sound paranoid.'

'You're the one who's claiming that four separate women have grudges against you for no reason. Not to mention Skye.'

'Do not bring my daughter into this.'

'You're going to drive her insane if you go on like this. Managing her, keeping her like a pet, making her date creeps like Brett Rickards just for the exposure.'

'What has she been telling you?'

'She hasn't told me anything. She won't speak an ill word of you, and that's not normal.' I'm working this through in my own head as I'm saying it, realizing just how true it is. 'What teenager doesn't have a bad word to say about her dad, ever? You've cowed her into idolizing you.'

'I made a real miscalculation inviting you into our lives. I thought you'd help her, but you've just encouraged her worst instincts.'

'She's nineteen. She doesn't need to be curated, she needs a life of her own, not a wing of your house.'

'You want me to send my suicidal daughter out into the world to live with strangers.'

'She's not suicidal. She's fucked up because you've controlled her entire life, and you've made her believe you're the only person who loves her or understands her.' The full weight of just how badly I misjudged her is crushing, now. Slitting her wrists in a house full of press was not a grab for attention, but a cry for help. She was trying to expose him to the world, maybe unconsciously, maybe hoping that I was an ally instead of just one more myth-maker for her father.

'And you're terrified of letting her out into the world in case she spills everything, in case she ruins your whole golden family charade. But it's already ruined. Let her go.'

'What will happen if I don't?'

'Then I'll find a way to publish what I know.'

We both know that this is likely an empty threat; I have evidence of nothing and no editors who will take my calls.

'And what exactly do you know?'

'That you didn't just have an affair with Bridget. You raped her, and nine months later she had Skye, and less than a year later she was dead.' I exhale all of this like a breath I've been holding for days.

'What?'

He looks caught off guard, and for a moment I doubt myself. Carol could have been lying.

'Is it true?'

'Of course it's not true. How can you even ask me that?' He sounds genuinely wounded, but something in me does not give. I do not believe his performance.

'You're lying.'

'My God, you're a piece of work, aren't you?' he says then, in mock-wonder. He's almost pressing me into the wall now, and maybe I want him to. Maybe I want to tip him over the edge. 'Always hungry for a narrative. Real plot twist, the way you've turned me from your hero into your antagonist. I assume your only source for this is my ex-wife?'

'There's a lot of sources out there assembling against you. I'm the least of your worries.'

'You know that I can ruin you. Financially. Professionally. In every possible way. I know you inside out and you are not impressive to me.'

'Let Skye go to college. Let her study whatever she wants. Let her live in dorms or with roommates like a normal nineteen-year-old. Stop punishing her because she's living proof of your filthiest secret.'

'Stop talking,' he says, and his hand is at my throat now and I'm frozen. I could struggle, I could push him away, but something in me wants to see this through, wants to know for sure. His grip tightens, his thumb and fingers pressing hard into the sinews of my neck, and I don't stop him. For a moment, I imagine dying.

He lets me go just as my vision is going dark at the edges. I'm still on the ground when he leaves, breathing hard and struggling to swallow, but not so hard that I don't hear the door slam. And the thought occurs to me very clearly: *finally, you've met Clark Conrad*.

Clark Conrad Is The Kind Of Abuser Hollywood Needs To Stop Protecting

The allegations against Conrad are true. Here is the proof.

Published July 2, 2016 on Reel.com

By Jessica Harris

Four months ago, Clark Conrad was accused of domestic abuse by his former girlfriend, Amabella Bunch. Bunch claimed that Conrad had physically assaulted her on multiple occasions, that he had been emotionally abusive throughout their relationship, and that a recent assault had left bruises on her face and neck.

This year alone, Conrad has won an Academy Award, relaunched the beloved television series that first made his name, and started his own production company. He has been rewarded in all the ways that this industry loves to reward its powerful men, and protected in all the ways this industry loves to protect its powerful men. Meanwhile, Bunch disappeared. Last week, she was found dead in her apartment, from what has now been confirmed as a drug overdose. Her allegations are available to read in full online.

Bunch was not the first woman to accuse Conrad of abusive, violent behaviour. But she was the first to be heard, because his other accusers were muzzled by a variety of means – some legal, some monetary, some purely devious. One woman sold her story exclusively to a tabloid, only to discover that their motivation was protecting Conrad, not publishing the truth. These women's stories are not mine to tell here, but I am going to tell my own.

I became romantically involved with Clark in March of this year, two months after I was assigned to interview him for the magazine Nest. Our relationship was passionate, intense and all-consuming, and for weeks I saw no bad in him at all. Like much of the American public, I had been besotted with Conrad for years, ever since Richard Loner first brooded his way onto my screen in the late nineties. Clark's interest in me was intoxicating, and blinded me to much of the truth about him, even as a journalist with some experience in this industry.

It was on the evening of June 27 that Clark put his hand around my throat and squeezed, hard enough to make me wonder if I was going to die. That night, I had told him I was ending our relationship, and confronted him with an allegation that had haunted me since I heard it. In 1997, Clark raped a costume assistant on the action movie Gone, which was filming on location in New Zealand. Her name was Bridget Meriweather, and she died less than a year after the movie wrapped, after having his child. I have no proof except that as soon as I heard this story, I knew in my bones that it was true.

Clark denied it. He threatened me. And then he pushed me into a wall, put his hand around my throat, and squeezed. His grip was hard enough that I came close to losing consciousness. I was hoarse for a full day afterwards, and struggled to swallow, but somehow he did not leave a mark. I suspect he knows by now how not to leave marks.

Clark Conrad is a violent man with a long pattern of abusing, muzzling and ruining women he no longer feels in control of. To most of America, he is still known as a movie star and a mensch. But he is an abuser who has benefited from a system that is designed to protect men and to silence women. I have been part of that system. I published two interviews with Clark celebrating him, his life and his career, fawning over his every word. And there is no denying that he is a talented actor. His entire existence is a performance.

Stop protecting Clark Conrad. Stop casting him. Stop idolizing him. Stop calling him the nicest guy in Hollywood. And start taking his accusers as seriously as you take him.

22

The article is live for less than fifteen minutes. It's more than enough.

It's short and disjointed and inelegant, in desperate need of an editor, and throughout the frantic half-hour of writing it I'm sure that there are things I'm forgetting, or omitting, but it doesn't matter. What matters is that it's out there, and it can't be taken back, and it can't be ignored, especially given the source. My login credentials for Reel were never revoked, after Cannes, and though it seemed impossible that the system would really let me publish the article, I also know that digital journalism has evolved too fast for old-school publishers to keep up, and that editorial hierarchy is nowhere near the top of the priority list for the people who build these systems. All I'm doing is exploiting an oversight.

I suspect that Reel's first move, after taking the article down, will be to claim that they were hacked. So I take a selfie of myself beside the headline on my laptop screen, and post it on my Twitter account with the words: 'Yes, I wrote it.'

The only part that I left out, the part I deleted and reinserted before ultimately deleting for good, was the truth about Skye. She would be known for ever as the product of rape, if only allegedly, and whatever becomes of her next she deserves more than this.

Going to Tom's is not fair. I'm not proud. But his is the only address I have in my head, the only place I can imagine feeling safe, and of course he buzzes me in right away. He answers the door in his bathrobe, hair damp from the shower, and I want to bury myself against him and let him save me. But I can't. I'm on this path now, and I won't take him with me.

And so we sit across from each other in his messy kitchen, our hands clasped around mugs of strong Tetley tea like we always drank at university, not touching. I tell him, and he doesn't question my judgement or my motives or my story, doesn't appear sceptical of the truth about Clark, doesn't doubt me for a moment.

'What are you going to do?' is the question he does ask me.

'I don't know.'

'I'm not even sure what happens in that situation. A reporter publishing a story without permission – I mean, it's a true fable for the digital age.'

'All these big legacy brands now run on a CMS that half their staff don't understand. It's amazing this doesn't happen more.'

'Has it ever happened before?'

I shrug.

'I may have done something truly unprecedented.' My bravado is shaky. The unspoken truth around the edges of all this, the truth neither of us will touch, is that this will likely be the last article I ever publish. That, at the very least, my life as I know it is over.

Tom's housemates are both thankfully out of town, and after flatly refusing to let him give me his bed, I sleep more deeply on his futon than I have in weeks. My sleep is so deep, my exhaustion so profound, that I pass out while it's still light outside and wake up in the dark, disoriented, flooded with panic until I remember where I am. And what I did.

My phone is in aeroplane mode. I'm not checking my emails or Twitter or the news, and maybe this makes me a true blockbuster hero, walking stoically away from the explosion I just caused without looking back at the fallout. Or maybe it makes me a coward, head in the sand.

Tom finds me out on the tiny deck as the first pastel flickers of dawn are rising, smoking.

'Since when...?' he asks, gesturing between me and the pack of Camels I found on the patio table.

'Seemed like the time to start again.'

The cigarette's not giving me the warm jolt it used to, though, and it's doing nothing to curb the curls of anxiety in my stomach. I let Tom finish it.

'I was thinking. We should go home to England.'

'*What?*'

'Yeah,' he says, as though he's trying to convince himself. 'He can't chase you all the way over there, right?'

'He probably could.' I don't know, in truth, the length of Clark's reach.

'Well, they're not going to extradite you back to the US for a civil case, if he sues you.'

'You've thought about this more than I have.'

'You haven't committed a crime. Reel gave you publishing access, it's not like you hacked them. The most anyone can do is sue, and if you're in England you'll be fine. Right?'

'You just got here. The very first show you got cast in actually got picked up, and it's a hit. Do you have any idea how rare that is? You'd be insane to walk away.'

'Jess, it's you.'

I look at him and wonder when he came to love me this much. How he possibly can when I have nothing to offer him, when I've sold out everything I ever was. He can't see it yet, that I'm a shell, but he will.

'No,' I tell him quietly. 'I won't let you do that for me. You deserve this. This career, this life. The glow.'

'What?'

I kiss him quickly, not letting myself linger, not letting this feel like anything but closure. Clark is still all over me, inside me, spilling out of my pores like something rotten. I feel toxic.

He makes me breakfast and I try to eat it. He tries to make conversation, tries to make suggestions, and I try not to snap at him. I know that I can't stay here for very much longer, but when I imagine what's next it's a blank space, an absence where my future should be. When he goes to answer the door, the moment of silence is endless.

'Um— Jess?'

I follow the sound of his voice, and find Skye Conrad standing in Tom's hallway, and my first thought is that Clark has sent her like an assassin. She's wearing all black, leggings and sweater and sneakers, and her hair is cut short.

'What are you doing here?' I ask, trying to see behind her to check for Clark or for Lenny. But she came here alone.

'You said you wanted to get out of town.'

'Yeah, but that was before—' Before I published an article calling your father an abusive rapist. 'How did you even find me here?'

She glances at Tom.

'This is your boyfriend, right?'

A shiver of guilt, as I remember the lie I told her so effortlessly back in Venice. Trying to convince her that there was nothing between me and Clark. I shake my head, glancing apologetically at Tom whose face is unreadable.

'You wanted to leave,' she says, and she sounds resolute, focused. 'I'm leaving. My car's outside.'

'Does Clark know you're going?'

She looks incredulously at me.

'You really think he'd let me go? You're more deluded than I thought. You should leave too, while you still can.'

I don't hesitate for long. Within ten minutes, I'm letting Tom hold me for too long as we say goodbye, and putting two bags that contain all my worldly possessions into the back of Skye's car. In the end, I abandoned most of my things at the Studio City apartment – books, toiletries, clothes I used to wear to junkets and premieres and parties. All just stuff, vestiges of a life that's now over. Let Clark burn all of it.

I watch the Hollywood sign disappear into the distance as we drive down the freeway, growing smaller and smaller until it's indistinguishable from the hills. Skye keeps quietly crying as she's driving, and pretending not to be, and I'm pretending not to see. Her one-hand grip on the steering wheel terrifyingly loose, her other hand wiping tears from her face, and if we make it to wherever we're going then we will have to work on this, we will have to figure out how to speak to each other.

At a gas station just north of Malibu, I try. We bought snacks that neither of us has any intention of eating, and now we're sitting in the parking lot with them spread out before us, at a stalemate.

'I didn't mention you in the article,' I tell her.

'I know.'

I steel myself to say something I would never have had the courage to consider a week ago. But now my nerves are already raw and I have nothing to lose.

'Bridget was your real mother. The woman who Clark—'

As it turns out, there are still things I can't say. But she knows. It's why she left.

'It takes a lot of strength to do what you're doing,' I try next. 'To get out. I know how much you relied on him, how he felt like your only family—'

'Just shut up,' she says quietly, and I do.

A couple of hours later as we're nearing Morro Bay, the sky begins to shift around us. I've heard about the microclimates in northern California before, how blazing sun can give way to mist within a mile, but watching it happen is disorienting. The road up ahead is consumed by what looks like a ground-level cloud, obscuring everything beyond, and though I glance nervously at Skye she has no reaction, driving directly into it as the world darkens.

'Fog isn't a bad place to hide,' I joke. But the truth is that this is creepy, and only gets more so as the sun goes down. We agreed to drive until we reach Monterey, where Skye says she has a friend, but it's another three hours away and I'm exhausted. I'm also afraid to fall asleep in the passenger seat, lest we wake up upside down in a ditch.

'Maybe we should find a motel,' I suggest, but she ignores me. And for the first time it occurs to me that I'm sharing a car with someone unstable, someone who could do me just as much harm as the people I'm running from. Maybe she really was sent to kill me, to finish us both off at once.

These anxious, jagged thoughts of death are familiar, they happen to me under stress and when I'm tired, and I have to hold them at bay.

'Skye?'

'It's fine,' she says. 'Let's just get to Monterey.' She sounds tense, an unfamiliar tone for her, and she's looking in her rear-view mirror more than seems necessary. Dread shuffles in my chest, and I stay silent.

It begins to rain, hard. Watching the windshield wipers clear their circular swathes again and again reminds me of being a child, watching this same endless pattern from the backseat. I'm dozing, half-lost in memory, and wake up with a jolt as the car abruptly picks up speed.

'What's happening?' I ask Skye, and then I see in the rear-view mirror. An unmistakable black SUV is following us,

Lenny in the driver seat just visible through the rain. Panic is rising, my chest tightening and I can't believe that this is really happening, they have really followed us all this way and now they will run us off the road.

Skye takes a sharp turn onto an exit ramp, getting off the freeway at the last possible minute and speeding into the darkness, and for a while I think we're free. But before long Lenny's headlights are back behind us, golden in the fog, and now we're driving towards the sea and soon there will be no more road.

'Just pull over,' I murmur finally, resigned. But she lets them pursue us all the way to the beach, finally coming to a stop inches from the ocean. The air is clearer here, the water glistening, and behind us Lenny's engine stops, and this is yet another moment in which I realize I have underestimated Skye. She wants them to think there's a possibility that she will drive this car into the sea, drown us both, make them keep their distance out of caution. It works.

'Skye!' Clark yells, and she winds down her window to respond but does not get out of the car.

'Leave us alone!'

'I just want to know that you're okay. You just disappeared, honey, you can't do that – I've been frantic.'

'You were never gonna let me go.'

'That's not true,' Clark says plaintively. 'If I thought that was what you really wanted, of course I'd let you leave. But sweetheart, where are you driving to? San Francisco? You're planning to, what, to get a job in Silicon Valley? You don't have a plan, you don't know what you want to do with your life—'

'How would you know?' she asks, and I want to tell her to stop engaging him, that the more she makes this a conversation, the more he will think he can win. Every conversation we ever had was a negotiation, a transaction.

He's closer now, a few feet from the car. I turn cautiously to look behind us and there he is, his hair tousled, his face a mask of pain. He sees me see him.

'Jessica,' he calls out now. 'Listen to me – you were right to publish that article. You were right. I needed someone to hold me accountable, because God knows nobody ever has, and it's you. You know me better than anyone.'

He thinks I will be swayed by this, that I will swoon, and who can blame him? From the corner of my eye I see Skye watching me, probably wondering too.

'I need you both,' he continues, his voice cracking in the wind. 'I want to be a better man, I want to take responsibility for the things I've done, and I can't do any of it without you.'

'Leave us alone,' Skye tells him again, and when he speaks next his tone has changed.

'Look, I don't want to do this. But honey, you're still in outpatient treatment, and if I tell them you've absconded they will have you held under a 5150. Every paper will get a hold of it, every blog, every news outlet. You've seen what happens to rising stars after a psychiatric hold – they are never known for anything else. I do not want that for you. You have too much potential.'

He is so clear to me now. So craven and small, so monstrous. He's moving closer, Skye's silence shredding his composure. 'Skye. Stop this charade, now.'

Beside me Skye is opening the glove box, and now there's a gun in her hand. I scrabble blindly for the door handle, pure adrenalin telling me to run, but Skye is already getting out of the car and she's pointing the gun at her own head.

'I am not your puppet,' she screams at Clark, whose face has drained of colour. 'I'm not some victim you can make disappear. *I'm not my mom.*'

I get out of the car too, numb, edging closer to her.

'If you don't get back in your car and drive back to LA, I will use this on myself. If anyone tries to come near us, if you try to follow us, or send us messages, I will use this on myself.' Her voice trembles. 'If I ever see you again, I will use this on myself.'

I believe her. And so does he.

'When you regret this decision, in a month or two, know that you can come home. Take some time, cool off, and when you're ready your suite will be there, untouched, waiting for you,' Clark tells her, as he's backing up gradually with hands in the air, as though he's the one at gunpoint. This will be my final image of him, the one that lasts, the one that feels true.

'Burn it to the ground,' Skye snaps, and keeps the gun at her temple until he's back in the SUV and Lenny's starting the ignition, his face impassive as ever. The things he must have seen.

After the sound of their engine has faded into the distant buzz of the freeway, I reach out and put my hand on Skye's arm. The bare skin of her wrist, just hard enough to feel her pulse there, to feel her alive. She doesn't shake me off.

EPILOGUE

The first night I ever spent in LA, I hiked for three hours up to the Hollywood sign as the sun went down, cicada song spiralling around me. I had been awake for twenty-seven hours, too wired to sleep on the flight from London, and arrived at the summit on a knife's edge between exhausted and exhilarated.

I didn't know until too late that the trail I picked brought me out directly behind the sign. Six-and-a-half miles of shadeless upward climbing all to look at the back of a landmark, a bruising anticlimax. But the sunset spread itself out over the city as I sat there behind the H, peaches and gold giving way to velvet darkness above the skyline's twinkling lights, and it felt like a show put on for me alone, a welcome parade. My Hollywood was born that night, aglow with promises, and only now that I'm a thousand miles away in the desert can I look back and clearly see the ending of it.

Fictional worlds have lost their hold on me, I realized yesterday when I started adding up how long it had been since I watched anything. Eleven days, including three on the road, the longest I've gone without screen time in my living memory. When Skye and I stopped at a roadside bar with a TV playing sitcom reruns I had to fight the urge to cover my eyes and ears, as though I have an allergy now. Maybe overexposure. Maybe I know too much for the artifice not to grate. Or maybe the bar was just too loud and my anxiety too close. We didn't stay long.

We've been driving east, since Monterey, our destination unclear and for now unimportant. Outside of Las Vegas we passed a billboard with Clark's face on it, stretched out above us: *Loner. Returning This Fall.* This ad was made and paid for long before I published my article, and maybe by next week it will be pulled down. Maybe all of this will do him some lasting damage. Or maybe the machine will keep on turning the way that it always has, and he will weather this storm just like he always does, and everybody will be calling Clark Conrad the nicest guy in Hollywood again by the autumn. *That poor guy*, they'll say, *I've never seen a smear campaign like it. I heard that journalist was a really crazy fan, couldn't handle it when he broke up with her.*

Skye and I still haven't quite found a rhythm, a way of talking that doesn't feel insane, but we're close. Her Hollywood is different from mine, her loss more gaping, but she brought me with her for a reason and it was not benevolence. We share something, in the wreckage Clark left behind, in the days we've spent on the road together, and though I made her promise to lose the gun once we end up somewhere permanent, I have stopped worrying that I'll wake up and find her dead.

The glow has receded. It began to fade months ago, with Skye's blood in the water, with Schlattman's eyes on me, with Bridget Meriweather's picture, with Carol's skittish story, with Clark's hands around my throat. It was never really there, in fact, but like any beloved fictional thing its loss leaves behind an ache, and in time I will find a way to live without it.